M

"I can't lose you," he muttered

"Damn it, I can't. You are the sky to me, Alexa. No matter what, you are still my sky."

She froze.

His words. She recognized them. So long ago—

With a sob, Alexa pulled back as much as she could, with his body still, unyieldingly, on hers. She tried, in the darkness of the boathouse, to see deep into eyes that were both familiar and unfamiliar.

"Oh, my Lord," she whispered hoarsely, tears cascading down her cheeks. "You *are* Cole."

Dear Harlequin Intrigue Reader,

Harlequin Intrigue has four new stories to blast you out of the winter doldrums. Look what we've got heating up for you this month.

Sylvie Kurtz brings you the first in her two-book miniseries FLESH AND BLOOD. Fifteen years ago, a burst of anger by the banks of the raging Red Thunder River changed the lives of two brothers forever. In *Remembering Red Thunder*, Sheriff Chance Conover struggles to regain the memory of his life, his wife and their unborn baby before a man out for revenge silences him permanently.

You can also look for the second book in the four-book continuity series MORIAH'S LANDING— *Howling in the Darkness* by B.J. Daniels. Jonah Ries has always sensed something was wrong in Moriah's Landing, but when he accidentally crashes Kat Ridgemont's online blind date, he realizes the tough yet fragile beauty has more to fear than even the town's superstitions.

In *Operation: Reunited* by Linda O. Johnston, Alexa Kenner is on the verge of marriage when she meets John O'Rourke, a man who eerily resembles her dead lover, Cole Rappaport, who died in a terrible explosion. Could they be one and the same?

And finally this month, one by one government witnesses who put away a mob associate have been killed, with only Tara Ford remaining. U.S. Deputy Marshal Brad Harrison vows to protect Tara by placing her *In His Safekeeping*— by Shawna Delacorte.

We hope you enjoy these books, and remember to come back next month for more selections from MORIAH'S LANDING and FLESH AND BLOOD!

Sincerely,

Denise O'Sullivan
Associate Senior Editor
Harlequin Intrigue

OPERATION:
REUNITED

LINDA O. JOHNSTON

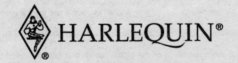

TORONTO • NEW YORK • LONDON
AMSTERDAM • PARIS • SYDNEY • HAMBURG
STOCKHOLM • ATHENS • TOKYO • MILAN • MADRID
PRAGUE • WARSAW • BUDAPEST • AUCKLAND

To my agent Paige Wheeler, because of her excellence,
her guidance and her friendship. To my editor
Allison Lyons, because of her thoroughness and
thoughtfulness, and because it's fun to work with her.
To Marcy Elias Rothman, because of her kindness,
her friendship and her helpful suggestions.
And to Fred, just because.

ISBN 0-373-22655-1

OPERATION: REUNITED

Copyright © 2002 by Linda O. Johnston

This edition published by arrangement with Harlequin Books S.A.

® and TM are trademarks of the publisher. Trademarks indicated with
® are registered in the United States Patent and Trademark Office, the
Canadian Trade Marks Office and in other countries.

Visit us at www.eHarlequin.com

Printed in U.S.A.

ABOUT THE AUTHOR

Linda O. Johnston's first published fiction appeared in *Ellery Queen's Mystery Magazine* and won the Robert L. Fish Memorial Award for "Best First Mystery Short Story of the Year." Now, several published short stories and novels later, Linda is recognized for her outstanding work in the romance genre.

A practicing attorney, Linda juggles her busy schedule between mornings of writing briefs, contracts and other legalese, and afternoons of creating memorable tales of paranormal, time travel, mystery, contemporary and romantic suspense. Armed with an undergraduate degree in journalism with an advertising emphasis from Pennsylvania State University, Linda began her versatile writing career running a small newspaper, then working in advertising and public relations, and later obtaining her J.D. degree from Duquesne University School of Law in Pittsburgh.

Linda belongs to Sisters in Crime and is actively involved with Romance Writers of America, participating in the Los Angeles, Orange County and Western Pennsylvania chapters. She lives near Universal Studios, Hollywood, with her husband, two sons and two cavalier King Charles spaniels.

Books by Linda O. Johnston

HARLEQUIN INTRIGUE
592—ALIAS MOMMY
624—MARRIAGE: CLASSIFIED
655—OPERATION: REUNITED

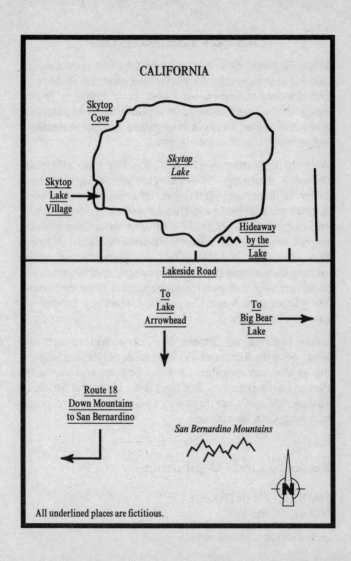

CALIFORNIA

Skytop
Cove

Skytop
Lake

Skytop
Lake
Village

Hideaway
by the
Lake

Lakeside Road

To
Lake
Arrowhead

To
Big Bear
Lake

Route 18
Down Mountains
to San Bernardino

San Bernardino Mountains

N

All underlined places are fictitious.

CAST OF CHARACTERS

Alexa Kenner—She became engaged to her business partner out of gratitude for his support after she lost the only man she ever loved. But has fear of her fiancé and his terrorist plot made her delusional…or is the handsome new guest at her inn really her dead lover?

Cole Rappaport—Saved after a bomb blast two years earlier, he was determined to remain out of Alexa's life to protect her. But has she been involved in the terrorist plot all along? He can only find out by paying her a visit…incognito. Enter *John O'Rourke,* home improvements salesman extraordinaire.

Vane Walters—A protégé of Cole's father, Vane had been like a brother to him. A very deadly brother…who is now engaged to the woman Cole loves.

Minos Flaherty—Vane's subordinate and handyman has an agenda of his own.

Forbes Bowman—Cole's gruff superior officer and friend, who saved his life.

Ed and Jill Fuller—Vane's guests at the inn claim to be from Bolivia, but their accents suggest somewhere farther away, and a lot less friendly.

Jessie Bradford—An officer in Cole's counterterrorist unit; his backup is necessary…and potentially lethal.

Allen Maygran—Jessie's equally deadly partner.

Dear Reader,

Books take a long time to write, longer yet to edit and publish.

Operation: Reunited was in process before the terrible events of September 11, 2001. When I began it, the idea of terrorist infiltration of the United States was unthinkable, a figment of my own imagination.

Now I know my imaginings were not so wild.

Operation: Reunited is a story of good overcoming evil and love conquering all—platitudes, yes, but ones that provide hope. We all know romances have happy endings despite the muddle in the middle. And we all need happy endings now and then.

I hope you enjoy *Operation: Reunited* for what it is intended to be—a romance, a respite and, hopefully, an enjoyable read.

Please visit me at my Web site: www.LindaO.Johnston.net.

Regards,

Linda O. Johnston

Chapter One

As Alexa Kenner picked up the glass container of Chapultapec red cayenne pepper, she glanced down the aisle toward the front of the gourmet food store. A dark-haired man in a deep green shirt strode by. He had the limber, confident gait of someone with no doubt about the world's need for what he would lend it. A familiar stride. A familiar man?

"Cole," Alexa whispered as her heartbeat accelerated. The pepper dropped from her shaking fingers, hitting the tile floor with a crash. Instantly, a fine crimson dust erupted everywhere, coating the aisle. Alexa felt it float into her sandals and between her toes. Her nose tickled, but she refused to sneeze.

Tears welled in her eyes that had nothing to do with the spilled spice.

They had everything to do with sorrow. Loss.

Desperation.

"Are you all right, miss? I'll have someone clean this up in a jiffy, don't you worry."

The words sounded distorted to Alexa, as if they had been murmured down a long tube. She didn't even turn to see if the person talking was male or female, an employee or a customer. Instead, she hurried down the aisle toward where she had seen the man.

Of course he hadn't been Cole. But she nevertheless felt drawn, as if entangled by a rope caught in a pulley. She had to take another look, just to show her jangled senses that there was no resemblance at all.

When she reached the end of the row of condiments and spices aligned on tall shelves, she glanced down the perpendicular aisle. A balding man in shorts wheeled his grocery cart toward the fruit counters. A young woman wrestled with her screaming child, trying to get him to resume his seat in the front of her cart.

No man in a green shirt.

It doesn't matter, Alexa chided herself. She had gotten herself into this situation. No miracle was going to occur to get her out of it. Seeing shadows of Cole was of no use.

She brushed off her jeans and feet, commanded her legs to lose their wobbliness, then walked toward where a young man in a long white apron was already sweeping pepper into a dustpan with a whisk broom. Fortunately, the container hadn't been large. She knelt beside him, picking up shards of glass carefully and placing them in the container he'd brought.

"I'm terribly sorry," she told the boy, whom she knew only as Benjy. "I'll be glad to pay for the damage." She stood as he finished cleaning.

"No need, Ms. Kenner. The manager wouldn't hear of it—especially not from a good customer like you." Standing, he grinned shyly. A small amount of teenage acne reddened his chin. "I don't even know what half these things are for." He gestured toward the tiers of seasonings with names like Jump Up & Kiss Me Chipotle Hot Sauce and Purple Haze Psychedelic Hot Sauce.

"Neither do I," admitted Alexa, "but I'm learning." The forced but friendly smile she turned on the boy froze. There, just starting down the aisle, was the man she had seen before.

She stared. She didn't mean to; she couldn't help it.

But it was just as she had expected, just as she had known. His resemblance to Cole was superficial.

Of course it was. Cole Rappaport was dead.

This man was good-looking, maybe even more handsome than the man she had once loved so completely—and lost so catastrophically. Cole's jaw had not been quite so broad, and he hadn't had a cleft in his chin. His cheekbones had not been nearly so well defined, and his nose had been wider. His brows had been shaggier and more arched, not such a straight, hawkish line. And, of course, his dark hair hadn't been nearly as long as this man's, and there had been no hint of silver at Cole's temples.

The man caught her stare. His eyes widened for a moment, as if he somehow recognized her. But she was certain that he was a stranger.

As he drew closer, his expression, unsurprisingly, showed no hint of recognition. His shirt was open at the throat, revealing the beginning of a thatch of hair as dark as that on his head but curlier. His sleeves were full, in the manner of an old-time swashbuckler—an analogy that suited his broad-shouldered, tall physique. His brown eyes, as dark as the German bock beer she used in her special beef stew, seemed quizzical. Cole's eyes had been a similar shade....

One brow was raised, as though he was amused that a woman he didn't know was staring so unabashedly. "Hello," he said. His voice was deeper, more gravelly, than Cole's had been. "Do I know you?"

"Only if you're Cole," she blurted, realizing how inane that must sound.

"Not especially," he said. "I like air-conditioning in summertime. But I'm always willing to have a pretty lady warm me up."

The amusement she thought she had seen on his face before was now a knowing, sexy smile. What was he talking about? And then she realized he thought she had suggested he might be *cold*. She flushed. He obviously thought she was flirting, when that was the farthest thing from her mind.

Still, she studied that smile carefully. Cole had had one that was similar. A smile so sexy, it had made her want to follow him to the nearest secluded place—a park, a hidden wall—and make torrid love with him.

A smile that had convinced her to do just that, over and over....

"Forget it," she said. "I'm sorry, but you misunderstood. I didn't mean to stare. You reminded me of someone."

"Someone you like, I hope."

"I did," she admitted quietly. "But he's dead."

"Oh. I'm sorry."

"It's okay. It happened a while ago." Two very long, very painful years ago. "Anyway, I apologize for staring." Alexa turned away quickly and began to study the nearest shelves, hating the feeling of desolation that gripped her insides. *Oh, Cole.*

"Excuse me," the man said.

Alexa couldn't help looking at him one more time as he edged past Benjy, who was mopping the floor. His gaze wandered over the shelves as he apparently looked for something. He carried a plastic store basket in which a few items had been placed: toothpaste, oranges, a couple of bags of blue-corn tortilla chips. In a moment, he plucked a bottle of mild taco sauce from a shelf, and then continued down the aisle. She must have been mistaken about his gait. Not that it appeared unconfident, but it was slower, more deliberate—different from Cole's world-challenging one. And Cole would have considered anyone using mild sauce on Mexican food wimpy.

The stranger turned back to her once more. "See you," he said with a wave.

In your dreams, Alexa thought. She sighed. She didn't dare let the man think she was coming on to him.

She didn't even want to consider the consequences, if Vane thought she was flirting. She had other, more risky reasons to tempt his ire.

She forced herself to pull her list from her pocket and study it. She still needed milk and feta cheese. *That* was all she should be thinking about. She concentrated once more on her shopping.

A few minutes later, though, the man was at the checkout beside hers. She looked around. The lines at the other open ones were longer. In fact, there were a lot of people around, mostly strangers, though she often knew the patrons in the Juarez Gourmet Grocery. The new Skytop Lake Village shop had been open only a few months, but was already wildly successful with locals.

Alexa didn't want to move to another line, but she felt embarrassed around this man. And upset. She had tried so hard to put Cole out of her mind….

Stay cool, she commanded herself, ignoring the way her breath caught in her throat. Abruptly, she drew her gaze away.

In the next line over, ready to check out, was Marian Shelton, one of her neighbors. "Hi, Alexa," Marian said.

"How's the B & B business?" Fiftyish, Marian wore her black, curly hair in a frizzled mop about her head.

"Not bad," Alexa lied.

"You own a bed-and-breakfast?" It was the stranger talking. She recognized that rumbling deep voice from moments ago.

She turned slowly, sucking in her breath for fortitude. She pasted a bright smile on her face. "Yes," she said.

"The Hideaway By The Lake," Marian said. "It's the most charming inn around, with the absolute best lake view. And it's all the better because of Alexa's restaurant. She serves gourmet food there, you know."

A few months ago, if a friend had talked up her establishment and her cooking, Alexa would have been thrilled. But now…things were different.

"That sounds great," the man said. He held out his hand. "My name is John O'Rourke. I'm here on a vacation, and to scout out a possible place for a new store. I'm in home improvements—sales, mainly."

"How do you do, Mr. O'Rourke," Alexa said formally. "I'm Alexa Kenner." She didn't want to be rude so she took his hand. It was warm, and his grip was firm. Reassuring, somehow.

But his look was anything but reassuring. There was a blatant sensuality in the way his eyes captivated hers, almost familiarly.

She pulled her hand, and her gaze, away quickly. "I'm happy to say my inn is pretty full right now." She didn't want him to ask about a room. She wouldn't want to have to tell him no—not in front of Marian, who knew she still had vacancies. Marian, two doors down on the same side of the street, was the kind of neighbor who counted cars in the driveway. She would believe there was room for several more—and therefore several more guests.

But Marian didn't know what was happening at the inn. No one knew, except for Vane.

Alexa couldn't rent a room to anyone. It wasn't just because of the way this man had started, by his very presence, to unnerve her.

"Oh." O'Rourke's tone was noncommittal. Maybe he hadn't been about to ask for a room. She felt relieved…didn't she?

Marian finished making her purchases and left, thank heaven, before she could try harder to promote her neighbor. Picking up a magazine from beside the checkout, Alexa pretended to study it.

Soon, it was her turn. When she had paid for all her groceries, she wheeled her cart toward the automatic glass door.

"Wait!"

Moving out of the way of someone entering the store, Alexa turned at the voice, which was now becoming familiar. Too familiar. "Yes, Mr. O'Rourke?"

He took two strides before he stood beside her. He gripped a white plastic grocery bag in one large hand. He was tall, as tall as Cole had been.

"I'm John," he corrected, startling her.

Of course he couldn't read her mind. He was just being friendly, asking her to call him by his first name.

"Alexa, rent me a room. Please. I'll need it for a week or two."

"But—"

"I don't want to beg, but I will. I came to Skytop Lake for the *lake*. I told the travel agent that before I left L.A., but she stuck me in a perfectly awful place in the woods that's a mile away from the water."

Alexa tried again. "The thing is, John—"

"Plus," he interrupted with a devilish grin that somehow reminded her she was a living, breathing woman, "I'm scouting for an inn where a professional organization of salesmen I belong to can hold a meeting in a few months. If I like your place, and I'm sure I will, I can bring you some more business."

Darn it all! Marian was standing outside the door as it opened and closed, chatting with another woman but keeping an eye on John and her. Could she hear them? Alexa could hardly say to this handsome, disconcerting man, right in front of her neighbor, that she didn't want any more business.

And she *did* want more business. Much different business from the guests she had.

There were a couple of rooms that remained empty. Over the past miserable months, she had insisted on renting a room, now and then, to someone from outside if she had a good reason: a former guest, a friend of a former guest, a neighbor's relative. That allowed the pretense, at least, that everything was normal.

Normal? For her, turmoil had become normal.

She glanced outside as the door opened again. No one stood out there to stop her.

Still...her nerves tensed. Half unconsciously, she reached for the ostentatious diamond on her left hand— the damnable symbol of all that was wrong. She wasn't considering this because the man reminded her of Cole, was she? He *wasn't* Cole. He couldn't help her. She had to help herself.

"You should know our rates first," she waffled, glancing as a couple of teenagers moved past them. She quoted an amount that was higher than normal, but wasn't too far out of line.

"Done!" he said with no hesitation, though she saw his eyes follow her fingers to her engagement ring. A hint of a scowl furrowed his broad forehead, and there was no hint of his earlier sensuality when he caught her glance this time.

Good. At least he wouldn't get the wrong idea. She needed no further complications in her life. Her life was much too complicated as it was.

At his request, she gave him the address and directions. "I'll check out of my other place and be there in an hour."

Before she could change her mind, John O'Rourke headed out the door. "Fine," Alexa said with forced enthusiasm to his retreating back. "See you then."

Oh, Lord, she thought as she wheeled her cart slowly out the door. What had she done?

Despite her resolve to be calm and forthright, her knees grew weak as she approached one of the two large SUVs that Vane had insisted they needed for the inn. It was parked in a crowded area in front of the gourmet food store, the last of a row of busy shops in Skytop Lake Village.

Vane sat sideways in the driver's seat talking animatedly with his prize minion, Minos Flaherty, who was seated behind him.

Alexa took a deep breath. This wouldn't be easy, but she had to say something now. It would be much too embarrassing to have an argument in front of John O'Rourke when he appeared to claim his room. And with so many people around here, Vane was unlikely to make a big scene.

Vane spotted her. He immediately stopped talking and slipped out the door. A smile lit his face as he approached.

Vane Walters was a man who would make any woman look twice. He was not quite six feet tall and worked out daily, and his attention to his physique showed in the proud way he held himself. He wore a blue button-down shirt tucked into blue jeans. His dirty blond hair was combed carefully to hide the fact that his hairline had begun to recede, and the deep lines that underscored his brown eyes when he grinned made it appear that he had a great sense of humor.

Perhaps he did—at the expense of other people. Alexa included.

"Hi, darling," he said, and gave her a kiss full on the mouth. She forced herself to respond, even though she knew his attentiveness was for show. Once, his kisses had stirred her—some. She had cared for him, a lot. He had been so kind, so supportive...so deceitful.

She had wished fervently lately that she could simply end their partnership—and their engagement—like any normal woman would. But things were far from simple. And she had been warned.

"Hi," she responded with forced cheerfulness, stepping ever so slightly back. "Would you mind helping me put the groceries in the car?"

"Minos!" Vane called.

The smaller but even more muscular man, whom Vane had hired only a few months earlier, was surprisingly graceful as he leapt from the car and began unloading the cart. Another shopper pulled into the neighboring parking space and got out of her car.

This was the moment for Alexa to speak. She took a deep breath. "Guess what?" she said brightly, ignoring the nervous unevenness of her voice. "We've a new guest arriving tonight."

"What?" Vane stepped back and stared.

She could see the anger that lurked behind his eyes.

But a woman was helping a child out of the car beside theirs, and Alexa saw Vane glance in their direction.

Quickly, Alexa gave an embellished version of what had happened in the store. She ached to flaunt her defiance, but that could be too dangerous. Instead, she acted defensive.

"He's only planning to stay for a few days," she lied. "I could hardly tell him to get lost right in front of Marian. I think she knows him." Sure, that was a fib, but maybe it would fit the man into the group of outside guests whose presence Vane might accept. "It'll be pleasant to have someone new stay with us for a little while." She looked tellingly toward the mother and child as they walked toward the stores. "It's an inn, for heaven's sake," she murmured under her breath. "Whatever is going on, surely it would be better for the place to continue to resemble a normal B & B."

Vane was ten years older than Alexa's thirty-one, but his features were youthful so he usually didn't appear much older than she. Right now, though, his scowl made him look every bit his age.

She'd been wrong. He was going to make a scene, Alexa suddenly realized. Right here. Maybe he would even threaten her, as he did when they were alone.

She couldn't deal with it. Not now. Not here.

Impulsively, she grabbed him and gave him as big a kiss as he had just given her. Stepping back, she forced herself to smile. "I'm sorry," she said, meaning it because he worried her, and not because she otherwise regretted what she had done. "I won't do it again without consulting you. But I think it's a good thing, to make the inn look as busy as it used to."

"We'll see," Vane said. "Now get in the car."

Alexa turned and opened the vehicle's door. This was one command—of too, too many—that she would obey.

WHAT THE HELL had he expected? Cole Rappaport watched through the windshield while that little scene played out, his hands fisted on the steering wheel of the luxury car he had borrowed for this assignment.

Alexa and Vane.

Oh, he had known the facts before he'd gotten here. They owned that inn together. They were engaged—the woman he had once loved so consumingly, so profoundly, that he'd considered giving up everything for her, and the man he had considered almost a brother.

But he had been out of their lives a long time. Had allowed them to think he had disintegrated in that damn explosion. For their own good, or so he had believed.

The sound he made into the stillness of the car was more a bark than a laugh.

He watched as Alexa stepped into the late-model SUV, the way her jeans stretched tight over her well-shaped behind. He was fifty times a fool for noticing, but she still looked good. Too good, though he had noticed small wrinkles of strain at the corners of her wide blue eyes. Maybe she had missed him.

Maybe she felt guilty.

Right. And maybe he was really John O'Rourke here on vacation.

When they had been together, her golden-brown hair with its reddish highlights had either been caught up in a tight bun at the back of her head, or, when they were alone, loose around her shoulders. Today, it had been drawn back into a plastic clip at the base of her long, graceful neck.

She was thinner than he recalled. She wore a navy

work shirt over her jeans. Had he ever seen her before in anything less than designer slacks and silk blouses? When she was clothed, that is. He had seen her in a *lot* less, once upon a time.

Even now, his body tensed in recollection of the passion they had once shared. But he pushed it aside. He had a job to do, and that was the only reason he was here.

And it was a damn important reason.

He watched their SUV drive away, Alexa in the passenger seat talking earnestly to her fiancé.

Her fiancé. The man who had a right to kiss her like that. Cole had to remind himself of that little fact over and over, allow it to slice away at all the corners inside him that had eroded every time he had allowed himself, over the past couple of years, to think of Alexa. He needed every edge within him to be hard and sharp now.

He hadn't planned on running into her just yet, but the chance meeting had worked to his advantage. And he would need a lot of advantages here to achieve all he had to.

She'd apparently thought she knew him—then realized her mistake. He hadn't expected her to think he was Cole Rappaport, not with all the reconstruction done on his face after the explosion. It made disguise unnecessary.

Still, there was just the smallest bit of hurt clenching at his guts—hurt that had nothing to do with the residual, persistent pain from his injuries. A closer look had told her he wasn't Cole. She *hadn't* recognized him.

With an irritated snort, he lifted his cell phone from its stand on the console and pressed a single button.

"Bowman," said the familiar, curt voice at the other end.

"It's me. I've got a room reserved at the Hideaway

By The Lake.'' Cole hated talking on cell phones; they weren't secure. There was a lot more he could say to his boss and mentor, Forbes Bowman—the man who had saved his life—but this wasn't the time.

"Great" came the reply. "You have fun, hear? And check in now and then so I know you're still alive." The words, delivered in a hearty, amiable tone, could have been one friend talking to another. But Cole knew they were serious.

"Thanks," he said. "Are you still looking into that sales data I asked for?"

"Yep," Forbes replied. "I'll pass it on when I get it."

Of course the information Cole had requested had nothing to do with sales—and everything to do with his work here. "Later," he finished. He pushed the End button and replaced the phone in its slot.

Since there was no lodge he needed to check out of, he had time to kill before showing up at the Hideaway By The Lake. He started the engine and drove around the Skytop Lake Village shopping center until he located a small convenience store. He got out and went inside.

Good. In a quiet corner far from the checkout stand, there was a public phone. It would, he hoped, suit his purposes later, when he wouldn't trust the cell phone for what he needed to report to Forbes.

He glanced at his watch.

Soon it would be time for him to check in. To see Alexa and Vane on their home turf. To delve into the secrets they had kept from him two years ago, and the secrets they were keeping now.

Then, the fun would begin.

Chapter Two

Alexa carried the last bag of groceries into her professional gourmet kitchen. "Thanks, Minos," she said to the man in the sleeveless T-shirt and torn jeans who had helped her.

Vane had disappeared as soon as they had pulled into the inn's garage. Alexa figured he'd gone to socialize with some of the guests. He was good at that.

"No problem," Minos said, hefting two bulging plastic bags onto the tile counter with ease. The short man with the large muscles looked at her with stern brown eyes beneath thick, dark brows, as though expecting her to say something else. To do something he would consider reportable to Vane.

Alexa hid her shudder. Between Minos and Vane, she felt under surveillance every moment of every day. *She* should be watching *them*. Not to mention all of the inn's guests, every one of them here, she was certain, for some undivulged but nefarious purpose.

She'd seen similar deceitfulness before.

And when she had, the consequences had been unimaginably dire. Her parents had nearly lost their freedom.

She had irrevocably, horribly, lost Cole.

Minos hadn't moved. At least he couldn't stare into

her thoughts. She swallowed her sigh. "I'm going to be starting dinner now," she said with feigned cheerfulness. "If you want to hang around, I'll put you to work mincing onions."

"I've got things to do," he said irritably.

She was certain he did—whatever Vane assigned to him. And Alexa was sure none of it would benefit the inn. Or her.

Or the world.

As Minos left, Alexa considered her duties of the moment. She did have to start cooking. She also had to make sure a room was ready for her new guest.

John O'Rourke. He seemed like a nice enough man. A home improvements salesman.

Why had he reminded her of Cole?

Well, she knew just how much good wishful thinking had done her. Zilch.

No knight in shining armor would come to save her from her dilemma. No Cole Rappaport, or even a surrogate, would arrive to make things right.

She would have to do it herself.

She had already tried once to run to the authorities. Mistake! She had learned a valuable lesson about who had more credibility: Vane or her. It wasn't her.

And Vane had shown her then how he still could ruin her parents' lives. Her life, too—even more than it already had been ruined.

Her options were limited, but she did have options.

She hoped.

PULLING THE CAR over to a curb, Cole glanced again at the directions Alexa had given him, then back up.

There it was, the Hideaway By The Lake. It was a large Swiss-style chalet with a peaked roof. The rails around the wide second-floor balcony were cut out in a uniform, gingerbread pattern.

Between the house and its neighbor was a tall bougainvillea hedge that lent privacy. Beyond, he glimpsed glistening blue water. A vacant lot next door was crowded with white pine trees.

"Nice," he grumbled. He'd had no doubt that it would be.

Alexa had had good taste. Or so he had believed, until he had learned of her perfidy. Her betrayal.

And her engagement to Vane Walters.

Cole instinctively studied the rest of the street. Residential. Lined with resort-style houses of varying sizes— A-frames, small stucco haciendas—and all well-maintained. Not too close together, and a lot of secluding landscaping in between.

Plenty of places for someone to hide, though from what he gathered, no one was bothering to stay out of sight.

Just like last time.

Exiting the car, he popped the trunk and pulled out his single carry-on bag. He'd traveled light. He expected to be here for a while, but had no intention of worrying about how he dressed. The weight in his bag came from his laptop computer, some special equipment—and the Beretta 9 mm semiautomatic secreted in a hidden compartment.

The front door was large—carved black walnut. It was locked. Cole rang the bell, and in a moment Alexa answered.

"Mr. O'Rourke," she said as she opened the door. He started to correct her, but she beat him to it. "John. Come in, please." She stepped back, continuing to hold the door.

"Thanks." He was highly conscious of her nearness as he skirted around her, his bag in his hand. The top of her head reached to just above his shoulder, and she looked almost childlike with her hair pulled back that way.

Almost. For there was no mistaking her sensuous curves in that casual outfit.

Then there was the subtle citrus scent that wafted about her. A familiar scent. Even after two years, she hadn't changed that, at least. It reminded him of seduction. It reminded him of *her*.

He gritted his teeth. Okay, so he couldn't be completely detached. She had been a desirable woman. She still was. He had seen it, felt it deep in his gut, earlier that day.

But he was a grown man. He would keep his lust in check. Unless there was some way to use it to further his goals....

Once, he had been determined to succeed, but he hadn't been so much of an SOB as to cold-bloodedly engage in seduction to gain an advantage. Now, he wasn't so sure.

"Is there something wrong, John?" Alexa asked.

He watched her anxious gaze take in the room in the direction he'd been staring, as though she feared she had missed cleaning some noxious piece of dirt.

"Not at all." He pasted his most innocuous salesman's smile on his face and looked down into her troubled eyes.

Soft blue eyes. They were missing the teasing twinkle he remembered. Or had she lost it over the years, because of what happened? That would be a shame.

"This place looks charming," he continued hastily, turning away.

He wasn't lying, this time. The inn *was* charming. Its

entry was a combination lodge-like living room and hotel reception area, with high wood-beamed ceilings and a long, tall cedar desk along one wall. The tangy aroma of burnt wood emerged from a huge stone fireplace at one end of the room, although no fire blazed there now.

As he approached the registration desk, he was greeted by a dog. It was a German shepherd—a young one, still gangly and waiting for his thin body to catch up with the size of his long legs and large paws. But the animal must already have been well trained. He made no watchdog noises. No growls at the intruder that was Cole. No, *guest*. He was a paying guest here.

A guest with an agenda that his host and hostess would abhor.

Alexa stooped gracefully to hug the squirming puppy. "John," she said, "meet Phantom."

Cole froze. Phantom.

That had been Alexa's nickname for *him*.

For a moment, his guard lowered like a tinted car window opening to reveal the recent past. How he wanted to bring her to her feet and into his arms. To tell her who he was, why he was here, and damn the consequences.

Except that she had betrayed him once. She might not realize it now, but she was betraying him again.

And he could not allow her to get away with it. The stakes could be too high.

"What an interesting name," he said, hearing how tight his voice sounded. He cleared his throat, as if an allergy had caused moisture there—and not emotion. Cole Rappaport didn't let emotion interfere with what he needed to accomplish. Ever.

"I once had a…friend I called Phantom," Alexa said as she rose. She stared with her assessing blue eyes as if sizing him up once more. Assuring herself he wasn't that very *friend.*

Did she know? How could she?

Putting his friendly, salesman look back on his face, Cole said cheerfully, "And what did that friend do that made you give him that nickname?"

"He disappeared," she said. "A lot." Her tone was matter-of-fact, betraying none of the bitterness of their past disagreements.

Ostensibly, Cole had been on leave from the army during the months they'd known each other. He hadn't been able to tell her the truth. Now and then, he'd had to disappear, to follow a lead or report in person. When he'd returned, she never hesitated to express her anger that he hadn't bothered to explain, or even to say goodbye. She had loved him then, with all the ardor he had ever dreamed of in a beautiful, sexy—demanding—woman.

At first, he would let her vent. After a while, he'd scoop her into his arms. That way she could unleash her passion in a much more enjoyable way. He still recalled her taste when he touched his tongue to her cheeks, stopping her salty tears with small, sensuous licks that turned into the most volatile sexual encounters....

God, how he had loved her! He had believed she was an innocent in all that was happening.

"That man must have been a fool," Cole forced John O'Rourke to reply to Alexa. He nearly choked on the double meaning of the words. He *had* been a fool. But Alexa thought she was speaking about someone else, someone who wasn't the man before her. He continued, "No man with any brains would ever disappear from a pretty woman like you."

"Thanks," she replied almost curtly. "Would you like

me to show you the room I have available, before you check in?''

''Why not?'' he said. And then he froze.

Entering through the open doorway at the far end of the living room was Vane Walters. He was followed by three men. All short or balding, unprepossessing. The kind of people who could disappear easily in a crowd.

But Cole didn't take the time to study them thoroughly...now. His eyes were glued on Vane's.

He didn't blurt out the invectives that sprang to his lips. He was too well-schooled for that.

Alexa's quick step forward abruptly shifted Cole's gaze to her. ''John O'Rourke,'' she said, ''I'd like you to meet my partner at the Hideaway, my fiancé, Vane Walters.''

Was there a tremor in her voice?

Cole didn't look down at her. ''Hi, Vane,'' he said in a hearty salesman's voice. He approached Vane with his hand out and his heart beating faster. Alexa had seemed to recognize him before seeing him closer, talking to him. Would Vane?

''Hello,'' Vane said. He didn't look pleased to see the man whose hand he shook, but neither was there recognition in his stare.

''You've got a great place,'' Cole said. ''I'm glad you had a room available. Alexa's going to show it to me now.''

''Fine,'' said Vane.

Cole saw a look pass between Alexa and Vane. He couldn't interpret it. But then Vane glanced back at Cole.

''I hope you enjoy your stay here, Mr. O'Rourke.''

''John,'' Cole corrected. ''I'm sure I will.''

And he was equally sure that Vane—and Alexa—

would rue the day John O'Rourke ever took a room at the Hideaway By The Lake.

"IT'S PERFECT." John O'Rourke stepped behind Alexa into the cubbyhole of a room that she had opened for him. He was so large that his shoulders, beneath his loose green shirt, seemed to stretch from one oak-paneled wall to the opposite, painted one. At least his head didn't touch the high ceiling. But the bed was a normal-size double with a plain pine headboard, and Alexa suspected his feet would hang off the end—not that she intended ever to find out.

"You're sure it's all right?" Alexa tried to sound hopeful, though her real hope was that he would hate it. She had had angry words with Vane again as she had come upstairs to make sure the room was ready. He had reminded her of his acute displeasure with her by his glare a few minutes earlier. Maybe she had been wrong in picking this particular small rebellion. She had much larger ones to plan.

But first she had to figure out a way to protect her parents.

"I don't have any rooms available with a lake view," she continued, "and this one looks out on the neighbor's property." She pointed toward the window with the lacy curtains she had sewn herself.

"That's fine. I mostly wanted to be near the lake so I can jog beside it. Is that the bathroom?" He pointed toward a closed wooden door.

He was standing near her. She could almost imagine she felt his body heat mingling with her own....

Where had that thought come from?

"Yes," she said abruptly. "Would you like to see it?" *Alone,* she thought. *I'm not going to go show it to you.*

She felt her face redden. The thought of John O'Rourke in the small shower stall, naked and dripping and utterly, masculinely, erotically filling it, made her think yet again of Cole Rappaport. Showering with him. Making long, slow, wet love with him in a similar shower stall up here, in this inn at Skytop Lake where they had stayed together.

Just before he had died. And hell had broken loose.

The bubble that was her euphorically sensuous recollection burst abruptly. She had to get hold of herself. Her mind had been spiraling into chaos ever since she had first spotted this man, just because his stride had somehow reminded her of Cole.

John crossed the room and peered into the bathroom. He turned back, a pleasant smile on his much-too-handsome face. "It's great. I'll take it."

"Good," she lied, wishing now she had never agreed to let him have a room. She needed all her senses to be sharp, her mind keen. "Come downstairs to fill out the paperwork, then you can get settled. I have to work on dinner."

"That's right—the lady in the food store said you have a gourmet restaurant here."

Oh, please, she thought. *I don't want to see you this evening.* But at least he would provide a respite from the other guests whom she was required to serve. Still, she said, "Yes, though there are other good restaurants in the area. Don't feel obligated to—"

"I wouldn't want to eat anywhere else," he said.

He followed her out of the room. Behind her on the stairs to the main floor, he asked, "What's for dinner?"

"It's Mexican." Maybe he didn't like spicy foods. "I usually do two main dishes. The specialty tonight is chile rellenos, my own recipe—very hot. I also have quesadillas with beef and jalapeño cheese. Both are served with a seasoned taco salad.''

''All spicy?''

''Yes.'' *Please,* thought Alexa. *Tell me how much you detest things that are hot.* But turning to look at him, she suspected that this man was himself very hot. Fiery. Especially if he was anything like Cole. And maybe that ran to his taste in food, as well.

''There's nothing I like better than food that puts hair on my chest.''

Involuntarily glancing up toward the shock of black, curly hair peeking from the open V of his shirt, Alexa smiled uncertainly. *But what about the sauce you bought?* Alexa wanted to ask. *It was mild.* She said nothing. Instead, she fled down the rest of the steps.

COLE HAD UNPACKED his few belongings, hanging a couple of shirts in the handsome, carved teak wardrobe along one wall, finding places to conceal his equipment. He had begun to settle into his room at the inn. This inn that held so many bittersweet memories. Alexa's inn.

Alexa's…and Vane's. He could not allow himself to forget that it belonged to the two of them.

The two of them, together, now. And before.

The man he had loved like a brother…and the woman he had loved more than life.

Fortunately, though the room was small, it had its own phone, so he had been able to use the modem in his laptop. Sitting on the bed, on top of the homey chenille bedspread, Cole glared at the screen.

Not that he was surprised, after his earlier phone call, at the contents of the encrypted e-mail from Forbes Bowman that he'd just deciphered. But it made his stay here even more necessary.

He had come to Skytop Lake because of the latest intelligence from his most reliable overseas contacts. According to rumor, the terrorist operation that had supposedly ended with the blast meant to kill Cole had apparently been resurrected—and the trail led straight here.

Reports of several field agents had been due today, concurrent with Cole's arrival. According to Forbes's e-mail, they had hit only dead ends. There was no information yet on any similar operations anywhere in the country. Either this inn was the only location, or the agency's sources were not yet coming through.

Last time, there had been at least half a dozen havens for foreign terrorist agents sent for training and preparation for dispersal to strategic facilities all over the U.S. Maybe more. All the havens had been a part of the Kenner Hotels—the elite chain that had been owned by Alexa's family.

The elite chain that no longer existed, thanks to the events of two years ago.

Back then, Cole had been undercover, seeking to learn the terrorists' goal. He hadn't succeeded. All he had known was that every one of the agents had been highly trained in handling and detonating explosives. His group had speculated that each was to destroy some key U.S. facility—probably triggered all at once. But he didn't know which facilities. Or why.

This time, he would find all the answers. He would succeed.

He had a starting point, for he knew now that Vane Walters was involved, as he had been two years ago.

So was Alexa Kenner.

Alexa. Cole felt his heart grow cold. She was still so breathtakingly beautiful.

So deadly.

Unconsciously, he touched the cosmetic surgery scar at the side of his face, beneath his hair.

"Why, Alexa?" he whispered into the stillness of his room. Had she been in love with Vane even then?

Cole would never have thought there was someone more important in Alexa's life two years ago. Not with the passion they had shared.

So much had happened between them, both in Santa Monica, and most especially here, at Skytop Lake. At this very inn, though it had been very different then. More run-down.

Why had she bought this place with Vane? So she could laugh at how she had tricked Cole? Had seduced the foolish man, made love with him...killed him?

"Damn!" Cole clenched his fists so tightly that his hands immediately cramped. He loosened them and stared at his fingers, at the small red scars, nearly invisible now, that he had also incurred in the explosion. Recalled how excruciating the physical pain had been. His hands still ached. So did much of the rest of his body.

Alexa and Vane didn't know he had survived. He hadn't told them because he thought their ignorance would protect them.

Instead, it had probably protected *him*. From them.

He glanced again at Forbes's e-mail message. It ended with "We're counting on you."

Forbes had been there for him when the compost had hit the fan two years ago. Had pulled him from the garage set ablaze by the explosion. Had saved his life, and had helped to save his sanity.

No, Cole would not let Forbes down. He typed in a return message to his friend, then set the encryption software.

"Will report back soon," he wrote to his boss. "With something useful."

Chapter Three

There were only eight tables in Alexa's dining room overlooking the lake, the better for her to provide individual attention to all her guests.

Before.

Now, when customers called from outside the inn, the majority were told there were no reservations available, for meals or for rooms. A few exceptions were made most evenings so the place would still resemble a public restaurant. But those people were all served early, at six o'clock. The inn's guests ate at seven.

Then, Vane was the one to move from table to elegantly set table, the consummate host. Alexa's role was to provide the food and serve it with a smile, then fade back into the kitchen.

That was all right with her, at least most of the time. She didn't want to socialize with their guests. Though she was filled with questions, she doubted any of them would answer—even those who spoke English.

Putting food on the eight tables kept her busy—especially that night. She'd had a college-age kid helping until a few months ago. Now, only Minos helped to wait tables. She didn't know where he was that evening, only that he was not at the inn.

She didn't miss him.

When John came downstairs, it was seven o'clock. She should, perhaps, have called him down earlier, since he had made it clear he intended to eat there that night. Perversely, she hadn't. She wanted to see Vane's reaction to having this guest join the rest.

At the time John arrived, all tables were occupied. Vane had just gone into the kitchen to open a bottle of wine.

Alexa approached John at the dining room door. "Sorry," she said. "I'm afraid we're full." She felt self-conscious in the long, lacy apron she wore over her black slacks and sleeveless sweater. Though she was a gourmet cook, she was far from a neat one.

"That's okay." His eyes ranged over her, making her feel even more uncomfortable. But he raised his brows as if in appreciation and smiled. "My compliments to the chef."

"You haven't eaten anything yet." She felt herself redden.

"I will." He approached one of the tables. "Mind if I join you?" he asked two of the B & B's guests, a young couple who sat at a table for four.

The two glanced at one another, then at the guests seated at the next table. Neither seemed certain what to do.

Apparently etiquette won out over whatever else warred inside them. "Please," said the man, gesturing toward an empty seat. His accent was heavy, but Alexa didn't know where he was from. His hair was dark, as was his complexion. Annoyance glowed from eyes too close together over a long, broad nose.

His female companion's mahogany eyes took in John,

who had dressed in a light blue sports shirt. She apparently liked what she saw, for she smiled.

The seductive smile annoyed Alexa. She was even more annoyed when John smiled back.

"I'm John O'Rourke." He held out his hand.

His new companions gave their names, Ed and Jill Fuller. That was how they had registered, but Alexa suspected that the names were false.

When Vane reentered the dining room, his gaze landed on John. His demeanor grew stiff as he approached the table. "Everything okay?" he asked, including John O'Rourke in his gaze.

But Alexa knew the question was for Vane's guests.

And if things were not okay with them, she knew who would pay. She tensed, recalling her earlier thought about wanting to see Vane's reaction. *Fool*, she chided herself. Had she thought he'd be pleased?

But he might have been less irritated if John had been sitting by himself.

Before Ed Fuller could respond, Jill said, "All is good. We are friends here, yes?"

"Absolutely." John winked at the woman.

It was Alexa's turn to go rigid, but even with her stiff shoulders, she went about serving the others in the dining room.

Alexa kept an eye on Vane, as he watched that particular table. Closely. Now and then he joined the group.

If only Alexa could eavesdrop. In the low rumble of dinner chatter from all the other tables, she only caught snatches as she took orders, served food and cleared dishes. Was Vane making mental notes, preparing to take out on Alexa later any displeasure registered by his guests?

"Where are you from?" she heard John ask Jill, when Vane was at the far side of the room.

"I am from Bolivia," she said very slowly and distinctly, in an accent that did not, in Alexa's estimation, resemble Spanish.

If John thought he was being lied to, he didn't show it. "You speak English well."

"Not so good," she replied with a self-deprecating smile that made it clear she enjoyed John's attention.

Her husband was clearly displeased when he jumped into the conversation. "We are learning here to speak good," he said, sounding defensive.

"I know how hard that can be," John said. "Learning different languages is not something I'm good at. And believe me, I've tried." His amiable grin encompassed both his companions. Ed Fuller's glare eased a little.

"How did you try?"

Jill's distinct and deliberate speech would have driven Alexa crazy if she'd been sitting with them. She gathered dirty soup bowls from a neighboring table, taking her time to prevent being obvious in her listening.

"I was a foreign exchange student in high school. I went to Switzerland, the French-speaking part. In return, my family had three different exchange students stay in our house for a few months at a time. I did a lot better helping them with their English than my host family did teaching me French." Again he grinned, this time with an embarrassed shrug of his very broad shoulders— shoulders Jill apparently noticed, for her admiring smile was more feline than friendly.

Alexa refrained from slinging a bowl at the woman. It wasn't her business if the guests chose to make fools of themselves. And a woman's flirting with a man, no matter how great-looking and sexy he was, right in front of her husband—well, that was definitely foolish.

Unless they weren't really married….

John took some taco chips that Alexa had baked from scratch, from a basket on the table. He barely looked at them as he dipped them in homemade salsa. That annoyed Alexa. She scooped up her handful of dishes and hurried into the kitchen. There, she ladled bowls of tortilla soup for John's table. She had made it spicy. Now, she considered adding even more chili pepper to John's. That would divert his attention from Jill Fuller.

Phantom was watching. In deference to keeping the food preparation sanitary, she blocked him into an adjoining room with a removable gate. As always, she spoke softly to him, and he greeted her in return by chuffing and dancing and wagging his tail.

"I'll give you a big hug later," she promised.

"Do you need any help, Alexa?" Vane stood in the doorway, his arms crossed. He appeared irritated.

She realized he wasn't really offering help, just criticism. She was too slow tonight.

She had to stop allowing John O'Rourke to distract her.

"No, thanks, Vane," she said. She picked up the tray with three soup bowls on it and hurried toward him. "I'm fine. Go ahead and entertain our guests."

But he didn't budge. As she approached him, he said through gritted teeth, "It appears that your friend O'Rourke is doing a good job of entertaining all by himself."

Waves of panic shot up Alexa's spine, but she stood still, balancing the awkward tray. "Yes," she said with a forced smile. "He's a salesman, and I guess salesmen like to talk."

"This one likes to ask questions. Too many questions. I think we'd better suggest that he find someplace else to stay."

In other words, *she* was to urge John to leave. Quickly.

"I don't think he intends to stay long, anyway." A little continued prevarication wouldn't hurt, she hoped. She could tell Vane later that she hadn't understood John's intentions.

But she liked having someone around who was here just because he wanted to be. As if this place were still an innocent inn.

As long as she was the only one Vane threatened, she wouldn't insist that John leave. But if the threats were ever leveled at the man she had encouraged to come here, she would get him out. Fast.

"I'll hold you responsible if any of the other guests feel uncomfortable with your friend, Alexa."

Vane's icy frown made her want to cringe, and she was relieved when he pivoted and left the kitchen.

Alexa put down the tray for a moment and sagged against the center island. Her legs were shaking. Damn! This was no way to live.

She *wouldn't* live this way much longer, she promised herself. As soon as she had what she needed to protect her parents and herself, she would escape.

Alexa would have sacrificed herself, and even her parents, if it would have done a damn bit of good. But it wouldn't. Vane had made that clear.

She picked up the tray once more and entered the dining room. Vane had joined some guests across the room and didn't even glance her way. Alexa served Jill Fuller a bowl of steaming soup first, Ed second and John last.

"This smells great," John said. "What kind is it?" She told him. He turned to his dinner companions. "Have you ever eaten tortilla soup before? I'm not sure what Bolivian cuisine is like.''

Ed Fuller appeared confused by John's question. Patiently, John rephrased it. Jill was the one to reply, but Alexa didn't hear her answer.

''Ms. Kenner?'' called a less heavily accented voice. Another guest, a few tables away, was holding up an empty wineglass. It was obvious what the man with the wrinkled face and demanding voice wanted, but Vane, seated at an adjoining table, just nodded curtly toward Alexa. Hiding her annoyance, she hurried to refill the customer's glass.

Alexa was too busy after that to do more than catch snatches of the conversation at John's table.

''This is a soup spoon,'' John said once, holding up the utensil. ''This is a teaspoon.'' The others at his table repeated the names.

He was teaching them English!

What did Alexa expect from a personable salesman? A former exchange student who could empathize with people who didn't understand the language in a strange country.

Several of Vane's guests spoke English well. Many didn't. Alexa suspected they all were terrorists, just like the last time. She had learned that after the fact, during the horror following Cole's death.

She had recognized the possibility this time, as soon as Vane started bringing in his own guests—all together, all foreign, all with identification that didn't seem to fit. But for the moment, there wasn't anything she could do about it—not without wrecking her parents' lives. What was left of her own, too.

She needed Vane's damn file.

She *would* find it. And more… Soon.

A short while later, Alexa prepared to bring a serving of chile rellenos to John and his companions. She glanced down at the plates. The filled chile peppers were mounded with spicy Mexican-style rice and covered with sizzling cheese.

John had claimed he liked spicy foods. If he didn't, that fact would come out now.

When she brought out the steaming dish, John was leaning over, conversing with two older men at the next table. It wasn't enough for him to make friends with the Fullers. He was branching out.

"And what brings you to Skytop Lake?" he asked the closer of the two.

"Ah...pleasure." The white-haired man with an underslung jaw had almost no accent. "I am here on holiday."

"And you're on vacation, too?" John said to the other man. "Where are you from?"

"New York" was the curt, precise reply that belied the answer. "Here comes your meal," the thin, wrinkled man added, looking toward Alexa.

John turned toward her, as she put the plate in front of him. "This looks wonderful," he told her. He inhaled deeply. "Smells wonderful, too."

"It *is* wonderful," she replied. "You'd better enjoy it."

He grinned and used his fork to cut off a hefty piece. He took a bite. She expected his eyes to water, but they didn't. She felt her eyebrows lift. Even *her* eyes watered when she had tasted the meal in the kitchen, and she was a true aficionado of spicy foods.

"It's great!" John said, and took another mouthful.

So what if he'd bought a mild salsa at the gourmet food shop? He obviously liked things hot.

Cole had liked things hot, too....

Alexa glanced around the room. Vane was staring at them. She didn't like the fractious gleam in his eye.

She escaped into the kitchen, greeting the eager Phantom, who wriggled behind his gate, with a quick pat before she washed her hands again.

When John had finished and signed for his meal, she expected him to go into the parlor with Vane and the rest of the guests. Instead, he joined her in the kitchen.

"You look as though you could use some help. How about a dishwasher? I work cheap."

"How cheap?"

"You can't get cheaper than free."

"But—" Before she could voice any objections, he had tied a plain, lace-free apron around his waist and dug into the pile of dishes mounded in and around the sink. "You don't need to get them spotless," she said resignedly. "Just scrape the visible food off and pile them into the dishwasher."

"Good. I have to admit, I'm not the world's best dishwasher, only its best home improvements salesman."

"And bull thrower." She felt her mouth quirk into a grin.

"Ah, you were listening in on some of my conversations in the dining room," he said with an arch smile. "I thought so."

As usual in his presence, Alexa flushed. "You don't want me to have eavesdropped. If I did, I'd know how nosy you are."

"Nosy? Me?" The tone of his deep voice feigned hurt.

"I heard more questions from you than on a TV game show."

"I'm darn good at games," he said with a raise of one straight, dark brow and a roguish curve to his lips.

"I'll bet you are." Had he meant the suggestive undercurrent to his words? Alexa was nearly certain he had.

How was she going to get through the rest of the evening here, with this man interrupting her work, her thoughts? Her kitchen was large, but his presence made it seem as tiny as his bedroom.

Hadn't she thought only a few minutes before how foolish it was for a married woman to flirt with another man in front of her husband? Whether she liked it or not, Alexa was engaged. Her fiancé was in the next room.

She glanced at the ring that weighed her hand down as if the stone it held was lead rather than a huge diamond. She didn't dare end the engagement yet. It would be playing with fire for her to defy Vane...now.

She would be playing with fire by flirting with John.

She couldn't exactly throw him out bodily. Nor did she want to touch that substantial body to try...did she? He wore navy trousers with his lighter blue shirt, and they looked great on him. His movements with the dirty dishes were decisive but deft. She had no fear that he'd fumble and drop them, despite the large size of his hands.

What would it feel like to have those hands stroking her...?

Why was she thinking such thoughts?

Whatever else Vane was, he had been a gentleman about not pushing her to have sex when she wanted nothing to do with him. And she'd wanted nothing at all to do with him for the months since he had seized control of their inn.

But John had reminded her of Cole. The very recollection of Cole dredged up yearning, libidinous feelings that she had kept hidden deep inside for ages.

Forcing her thoughts back to reality, she continued

cleaning, trying to pretend John wasn't there. That was hard to do, as he helped her stack dishes in the industrial-size dishwasher.

His curiosity had seemed unbridled as he had tossed questions to Vane's guests. Vane had noticed, which wasn't good. John had also been kind to work with the couple at his table, teaching them English.

John O'Rourke, surprisingly sexy home improvements salesman, was a man of many facets.

Eventually, they were finished with the dishes. "Thank you," she said.

"Anytime." He went to the shelves where she kept seasonings, and eyed them. "Looks like you're partial to hot stuff."

"The hotter the better," she said.

It was his turn to look at her in surprise. He leered, then laughed. "A woman after my own heart," he said, then left the kitchen.

ALEXA TOOK HER TIME putting the mounds of cookware away, making lists of dishes for the next day's meals and ensuring she had the ingredients…ordinary activities. Or activities that would have been ordinary had the circumstances been normal.

The truth was, she was trapped here, at her own bed-and-breakfast. She knew Vane was involved in something at best illegal, at worst malevolent. The guests—possibly terrorists—had all been invited by him…except one. And that guest was a puzzle, too.

Surrounded by people, Alexa was alone. She could trust no one. She could rely only on herself.

When she couldn't think of further excuses to stay in the kitchen, she released Phantom from behind the gate.

She knelt to give the cute, intense puppy a big hug, then rose. "Come on," she said, leading him out.

She hadn't intended to go into the parlor. She did not want to mingle with the people Vane had brought here. But she spied John in a hard-backed seat in the midst of them. They were grouped on the overstuffed sofa and assortment of chairs, all turned to face one wall so they could watch television—all the better to perfect their use of U.S. customs and language, she surmised. They congregated together like this a lot.

For just a moment, she leaned on the doorjamb to observe—because she was curious, she told herself, and not because she had any interest in studying John. Phantom lay at her feet. The crowd had the TV tuned to a quiz show, something called "Millions on Your Mind"—a clone of several other popular programs. Cheers and catcalls erupted from the small crowd of viewers in her house. What were they up to?

"It's koa wood," cried John, his large frame raised from the chair. "From Hawaii. That's the answer." He lifted his hands and swatted the air, as if he were somehow tossing his knowledge to the contestant on the TV screen.

"Are you certain?" asked Jill, who sat beside him—of course. "Ko-a?"

"Yes. It's a great shade of golden red when it's polished, and has a unique grain. That's definitely it."

Alexa felt the chile rellenos that she had hurriedly downed in the kitchen begin to churn in her stomach. Koa wood. *Wood.*

Cole Rappaport had been an expert on trees. When they had come here to Skytop Lake, he had pointed out the various types of pine trees, including ponderosa, Coulter and white, plus some of the most common de-

ciduous trees—Pacific dogwood, white alder, California
black oak. He had been able to tell them apart by their
size and shape, their bark, their leaves. Plus, he had described what their grain was like inside.

Cole would have known the answer to this quiz show
question, too. Cole knew everything about trees.

An icy shiver passed through Alexa. She studied John
once more. Yes, she still saw some resemblance to Cole,
but it was all superficial—height, build. And handsome?
Oh, yes. Definitely. Incredibly. But he didn't look like
Cole.

And Cole, whether she could accept it or not, was
dead.

ALEXA COULDN'T SLEEP that night. Instead, she stood
outside her bedroom, on the balcony at the rear that ran
the width of the B & B's second story and matched the
one at the front of the house. She did not bother to flip
on its light, preferring to stay in the dark.

Preferring not to advertise her presence, for she did not
want any uninvited company—namely Vane.

She knew she lost money by not making available to
guests one of the few bedrooms that opened onto the
balcony, with its lake view. Vane had argued with her
about it from the very first. But she had been firm. Keeping it to herself was worth any cost…especially now.

It gave her peace, or at least as much peace as possible
during this incredibly difficult time.

She leaned on the rail and watched lights from surrounding residences play along the patches of rippling
water visible through the trees. The air was fragrant with
the scent of pine blowing in the mountaintop breeze. She
shivered a little in the coolness, gathering her long terry-
cloth robe more closely about her.

"Beautiful view," said a deep masculine voice, startling her.

She pivoted. John O'Rourke had just come through the door to the center hallway of the B & B's upper floor. He was still dressed in the clothing he'd worn at supper.

And he was looking at her, not the lake.

Alexa pretended not to notice. "Yes, it is."

Her blessed solitude had been abruptly terminated. But to her surprise, she didn't mind.

He joined her at the rail, clasping his hands together and leaning on his arms. She was aware of his closeness. The warmth from his body radiated toward her—or was it her own sexual awareness of this gorgeous, sensual man that caused her to burn?

She was also aware of how he stared deeply into the darkness, as if trying to see into the myriad shadows between the trees and the house. What was he looking for?

"You can't sleep?" he asked without looking at her. Another of his many questions.

She shook her head. "I've a lot on my mind. And you?"

"The same." He glanced at her, but only momentarily. "I'll tell you mine if you'll tell me yours."

"Tell you what?" She felt suddenly jittery. What did he want to know? And why did he stare at the neighborhood like that, as if expecting to see something that didn't belong?

"Whatever's keeping you awake."

She made herself laugh. Attempting to regain the teasing familiarity they had shared as they had worked on the dinner dishes, she answered flippantly, "A guilty conscience."

John turned to her so abruptly that she took a step backward, her hands up for protection. In the faint light from the neighboring properties, she had no trouble making out the sharpness to his glare.

"And just why would that be?" His wide lips softened just a bit at the edges, as if he struggled to smile, to soften the harshness of his question.

Her attempt at levity so obviously unsuccessful, Alexa shrugged beneath her robe. She lowered her hands and looked out again over the shimmering water of the lake. "Just a figure of speech," she replied softly.

Why had he gotten so upset?

John suddenly grasped Alexa's arms, turning her to face him. His grip was firm, insistent, just short of hurting her. His hands released her quickly, but his gaze didn't. His eyes seemed to glow in the faint light on the balcony, as if they had a source of illumination of their own.

"Alexa," he said in a surprisingly soft and sympathetic voice, "I...I sense something here. Something not quite right. If you'd like to talk about it, I'm a good listener."

"You're imagining things," she said quickly.

"Am I?"

For a brief, crazy moment, she considered blurting out everything. What had happened two years ago. How the terrors of the past had somehow been resurrected right here, at the haven she had turned to in an attempt to put it all behind her.

How she feared what Vane was up to. How alone she felt, how responsible and scared.

How badly she missed Cole Rappaport.

She bit her bottom lip to prevent it all from spilling from her. She looked up into John's curious and kind gaze.

He was a salesman. A people person. He seemed outgoing, yet full of empathy.

Could he help her?

No, shouted a voice inside her. *You're still mistaking him for Cole. He's not here to save you.*

You have to do that yourself.

She *was* alone here, in the midst of all these people. And she didn't dare forget it.

"There's nothing," Alexa said firmly, though she glanced away from the inquisitiveness and sympathy in John's eyes. "Nothing at all."

"If you change your mind," John said, "all you have to do is—"

"Alexa!"

She turned to the glass door to the house. It slid open, and Vane stood there, fully dressed, as if he had been out somewhere.

"I've been looking for you," he said, his tone almost accusatory.

"Sorry," she said. She glanced toward John, intending it to be firm but apologetic. Hoping, for her own sake, to see in his continued stare the sympathy she had noticed before.

Instead, his glare had turned furious. But why? Alexa shivered as she turned to accompany her fiancé back into the house, but it wasn't the night air that chilled her.

Chapter Four

Cole got out of his borrowed car and stretched his jeans-clad legs.

The area around Skytop Lake lived up to its name today. It was August, well into summer, and the mountaintop community that extended high into the air was baked by the brilliant sun.

Resting one arm, bare beneath his T-shirt, against the vehicle's roof, Cole squinted, using the opportunity to glance around the Skytop Lake Village shopping center—including the entrances to the blacktop parking lot.

He recognized no one, saw no familiar vehicles. Good. That was no guarantee he hadn't been noticed, that he wasn't being followed, but he would remain alert.

He glanced at the calm, sparkling lake, visible between buildings, then entered the convenience store where he'd checked out the pay phone the day before. Its air-conditioning was working overtime so the entire store seemed as cool as the inside of the glass-fronted refrigeration units lining the walls. The place was nearly empty, and the phone was not in use. This must be his lucky day.

He made a skeptical noise that only he, and not the long-haired teenage girl behind the register, could hear.

Luck? He had run out of it at least two years earlier. Now, he operated on instinct and wiles.

He shunned all feeling. Feeling meant pain.

Pain for the loss of the man he had once considered a brother: Vane.

Pain at seeing Alexa again. Knowing what she was. Wanting her, anyway, with a deep, gut-wrenching desire.

He strode single-mindedly toward the pay phone, punched in the numbers for his credit card and waited.

"Bowman."

"It's me, Forbes. I'm on a pay phone—not secure, but unlikely to be tapped."

"Good. What have you found out?"

Cole could picture his friend and mentor sitting at his desk in his office in Washington, D.C.

Not the Pentagon, though their elite counterterrorist detachment had evolved as a Special Forces Unit that incorporated agents from all military branches. It was smaller, sleeker and more secretive than the elusive Delta Force, with the mission of infiltrating terrorist groups to terminate them. Despite being military, its members were constantly so far undercover that they seldom wore uniforms.

They called their group, simply, the Unit.

Forbes had insisted on a small, inconspicuous rented office for the Unit along E Street, between the areas that housed the FBI and the White House. "The better to keep us humble and alert," Forbes had said when he had first shown it to Cole.

"I haven't found out much yet," Cole replied now to his boss's question. "I'm still getting the layout of the place. The inn is fairly small. I'll need to hack into the computer to get information about the guests, but I suspect it's all a cover, anyway."

"How many are there?" Forbes's voice was gruff and in-your-face, as always. Cole's silver-haired mentor was nearing retirement age, though he was likely to be hauled from the Unit screaming and kicking—using the most injurious of self-defense maneuvers. As old as he was, he would do damage to guys much younger. Forbes was a large man—nobody's fool, nobody's wimp.

"Sixteen, I think," Cole said. "At least, that's how many appeared for dinner last night."

"And was it a good meal?" Forbes asked sarcastically.

"The best." The food *had* been great. It had been cooked by Alexa. Her graceful, slender hands had prepared it and served it. Hands he recalled touching him, once upon a time, so erotically—

He shifted and leaned against the wall.

"You still there?" Forbes demanded.

"Sure." Cole forcibly refocused his thoughts. "I talked to a few, and most spoke excellent English. I happened to sit at a table with a couple of exceptions. They claimed to be from Bolivia."

"Bolivia?" Forbes snorted.

"More like Libya. Anyway, their training is well under way. I didn't see anyone using utensils in anything other than the good old U.S.A. method of both cutting food and eating with the right hand. I joined the group for television afterward, and some even knew the language well enough to guess at game show answers."

He had also seen Alexa at the door, and had lived dangerously. Tempted fate, and her memory.

From the corner of his eye, he had seen her grow pale when he had answered a question about a tree. Did she remember Cole Rappaport's knowledge about trees? Did she somehow associate John O'Rourke, home improvements salesman extraordinaire, with the man she had helped to kill?

"Damn." Forbes's voice interrupted his thoughts. "If those suspects are doing that well, it means they're nearly ready."

"Could be. You got anything for me? Has anyone else reported finding other locations yet?"

"Not yet. You're on your own. It all depends on you."

"How can that be?" Cole demanded. "After last time, we know there has to be a host of agents ready to go underground."

"Maybe they changed tactics," Forbes said. "Numbers got them nowhere, after all."

"But the intelligence I learned in the field—"

"Never mind what's going on elsewhere," Forbes insisted. "I'll handle that. You just figure out what's happening there, hear?"

"Yes, I hear you. What about backup? Are you sending anyone here from the Unit to follow this crowd when they disperse? I already told Maygran and Bradford to expect your call."

Colonel Jessie Bradford and Major Allen Maygran were a couple of Cole's most trusted co-agents in the Special Forces Unit. They were among the very few who knew who he really was, for Cole used yet another alias within the Unit. Both had only recently joined other special operations military units. Vane would not know them.

"I've told you before to let me handle the details." Forbes did not sound pleased, although he seldom did. "But, yes, I'm working on getting together an inconspicuous crew to join you there soon."

"Good." Cole drew in his breath suddenly, as a familiar figure walked into the convenience store: Minos

Flaherty. The squat, muscular thug had not been at the inn last night, and Cole hadn't been in a position to figure out where he may have gone. He had half hoped that the guy had disappeared for good—but only if he had taken a long dive over a short Skytop cliff. If he had simply disappeared, as all the guests were expected to do soon, it could mean that the operation was commencing before Cole was ready to deal with it.

"Hey, you there? Er, John?" Forbes stumbled over Cole's name on this assignment.

"I'm here." Cole kept his voice low. "I've got to leave, though."

"Someone there?" Forbes's tone was urgent.

"Yes. I'll be in touch."

"Do that. And watch your butt." Cole heard a *click* on the other end.

His butt? Oh, yes. Cole had every intention of protecting that and every other part of his body.

Alexa's lovely face loomed suddenly in his mind, and he shut it out.

But for an aching moment, he realized that the most vulnerable part of him could still be his damn, foolish heart.

ALEXA OPENED THE DOOR from the kitchen to the inn's backyard—and the ground-floor vista overlooking the gorgeous blue splendor of Skytop Lake. At the shore, a long dock extended into the water. The inn's motorboat was tied alongside.

Around the lake, evergreen trees rose in thick glades covering the sides of the surrounding mountain ridges. Many trees were ponderosa pines. Cole had taught her that, on their wonderful, fateful weekend here. The last time they had been together....

She inhaled deeply. The heated air was so damp that she nearly had to take a sip of it.

"Come on, Phantom," she called behind her. The lanky German shepherd pup sped by her and out the door. He ran to the side of the house, out of her field of vision. "Wait!" she called. Phantom didn't return but started to bark.

The noise seemed magnified near the water, which also carried sounds of motorboats in the distance. Alexa ran along the top of the down-sloped lawn to the area where the noisy pup had disappeared. And stopped.

Phantom was barking because there was an intruder. No, not an intruder—a guest.

John was on the lawn beside the inn. He had stooped, and his hand was out toward Phantom, who hadn't yet stopped barking, though he had previously met John. John grinned and made soothing sounds. His substantial biceps flexed as he continued to reach toward the excited dog.

Alexa hurried to join them. "Enough," she scolded Phantom. "Sorry," she said to John. "He's trained not to bark much inside, but the outdoors is fair game." She knelt and gathered the pup to her. Only then did he stop barking. Instead, he struggled in Alexa's grasp, turning in her arms to slurp at her chin with his long tongue. Alexa laughed, then stood.

"I didn't mean to get his dander up."

John rose, too. His white T-shirt hugged every bulge of his well-formed chest. Alexa pretended not to stare at John but at his shirt. It had an outline of a mountain on it, and the logo read Skytop Lake. Reach for the Stars.

She wanted to reach for *him*. Especially with the way his deep brown eyes moved down her appreciatively, obviously taking in the fact that she, too, wore a T-shirt. Hers was over shorts, and his gaze lingered on her legs.

His eyes returned to her face, and she looked away quickly, ignoring the oozing warmth spreading through her, a heat that had nothing to do with summer in the mountains.

"He thinks he's a watchdog," Alexa said quickly, bending down to take Phantom's collar. She was curious as to what John was doing here, practically standing in the flower bed, but figured he was a paying guest and had the right to be anywhere on the grounds he wanted— or at least any public place. "If you were heading for the lake, there's a paved path on the other side of the house."

"I know. I went there at sunrise this morning to jog beside the lake."

"You'd said that was why you wanted to be here," Alexa acknowledged. She pictured this large man clad in a similar outfit to what he was wearing now, muscles straining as he ran. Sweat would bead on John, for even at dawn the summer air would be warm and humid.

She recalled how Cole had looked after an early-morning run here: damp and well-toned and as sexy as sin. She swallowed. *Stop thinking of Cole,* she ordered herself. But she might as well tell her lungs to stop breathing.

"I'm out here now because I can't resist an opportunity," John said.

"For what?"

"To pitch home improvements. Your inn is great. I love the chalet style. But did you realize it could use a coat of paint?"

Alexa nearly choked. This guy really was a home improvements salesman. No matter how good he looked, no matter how much he knew about tree trivia, he wasn't Cole.

Cole had been in the military. He'd had a can-do attitude. He wouldn't have told her that the inn needed paint. He'd have bought buckets and brushes and begun painting.

When she had been here with Cole, this place had needed more than a coat of paint, but it hadn't belonged to her.

"I'm aware it needs a little work," she answered dryly. Vane and she had fixed it up when they had first bought it a year-and-a-half ago. Had kept it up, too—for a while.

Then Vane had lost interest in the inn, at least as anything other than a place to further his scheme. He discouraged Alexa from spending money on it.

"Actually," she continued, hearing the defiance in her tone, "I plan to paint it at the end of the summer." She wasn't certain where that had come from. This place was hers, even if Vane was her partner.

But the likelihood was that to survive, she would have to leave it behind.

"Maybe I can come back and help," John said. "I enjoy painting. But this place is really nice. Have you ever considered expanding? Opening a chain of hotels?"

Alexa felt herself blanch. She stared at John. Did he know who she was? Who her parents were? Or was it an innocent enquiry?

"My family used to own a hotel chain," she said. "It got too…unmanageable. They're down to one now, in Arizona. I want to keep things simple, too." If only they *were* simple.

"Sorry. I didn't mean to pry." John took a step toward her. "Alexa, I still get the feeling that there's something wrong. If you ever want a shoulder to cry on, I've got two I can lend.''

Two very broad, substantial shoulders. And, heavens, how much Alexa wanted to take him up on his offer. Her eyes moistened. She hadn't allowed herself to cry for a long, long time.

But she caught herself. Almost laughed aloud. This was a very nice man. Kind and compassionate, a people person by profession.

But she could not lean on anyone.

And care for someone? She nearly snorted aloud. She had cared for Cole—deeply—and he had died. She had allowed herself to care, just a little, for Vane, and he had proven to be a monster.

''Thanks,'' she said brightly. ''I'll remember that.''

Phantom suddenly stood at attention. Alexa looked in the direction of his gaze. Toward the lake.

Minos Flaherty stood on their dock. He was back, damn it.

What was worse, he was staring straight at them. Vane would get a report.

And Alexa was certain she would pay for this very brief, very innocent, interlude with the kind and sexy John O'Rourke. At best, he might threaten her parents again. At worst, he would harm them, or her...or both.

COLE DID NOT FOLLOW ALEXA into the house right away. He watched as Minos Flaherty strode up the grassy slope directly toward him.

Cole didn't like the guy. Didn't trust him.

But John O'Rourke liked everyone. And so, Cole plastered a welcoming smile on his face. ''Hi,'' he called.

The short man didn't return the smile. He just nodded.

He seemed to be sizing John up. He didn't appear impressed.

That made Cole want to have some fun at the truncated thug's expense. He pointed up toward the house. "Are you the handyman here? You might want to recommend a new paint job. I was just discussing it with Alexa."

Startled, he realized he was behaving as if Alexa had needed an excuse to be with him. As if she needed protection.

But that was ridiculous. She had to be part of the plot.

"I'll tell Vane you said so." Minos glanced toward the structure looming beside him and grimaced, as though the thought of fixing it up gave him ulcers.

"Thanks. And if you want any other suggestions about improvements—" He didn't get to finish, as Minos disappeared behind the inn.

Cole stifled his laugh. He walked toward the B & B's front entrance and went in.

His laughter turned to bitter bile as he saw Alexa held tightly at Vane Walters's side. They stood by the inn's registration desk. Phantom explored the adjoining parlor, his nose to the rug.

Vane was talking with some of the guests, a middle-aged couple who had been at the far side of the room at dinner the previous night. He turned toward Cole. "Oh, Mr. O'Rourke," he said. "Do you know this area well? I was just telling the Smiths, here, about Skytop Lake Village."

"I know my way around," Cole replied coolly, studiously avoiding Alexa's eyes.

That attitude would not do. John O'Rourke, home improvements glad-hander, would never sulk.

"I know how to get there, at least," he continued in a lighter tone. "That was where I ran into your very kind fiancée yesterday.'' He smiled warmly at Alexa. She did not smile back.

''Yes, she has a habit of picking up strays.'' Vane softened his insult by grinning and squeezing Alexa tighter. Her return expression was something less than a smile. ''Oh, come on, darling. You know how much I like your little habits.'' He pulled her close and gave her a long, sexy kiss full on the lips.

Cole fought the urge to haul her out of his arms and punch Vane right on that overactive mouth. Amused chuckles arose from the throats of the Smiths, distracting Cole.

Alexa did not slap the guy. Back away. Even protest.

Why should she? They were engaged. She probably enjoyed it.

When the kiss was over, Alexa still didn't smile as she continued to stand next to her intended. Her lovely complexion had turned pink. From embarrassment?

Maybe. But there was also an expression in her large blue eyes that Cole did not recognize. It wasn't anger, for he had experienced that. But it certainly wasn't lust. Or love. For he had experienced that, too....

''We are going to take the Smiths and some of the other guests on a tour of the area, John,'' Alexa said. Her voice was close to a monotone, as if she had extracted all emotion from it. ''Would you like to join us?''

''Thanks, not today,'' he said quickly. ''I'm going to do some more exploring around the lake.''

He nearly kicked himself. The more time he spent with the crowd of clowns posing as guests, the more he might be able to learn.

But he had an urge to put as much distance as he could between himself and the happy couple, his assignment notwithstanding.

Besides, if he was fortunate, everyone else would go. And he could do a little exploring—*not* around the lake.

"Fine," Vane said. "Maybe another time."

"Sure. Touring with you two would be fun." As much fun as walking barefoot on razor blades.

He remembered when it had been fun to be with them, when he and Vane had been stationed in Santa Monica. That was where he had met Alexa.

Had fallen in love with her.

The biggest mistake of his life.

Some other guests descended the stairs beside the reception area, chattering excitedly. Jill Fuller's dark eyes lit immediately on Cole. She approached him, her full hips, beneath tight white pants, swinging suggestively. "John," she said, "are you coming on our tour? You must sit beside me, help me with my not-so-good English."

Her purported husband, Ed, was right behind her. His wide nose was wrinkled, as if he smelled something foul. "Yes, John," he said with much less enthusiasm. "We would be pleased for your company." If this scowl was his pleasure mode, Cole wondered what displeasure looked like.

"Sorry," he said. "I'm not doing the tour thing right now. My day's all booked up with solitude and contemplating the lake." He winked at Jill. "If you don't recognize those long words, I'll be glad to explain them."

"I will explain them," Ed said, taking her by the arm and leading her toward the front door, where the other guests were gathered.

"Time to go, Alexa," Vane said. "Sorry you won't be with us, John," he said to Cole. "We're going to have a great time. Aren't we, sweetheart?" He nudged Alexa, whose hand he held. Her left hand. The one on which she wore her engagement ring.

"Absolutely," she said. She sounded as if she meant it this time. But something in her look made him wonder what she was really thinking.

Nothing he would like, Cole was certain. But he still felt a pang of being left out, as he watched Alexa and Vane usher their guests into two nearly matching SUVs. Minos was with them, and he got into the driver's seat of one. Surprisingly, Alexa joined him. Vane got into the second vehicle.

Once, they had toured Venice Beach together—Alexa, Vane and him. Several times, they had shopped along the Third Street Promenade in Santa Monica. They had been inseparable.

Sure, he and Vane had had a job to do. Or at least Cole had. But he had been happier than he'd ever been before, and, certainly, since.

He watched as the two vehicles drove away, feeling strangely, sadly alone.

But he was always alone. He had to work alone. And his nostalgia for these two people and what had been...

Remember who they are. What they did.

They had betrayed him. They had been responsible for the explosion that had nearly killed him.

And if he really wanted to make sure he retained only ill feelings toward them, he only had to remember the worst of all.

The two of them were terrorists. And they were responsible for the murder of his father.

Chapter Five

Cole could have used the precious pocket of time alone at the inn to hack into the computer at the reception desk. But the computer was out in the open and therefore vulnerable. That suggested that nothing interesting was likely to be stored in it.

In fact, he figured that the likelihood of his finding anything useful anywhere accessible at the inn was slim, if not nil. Otherwise, why *would* they have left him alone here?

He had been using his cover as a home improvements salesman to good advantage, acting as if he were drumming up business by scouting out repairs and upgrades that needed to be done. Instead, he'd been looking for security devices such as hidden cameras. He'd found none.

He had, however, located bugging devices in nearly all the phones, including the one in his room. That didn't matter, since he had no intention of making any classified calls from here.

He also figured that there was a chance that Vane's arrogance would allow him to believe his plan so infallible that whether someone infiltrated his domain and gathered information didn't matter. Consequently, Cole had to at least check out every inch of the inn he could, particularly those areas occupied by his primary suspects.

He started with *her* room. Alexa's.

The lock was easy to pick. An amateur could have done it. And Cole was no amateur.

Standing on the floral area rug that covered the center of the polished cherry-wood floor, he looked around.

Her quarters were not much larger than his guest room, but the furnishings were not so impersonal. Her bed was made of plain, planked pine, swathed in a hand-sewn quilt in an intricate braid pattern. The matching rocker's flounced seat cover picked up the same colors of pink, white and navy.

On the wall were framed wildlife photographs, probably taken around this area: a bald eagle, perched majestically at the top of a white fir. A raccoon, washing its meal at the lakeshore.

Her simple taste hadn't changed. He had found it enchanting, once. He had found everything about her enchanting.

He still did....

No. Sure, she was still lovely. Appealing. Sexier than a centerfold. But he had to keep remembering exactly who, and what, she was.... Rather than remembering her vaguely citrus scent. It hadn't changed either. It hung in the air—

Damn! He was out of control.

Cole exhaled slowly, gathering his resolve. He frowned, looking around. He walked deliberately to her pine desk. Atop it was a computer, which he turned on. Before checking its files, he rummaged through her drawers. Maybe here he would find some answers.

But he suspected his search would lead him only to more questions.

"Explain it all, Alexa," he growled softly. No one would hear in the empty inn even if he yelled, but he was, after all, involved in a covert investigation. And being surreptitious was a hard habit to break.

He found nothing useful in Alexa's precisely organized drawers, not even any bookwork for the inn. Maybe it was all on the computer.

He anticipated a password to get into its folders. None was requested.

Discovering some of the B & B's financial records in a spreadsheet file, he scanned them. Nothing untoward there…except that no records were more recent than five months ago. The inn had been doing well then. Alexa and Vane had, it seemed, scrupulously shared the net proceeds.

Where were the records for the past few months?

He shut down the computer and headed once more for the hall, locking her door behind him.

He'd found it curious that Alexa and Vane did not share a bedroom. When Alexa and he had been all but engaged, they had spent every possible night together. Here she was, pledged to marry the man she'd conspired with for years. She lived under the same roof with him, but not in the same room.

Why?

"Why, indeed?" he whispered into the stillness of the knotty-pine paneled upstairs hallway. He wasn't here to learn about their love life. He wasn't even here to investigate what had happened two years ago, except as it related to today's plot.

If he could prove that his one-time friend and his one-time lover had conspired to kill his father, to kill *him,* so much the better. But that was insignificant in today's larger picture.

For there was something going on with much wider repercussions. Two years ago, there had been similar "guests" in Kenner Hotels all over the country. As now, rumors had begun circulating in the intelligence community that the "guests" were terrorist agents skilled with explosives and about to be planted underground in strategic locations throughout the U.S. Cole and Vane had gone there to investigate...or at least Cole had.

He hadn't counted on falling in love with the owners' daughter. But he had been so sure she was naively unaware of what was going on.

He'd been the naive one.

The only light in the hallway now came through the sliding glass door at its end—the door to the balcony overlooking the lake, where he had stood with Alexa last evening. Where he had wanted to take her into his arms and kiss her until her head spun, until she begged him to take her inside and make fiery love with her all night long....

The balcony where Vane had appeared.

Ignoring the way his gut constricted, Cole studied his surroundings. There were numbers on some of the doors: the guest bedrooms. One day, he would go through each of their belongings. But not today. Today he would get into Vane's room, at the end of the hall; he had seen Vane emerge from it earlier.

And then he would look for the room occupied by that ugly piece of crud, Minos.

Vane's door appeared more substantial than the others. And, of course, it was locked.

Cole started to pick the lock. It was more complicated than Alexa's. This was going to take time.

He knelt and withdrew his lock-pick set from his side

pocket. As he unrolled it, he heard a whisper of noise from downstairs.

Someone was here. That someone didn't want anyone to know it.

That could be another explanation for why he had been left alone here. He *hadn't*—at least not for long.

Silently, swiftly, Cole slipped his instruments back into his pocket and edged down the hall to his room. He had left the door ajar. He had also used a commercial spray to ensure that its hinges did not squeak. He slipped inside and, quietly, traded his lock-picking tools for his Beretta—in a shoulder holster beneath the blue denim jacket he hastily donned.

Then, he went back into the hall.

No one was there.

His back against the wall, he crept along it to the stairway. He looked down. No one. He waited.

No more sounds. But someone was there. He had heard it before. He *felt* it now.

If he were here as Cole Rappaport, he would sneak down, surprise whoever it was. But without knowing the identity of the intruder, such secrecy was unwarranted. It was better that he not break his cover—for now.

And in his openness, he would maintain the element of surprise. Who would suspect genial John O'Rourke of covert activity?

"Hello?" he yelled into the silence of the stairwell. "Is anyone there?"

Nothing. Cole began tromping downstairs, making noise.

His hand steadied on the gun hilt beneath his jacket.

He heard another noise. "Hello?" he called again.

Still no answer. Cole ignored the unease running in

arpeggios up and down his spine. He allowed his training to take over: Cool. Alert.

Ready.

He paused at the bottom of the stairs and listened again. His fingers flexed on his weapon, prepared to draw it—

"Hello, Mr. O'Rourke."

He whirled.

Minos Flaherty strode from the door to the kitchen, behind where the stairway rose. He stared evenly at Cole.

"I thought you left with the tour group." Cole managed a hearty John O'Rourke voice, even a John O'Rourke smile.

Pretending to scratch an itch on his chest, he remained ready to draw his gun.

"I went with them," the man replied. "But I came back. I had other business to take care of…here."

Their eyes locked. Cole suddenly had the sense that *he* was Minos's "other business." And that it meant more than spying on him.

Had his cover been blown?

Cole crossed his arms nonchalantly, keeping his right hand poised over his gun. "Anything I can help you with?" he asked in his best salesman voice.

Minos's eyes narrowed without moving from Cole's. Cole continued to smile, even as Minos's hand began to move along his side, as if to find something hidden on him—

"John!"

Cole turned his head at the sound of his alter ego's name. Jill Fuller stood just inside the inn's front door.

"What are you doing here?" Cole asked.

She sashayed suggestively into the reception area. "I came back," she said. "I knew you were here all alone,

poor man, and—'' Her brilliant smile sagged as her gaze
lit on something over his shoulder. Some*one*. Minos.

"I came because I do not feel good," she muttered.
The look she tossed at Minos was full of irritation.

Cole, too, looked toward Minos. His expression was
more enraged than irritated. Cole wondered if he should
thank the flirtatious woman for the distraction.

And he would definitely watch his butt more carefully
from now on.

TAKING THE GUESTS AROUND Skytop sightseeing had
used up more time that day than Alexa had anticipated.
She hadn't wanted to go. Vane knew that, which was
why he had insisted on it.

After they reached Skytop Lake Village, she'd had to
drive one of the cars, for Minos had disappeared. *He* was
allowed to beg off. Alexa wasn't. Another matter to add
to her growing list of resentments about which she could
do nothing but stew…for now.

On her return, she had excused herself, telling Vane
she had to get dinner ready. He could hardly argue with
that. It was *his* guests she needed to feed.

She had hurried to the kitchen. She didn't take time to
change clothes, but remained in her beige denim skirt and
short-sleeved blouse, pausing to throw a frilled apron
over them. Now, she leaned against her metal-topped
center island, thinking.

The menu she previously had decided on for dinner
would take too long to prepare. Instead, she settled on a
relatively simple meal: spinach salad plus a baked potato
bar. As toppings for the potatoes, she would serve
whipped garlic butter, tiny meatballs in a creamy Italian
basil sauce, white sauce with capers, and crumbled feta
cheese. Guests could take their pick.

She had all the spices and other ingredients tucked away in pantry and refrigerator, for most were staples of her cooking.

She washed the potatoes. Standing at the sink, she thought of John, who had helped with the dishes last night and again this morning after breakfast.

He hadn't gone sightseeing with them. Where was he now?

Why did she care?

She sighed. He wasn't Cole. She knew that. He wasn't at all like Cole, despite what she had thought at first—except for his sexiness. Who would have thought a salesman, especially one she'd just met, could play such havoc with her hormones?

But more important, he did seem to be a very kind man. Someone who could be a friend.

"I could use a friend," she murmured.

A bark sounded from the next room. Phantom frisked behind his gate, then barked again.

"I know, I already have a friend," she said laughingly. She wrapped the potatoes in foil, then popped them into the oven. They would bake as she prepared the rest.

As she returned to the sink, she glanced out the window toward the lake. She drew in her breath. There was John, sitting cross-legged on the end of the dock, staring up toward the inn.

His pose almost brought tears to Alexa's eyes. Cole had liked to sit the same way. His back had been just as ramrod straight, and he had often gripped his ankles in the identical manner.

The potatoes were cooking. Alexa could make time for a break, though she would need to bustle when she came back in.

Without pondering the wisdom of what she was doing,

she hung her apron on the hook beside the door, put Phantom on his leash and went outside. She didn't return John's wave, but hurried, with her pup, down the paved path toward the lake.

She tied the excited Phantom on one of the dock's posts, stepped out onto the planking, then halted.

The late afternoon was gorgeous. The sky's brilliant blue was reflected in the water, and so were the surrounding mountains and shoreline homes. The hum of motors broke the stillness, and a boat with a water-skier in tow traversed the middle of the lake.

"Hi." John greeted her, standing. He was dressed in tight jeans and a clinging T-shirt. Lord, the man managed to remind her of sex just by being here!

"Hi," she said, after clearing her throat. "Did you have fun exploring the lake today?"

"Not as much as I would have liked. Mrs. Fuller came back. She wanted company."

If the shameless woman had been nearby, Alexa would probably have pulled her hair out, strand by strand by pretty, dark strand.

Why did she feel so jealous? No matter what else Mrs. Fuller was, the woman was at least purporting to be married. Alexa was engaged. And even if she could extract herself—*when* she could extract herself—she had learned the hard way that involvement with a man, any man, wasn't worth the pain.

"I'm sure the two of you had fun," Alexa said, forcing a sly smile. "Or at least Mrs. Fuller did."

"Are you implying that I'm easy, Ms. Kenner?" John's tone pretended hurt. "You wound me."

"No," she replied. "I'm not implying that *you're* easy, only that Mrs. Fuller wishes you were."

"I think we both have Mrs. Fuller's number."

Alexa joined him in laughter.

"The thing is," he continued, "I really do want to see the lake. Do you allow guests to borrow your boat?" He gestured toward the small motorboat tied alongside the dock.

She would have. Vane didn't.

Of course, there was a solution.... "No, but I'd be glad to take you around the lake."

Damn! How could she be so impulsive? She opened her mouth to retract the invitation, but before she could, John stepped toward her. His expression radiated concern—and his eyes bored into hers.

Deep, dark, liquid-brown eyes. Smoldering eyes that seemed to see her worries, her fright, her loneliness.

She froze, feeling her lower lip tremble. She bit down hard to stop it.

"I'd like that, Alexa. But I don't want to cause trouble for you."

"Trouble?" Her voice was an octave too high, and she pulled her gaze away from his.

"I may be wrong, but it looks to me like your fiancé keeps you on a tight leash."

She chuckled grimly, then glanced back toward where she had left her pup. "Leashes are for beloved pets," she said. "I'm hardly that." She swallowed hard. She was beginning to reveal too much.

"Alexa?"

She swung back to face him, only to find that he had drawn even closer. Too close.

Staring at him, she could see, through his snug white T-shirt, the outline of the tight muscles of his broad chest.

She could reach out and grasp his hand. The hand of a would-be friend. The strong, substantial hand of a sensuous, too-attractive man.

She was tempted to take her own step forward—right into his arms....

What was she thinking? They were on the dock. In plain view of the neighbors. In plain view of the inn's guests.

Of Vane.

She took several hasty steps backward. "I don't know what you're talking about, John, but I wish you'd stop."

"I can't," he said, so gently that she just had to look at him again.

She saw sympathy in his expression, and something else. Determination? Resolve?

Anger?

"When will you take me on that boat tour?" he continued.

Never, she thought. But her insubordinate mouth said, "As soon as I can get away."

"Without anyone knowing." He nodded as if he understood the situation.

How could he? "But—" she began.

He held up his hand. "It's okay. When the time comes, just let me know. I'll be ready."

He edged past her on the dock, stooped to pat Phantom, then hurried up the walkway toward the inn.

Alexa followed, but not right away. She had to catch her breath first.

That man was driving her nuts, and she didn't even know him. Didn't want to know him.

And damn his sexy hide...he still somehow reminded her of Cole.

She untied Phantom. Together they returned to her kitchen. She shut him behind the gate again and took a deep breath. She had a lot to do and not much time to do it. Still...

Perversely, Alexa checked her freezer and drew out a package. She'd decided to add crabmeat dijonnaise to the toppings guests could put on their potatoes. She would watch John, see how much he enjoyed it.

And if he avoided it? So what? It wouldn't mean anything.

But Cole Rappaport had been allergic to crabmeat.

"GREAT DINNER," Cole told Alexa as he stood at the long oak sideboard in the filled dining room.

"Thanks. I'm glad you're enjoying it." She appeared a little nervous as she surveyed the crowd of seated guests. This evening, she wasn't wearing an apron over her long, forest-green dress. The knit dress itself was shapeless, but it announced that Alexa had a shape beneath it—a very sexy, very female shape.

Vane was eyeing them from the table with the three male guests Cole had first seen him with. Otherwise, would Cole have dared to edge up closer to Alexa, bask in the warmth from her body—feel those delicious curves against him?

Of course not. He was thinking again with his libido and not with his mind.

Remember what she's done, he told himself. *Why you're here.*

He'd figured, with her feigned nervousness, that Alexa had again assumed the role of innocent bystander, or victim. To get her to divulge something helpful, Cole was playing along.

Or was it that he hoped her innocence really wasn't an act?

If so, he was a fool for the second time.

Trying to pay attention to his meal, Cole took a baked

potato. He heaped crabmeat topping onto it, along with crumbled cheese.

Though Alexa had blurted out that first day that John O'Rourke reminded her of Cole, he didn't believe she still thought they could be one and the same. And yet…could this be a test?

He put a dinner roll on the side of his plate.

If he refused the crabmeat or grew violently sick to his stomach after eating it, Alexa would become even more suspicious.

He had accidentally eaten some at the dining room at the Kenner Santa Monica Hotel when he had first met her. She had seen him bolt to the rest room, had helped him to his room at the hotel afterward when, pale and shaky, he could barely stand.

Fortunately, he had discovered a medicine in the past two years that prevented such reactions. Equally fortunate, he had remembered to take his daily pill.

"Can I serve you something else?" Alexa asked him. "More salad?" He couldn't read her expression—quizzical? Taunting? Regretful?

"Yes. Please." He watched as she bent to use the tongs to add a heaping serving of salad to his dish…the way that damn dress outlined every curve. She was so close to him….

He inhaled the soft essence of citrus above the stronger aroma of the food.

He turned away as soon as she was finished—and caught Minos's eye. The other man scowled and looked away.

After Cole's encounter earlier with Minos, he had been reminded to stay alert. That powerful little man had appeared to have more than housework on his mind. A lot more.

And it didn't involve becoming John O'Rourke's best buddy.

Tonight, Minos presided over one of the tables near the Fullers. Pretending to be oblivious to the other man's hostile watchfulness, Cole headed in that direction.

He hadn't planned on sitting again with Ed and Jill Fuller, but both welcomed him to their table—even Ed. Did he have any idea that his wife had attempted to seduce Cole that very afternoon?

Jill wore a skimpy red dress that night. Her ample cleavage was very much in evidence, especially as she made a point of reaching for the salt and pepper.

Her overt display wasn't half as sexy as Alexa's assets merely suggested by her outfit.

A hum of conversation from the other seven tables filled the room. "I hope you're feeling better this evening," Cole said to Jill.

Irritation swept over her attractive and exotic features, but disappeared quickly. "I was just tired," she said. "I went to bed when I came back here." Her dark eyes flashed, as if reminding him he could have joined her.

Ed was dressed in a cotton shirt in a shade of brown that complemented his swarthy features. He seemed oblivious to the interplay fomented by his wife.

Or was her flirtation related to their purpose in being here? Was she rehearsing for a performance yet to come?

"So where are you going after you leave here?" Cole asked. "Home to—er, Bolivia? Or are you touring more of the States?"

"We will see more here," Ed said.

"Really? Where? I'm thinking of spending more time on the road before going home. Maybe I could join you."

"Oh, yes," said Jill, at the same time Ed said, "I do not think so."

Cole laughed. "Well, tell me where, so I can be sure either to tag along or avoid it." Not that he expected his answers to come so easily.

The Fullers looked at one another. Ed's expression was angry; Jill appeared chastised. Neither spoke. Instead, they glanced toward Vane.

Dressed in slacks and sport coat for dinner, their host now stood near the sideboard, beside Alexa. Didn't she ever get to eat?

Maybe she didn't want to eat here, with her guests.

Vane must have caught the Fullers' gazes, for, with an arm around Alexa, he maneuvered them toward the table occupied by Cole and his companions. "How are you enjoying your dinner tonight?" Vane asked jovially, as if he had had something to do with cooking it.

"It is quite good," Jill said, taking a petite bite of salad.

"Wonderful," Cole said, giving an effusive John O'Rourke-style compliment.

"My Alexa here is a great cook, isn't she?" Vane hugged her tighter. Alexa's smile was tepid. "She does everything well, don't you, darling?" Vane turned her and gave her a long and sexy kiss.

Cole watched as Alexa's arm, nearly bare beneath her short-sleeved dress, stiffened at her side, her fists clenched.

That damn diamond ring seemed to sparkle expressly to torment Cole.

Vane drew her even closer, nibbling at her ear—or was he whispering words of love to her? Her stiffness seemed to vanish, and she hugged him back.

Cole was even more glad he had taken his medicine. Otherwise, this sweet little love scene would have made him sick to his stomach.

When they finally drew apart, some of the inn's guests broke into applause.

Alexa's lovely cheeks turned pink. She bowed her head in what appeared to be shy embarrassment and left the room.

That night, Cole did not attempt to help Alexa with the dishes. He sat with the other guests as, once again, they tried to guess the answers on the TV quiz show.

This time, he did not participate.

Much later, when he couldn't sleep, he considered going once more to the quiet, picturesque balcony overlooking the moonlight-bathed water.

Would Alexa be there?

He had learned to ignore the myriad aches that remained as a reminder of the explosion that had nearly killed him. But now, as he lay in bed, they were accompanied by other aches, like the one in his groin as he thought of Alexa.

Yet the sharper pain, as he remembered the kiss she had shared with Vane, wasn't physical.

He turned over and closed his eyes.

Chapter Six

The rain was only a heavy midnight mist. The wind that accompanied it was more brutal, whipping the surface of the lake, frothing it at the dimly lit shoreline. Alexa's boat rocked beside the dock, which creaked in protest at the disturbance.

The whistle of the wind, combined with the soft patter of rain on the rustling leaves, crescendoed in Alexa's ears, adding to her despair.

Standing by the balcony railing, she hugged her long, quilted floral robe about her. But it wasn't the rain and the unremitting wind off the lake that chilled her so profoundly.

"How can I do this?" she whispered to Phantom, who lay at her feet. He whined in response, clearly sensing her malaise, though the pup had no answer.

But she had her own answer. She could do it because she had to. She would continue to act out the charade with Vane, because he had given her no choice—for now.

He had reiterated his threats concisely into her ear during that little scene at dinner. As a result, she'd had to pretend gaiety. She'd had to pretend to respond to him.

Her skin still stung from the scrubbing she had given herself in the privacy of her shower this evening.

She couldn't even fantasize any longer that John was Cole incarnate. He'd dug right in to the crabmeat at supper. Later, he had watched TV with the group for a while, and although he was unusually quiet, he hadn't appeared to suffer from an allergic reaction.

He wasn't Cole. Cole was dead.

"Alexa?"

She whirled at the sound of the masculine voice. But it was not the one she had hoped to hear. Vane stood just outside the sliding glass door to the hallway. He was still dressed in the same trousers and jacket he'd had on at dinner.

She didn't say anything, but returned her gaze to the bleakness of the vista before her. Phantom, who had also risen at the voice, sat at attention, leaning on her leg.

In a moment, Vane's shoulder touched hers on the opposite side from where Phantom sat. She steeled herself not to pull away.

"Miserable night," he said. "What are you doing out here?"

"Enjoying the view." *It fits my mood.*

"I wanted to let you know I'm going down the mountain tomorrow for the day. Minos will be around here, though he has some errands to run."

"Okay." She kept her tone neutral—though inside she wanted to rejoice for the respite. But not enough of a respite. She couldn't count on being alone at the inn for any period of time.

"You'll be here when I get back." It wasn't a question but a command.

"Mmm-hmm." She doubted he heard her unenthusiastic response over the whipping wind, but didn't care.

He grabbed her hand as it rested on the damp railing,

and squeezed it. "I said, you'll be here. If you aren't, all I have to do is—"

She yanked her hand away and faced him, her shoulders stiff. "Show your damn file to your damn government friends in high places," she spat. "You've made that abundantly clear. They'll believe you, not me."

He was the one with connections. Her parents were alleged terrorist conspirators. Never mind that he had manufactured the evidence against them. It looked real, and it could put her parents—and possibly her—away for life.

How could she have been so gullible? Two years ago, when her parents had been accused of conspiracy in the concealment of terrorists at the Kenner Hotels, Vane had stuck up for them. Claimed there wasn't enough evidence against them. Convinced the authorities to drop their investigation of the Kenners.

With nothing new to report, the media quickly lost interest. Alexa's parents decided to scale down, sell all but one of their hotels, get on with their lives.

She did, too. And when Vane suggested a partnership, she had jumped at it.

How was she to know that this inn was to be a front? Or that he had forged damaging, and very real-looking, documents, creating a handy file to tie her parents to the terrorist conspiracy. He was now ready to "find" it if at any time she didn't do as he said. Because deaths had resulted from the alleged conspiracy—Cole's and hotel manager Warren Geari's—she couldn't even count on a statute of limitations to protect her parents.

"Yes," she continued icily, "I will be here." She paused, feeling her chest heave in fury. "Besides, this is my inn. I won't leave it because I won't give you the satisfaction."

That was a lie. As much as she hated to, she *would* leave it, when she could. To survive.

Once again, she turned to face the lake. The rain fell more heavily now, as if the heavens wept in sympathy for her plight. But she knew better. No one knew and no one cared what happened to her—not the heavens or anyone else.

She would handle this alone. Somehow.

"I'm sorry, Alexa," Vane said, his voice audible over the wind. He had come closer again but was not touching her. "You know I really love you, don't you? I have for a long time. But there are things going on, things you don't understand. It'll all be over soon, I promise. When it is, we'll travel, anywhere you want. We'll have money and power and—" He stopped abruptly, as if he had said too much.

He didn't love her. He was obsessed. Still, this could be an opportunity to learn something important. Inhaling deeply to marshal her wiles, Alexa turned toward him. He had hunched his shoulders, but the rain still dampened his deceptively guileless face.

"That would be nice, Vane. I would like to get away for a little while. But without real, paying guests, how can we afford to?" The inn's income right now consisted of what she was charging John.

"Oh, they'll pay off, my darling. Don't you worry." There was something ruthless in his smile. At the moment, he no longer looked like the boyish man who had, she believed, come to her rescue two years ago, but more like the devil in disguise.

As he always had been.

"Please tell me what this is all about," she begged. "I want to understand. Maybe I can even help." *When the Pacific flows upward into Skytop Lake,* she thought.

Whatever the plot he was involved with, she wanted no part of it. But if he *thought* she did…

"I can't tell you now, Alexa. It's too sensitive. I'm part of a greater system. I report to others, and if I were to reveal any of it now, I'd be— Never mind. When the time comes, you'll know what it was and how I helped implement it." There was a radiance in his eyes that hinted of madness.

She hid her shudder in a smile. "I wish you'd trust me, Vane."

"I would if I could," he said. "But it's too dangerous."

For a moment, something resembling sadness shadowed his face, and she focused on the growing abundance of lines she saw there. He seemed to be aging before her eyes. She could almost feel sorry for him.

Almost.

But he wasn't going to talk, damn it. He'd known what was happening from the first. He had the information that Cole had died attempting to get. And there was nothing she could do to extract it.

"It's raining harder, Alexa," he said. "Let's go in."

"All right." She could be miserable in the solitude of her own room just as well as out here in the dampness.

Phantom accompanied her to the sliding glass door to her room.

So did Vane. "Can I come in?" he asked.

She felt fury flood her as her eyes opened wide. She knew what he was asking. *No,* she wanted to shout. *Don't even think of touching me, ever again.* She couldn't bear it.

But she forced herself to remain silent as she pretended, for a moment, to consider it. Her body trembled, not with lust, but with the effort of hiding her anger.

You son of a bitch. The words nearly burst from her.

There had been a time, when they had first moved here together, that she had given in to his urging. She hadn't cared much what happened to her, and he had, she'd believed, been kind to her. To her parents. She had even agreed, out of gratitude, to their engagement.

She had always felt detached from their lovemaking, although at times the warmth and nearness of another body had felt welcome.

She would never again feel the passion she had shared with Cole. That was a given.

Cole was gone.

And now she knew that the reason he'd died involved Vane and his plotting.

Share her body again with Cole's killer?

Masking her icy rage, she turned back toward Vane. His expression was heated, beseeching, and she had an urge to rake her nails down his face. Alexa had never before had such a strong instinct for violence.

"I'm sorry, Vane," she forced herself to say calmly. "I just can't right now."

His pleading, hopeful expression vanished, replaced by fury. "Fine. Not tonight. But I'm setting our wedding date, Alexa—and soon. I just need to check into a few things, then I'll tell you. I've had enough of your putting it off. We're engaged, and we will get married within the next couple of months, I promise you."

Couple of months? "And I've had enough of your threats," she dared to retort. "How can any marriage be based on lies and coercion and—"

She stopped herself. She'd been about to say "hate." But if she did, she might never be able to go back.

Might even sign her parents'—and her own—arrest warrants.

"—and fear," she finished.

His angry gaze did not waver. He did not attempt to soothe her. Apparently, he *wanted* her to fear him.

She shook her head sadly. "I don't understand you, Vane. Go ahead. Set the damn wedding date."

Before he could respond, she hurried into her room, Phantom right behind her. She slid the door shut and lowered the miniblinds.

For a moment, she just stood there. And then she knelt on the floor, hugging Phantom as she cried.

PERHAPS AN OUTING—*THIS* outing—was another small rebellion. But one necessary to Alexa's self-esteem. And her sanity. She had to get away, if only briefly. If she'd been able to count on a long enough window of opportunity alone at the inn to accomplish something, she'd have hung around, taken advantage. But she couldn't.

Puttering in the kitchen the next morning, she planned the day with a bittersweet smile on her face.

She had seen Vane off after breakfast. Minos, too—though she knew he'd be back soon. They each drove one of the SUVs. Most of the inn's guests rode with them, though Alexa had heard that Minos was going to drop his riders off somewhere to shop.

"We're going to have a great time," she told Phantom. The pup stood up from under a counter and wagged his tail.

"I'm sure we are," said a voice from the doorway. John walked in. He had dressed for their outing in one of his muscle-hugging white T-shirts that contrasted well with his longish, dark hair. Blue jeans rode low on his slim hips and outlined his thighs.

Alexa hadn't felt a bit of sexual attraction to Vane last night on the balcony. She'd once believed she would never feel lust again.

But John brought it out. Oh, yes, he did.

Maybe her plans for the day weren't such a good idea. Sure, she hadn't told Vane she wouldn't leave the inn, only that she'd be here when he returned.

But spending the day alone with a sexy stranger... Even if it didn't directly defy her fiancé's orders, he wouldn't like it.

Would Minos call Vane on the cell phone to report that she wasn't there? Come looking for her?

"I didn't give you much notice," she hedged to John. She had taken him aside when he'd appeared for breakfast that morning and issued an invitation. "If you have other plans, maybe we could do this another day."

"No, this is great. When I'm on vacation, I like to be flexible. And as I've told you before, I've wanted to take a boat ride around the lake. Can I help with anything?" John opened his arms toward the counter, where Alexa had piled the fixings for their picnic lunch. His muscles flexed at his motion, and Alexa tried not to stare.

"No, thanks. I just need to wrap these things, then I'll be ready."

Alexa had learned, with a lot of practice, to be efficient in the kitchen. Getting a picnic lunch assembled and wrapped was a piece of cake—figuratively and literally— for she had included a couple of slices of devil's food cake she had baked for dessert that night.

She had removed her ring and tucked it away before she left her room that morning. A picnic and a dip in the lake were too risky. She could lose it.

She *wanted* to lose it. But not by accident.

"Okay," she said to John. "You can carry this—" She pointed to the traditional wicker basket she had filled.

"My pleasure." He grinned as he lifted it effortlessly.

His dark eyes glinted as if the pleasure he anticipated involved an appetite that wasn't for food.

Heavens, Alexa thought, feeling warmth redden her face. She only hoped she hadn't brought even more trouble on herself than she could handle.

Last night's rain had cleaned the sky. It glowed a brilliant blue, reflected in Skytop Lake. As a responsible boat owner and host, Alexa grabbed life vests and oars from the tiny boathouse on the land side of the dock. She guided Phantom aboard and showed John where to settle the picnic basket.

The boat wasn't huge, but it was large enough to have a tiny galley and a head below. Alexa loved it. She had christened it the *Skytop Scalawag.* Last summer, she had taken it out almost daily, sometimes with Vane and guests of the inn.

But last summer seemed so long ago, long before Vane had shown his true colors.

At the helm, Alexa turned the key. The boat's inboard motor purred to life. John untied the lines that secured them to the dock. His lithe, substantial body moved with practiced grace, as if he had done this many times before.

Maybe Alexa would learn where, get to know him better on their outing.

And maybe she was being an idiot. This was only to be one enjoyable day, a relaxing interlude in a life fraught with tension.

Perhaps this expedition was a venture in utter foolishness. She could think of a million reasons she shouldn't be doing this, and only one reason she should—because she *wanted* to.

It had been a long time since she had done anything just for fun.

She carefully backed the *Scalawag* away from the

dock, then headed west, intending to make a slow clockwise circle around the lake. John sat beside her in the passenger's seat and Phantom lay at Alexa's feet.

"Tell me about Skytop Lake," John said over the even hum of the engine. The ride was smooth on the placid water. A breeze slipped over the windshield and batted them.

Alexa went into her tour-guide mode, explaining how this small body of water had formed naturally in the San Bernardino Mountains, unlike its more elite and well-known neighbor to the south, Lake Arrowhead. It was also less touristy than another, larger nearby lake, Big Bear. It was lined with homes, some occupied all year round, and others vacation getaways for people from the Los Angeles area. Surrounded by thickly forested slopes, it was one of the most picturesque places Alexa had ever seen.

"You sound fond of Skytop," John observed during a lull in her narration.

"You could say that," she said with a grin that fell as she turned away, ostensibly to check out a boat passing on their starboard side.

She forbore to mention how she had fallen in love with it when she had visited just over two years ago—when she had come here with the only man she had ever loved, Cole Rappaport.

Or how she had fled into the mountains after his death, after the near ruination of her family, only to find that the troubles of down below had followed her here.

Along the shore, she pointed out older homes and some commercial and retail areas, including Skytop Lake Village.

And then they reached the location she had planned for their picnic: Skytop Cove.

The cove was a local park, its dock and picnic area maintained by tax dollars. Its small beach was cordoned off from boat traffic.

Two other boats were tied to the dock. Once again, John helped with the ropes, after Alexa guided the *Scalawag* to a mooring. He went below for the basket, and Alexa, Phantom at her heels, staked out a picnic table.

"So what's our feast to be?" John asked as he helped lay a checkered cloth over the table.

"I hope you like tuna salad and greens in pita bread," Alexa replied.

"I love it."

"How about homemade potato salad and fruit wedges? Oh, and devil's food cake."

"I'm going to pay for this vacation by a month of extra workouts in the gym," John said. The light breeze off the lake ruffled his hair, pushed his T-shirt more tightly against his all-male chest. Alexa wondered if she should have sat beside him instead of across from him. It was hard not to stare at such a delicious-looking man.

She didn't try to stop herself from looking at him.

What was worse, he was blatantly staring at her, as well, his dark eyes shooting signals of sensual awareness. She should have felt uncomfortable. Instead, what she felt was overwhelming desire.

Neither said much as they ate. A family with two children occupied another table. At first Alexa wasn't sure who belonged to the dock's other boat, for she didn't see anyone else. But in a short while, two jovially chatting couples in outdoor gear appeared. They'd apparently been hiking along the trail that began at the end of the cove's beach and led up onto the nearest forested mountain. All four got into the second boat and left.

"Tell me about your home improvement business,"

Alexa finally said, needing to start a simple and casual conversation to counter the complex sensations this man's presence engendered. "You said you wanted to open a store?"

"Right now, I'm just thinking about it. And I really like this place. In fact, I've contacted some friends in the business who are going to come up in a couple of days. If you've room for them at the Hideaway, that would be great. I want to show it off as a possible place for a future sales conference."

"Oh," Alexa said. "I'll check." She knew she didn't sound enthused, but she couldn't promise anything.

Maybe Vane's guests would leave soon. She hoped.

Except that she hated to think what they would be up to after they were gone.

Out of the blue, John, his eyes steadily regarding hers, said, "If you were my fiancée, I doubt I'd like you to be off with some other guy, even as a tour guide. Does Vane mind?"

Alexa blinked, unsure how to answer. She decided on the truth, or at least part of it. "Probably. But our engagement is sort of a trial. We haven't set a wedding date."

I haven't agreed to one, Alexa told herself fiercely. But...*two months.* She shuddered.

"Vane looked pretty certain last night."

Alexa stood. "I've eaten enough. Are you ready for a swim?" She didn't like the direction of their conversation.

"Sure."

She plucked up a couple of towels she had placed on the picnic bench and hurried toward the tiny beach, Phantom right beside her. There, she pulled off her knit top and jeans. Underneath, she had worn a one-piece bathing suit. She had purposely not worn her bikini. This one was much less suggestive.

But she recalled how John kept studying her while she was fully dressed....

She sped into the water. Phantom ran back and forth at the shore, barking.

The water was cooler than the heated summer air of early afternoon. Alexa stood waist-deep on the sandy bottom and waited until she got used to the temperature.

That gave her the opportunity to watch John peel off his jeans, revealing a snug swimsuit and powerful thigh muscles. Lord, the man was built! She supposed it was from doing home improvement work, as well as working out in the gym he'd mentioned.

He didn't take off his T-shirt. Maybe he sunburned easily, though she doubted it, with his dark hair and deep complexion. It didn't matter. She got the idea of his physique even when he was fully dressed, and now he was partially unclad....

This was a terrible idea, Alexa decided. Her temporary escape was only going to lead to more trouble.

Or frustration.

But he didn't swim. Instead, he dunked himself in the water, wetting his hair, his body. His shirt plastered tightly to his sculptured chest. She found it impossible to avert her eyes as he stood in the water beside her.

"If you ever want to get away for a while, Alexa, let me know," he said solemnly. "And if you want to talk about anything, well, salesmen are good listeners as well as talkers."

He had offered his ear, his support, before. Obviously, she was not a good actress, for her sorrow must be showing.

"Thanks," she said simply. "I'll keep that in mind."

"While you're at it, keep this in mind, too." He leaned toward her and pulled her close.

She could have turned the situation into something light and playful by splashing him.

But she didn't. Instead, she allowed him to draw her against him in the cool water that seemed quickly to warm from their body heat.

His damp chest pressed against her barely clothed body, and she felt the proof that he was as aroused as she.

She wanted him to kiss her. Now.

But John suddenly drew away, and she nearly crumpled. "Sorry," he said lightly, although his chest heaved. "I got carried away."

She wasn't sorry, though she should have been. Alexa sighed, as he pushed off from the sandy bottom and swam away.

She heard childish voices from the picnic area and glanced guiltily in that direction. Fortunately, no one was looking toward her.

She swam around in the cool water. After a little while, she emerged from the lake, dried herself and dressed. Only then did she call out, "John, I need to get back to start dinner. Can we go now?"

He joined her on the beach.

She talked softly to Phantom, without facing John. She didn't look at his near-naked body, didn't want to be affected by it again.

Didn't want to let him see how embarrassed she felt.

But he knew, anyway. "Alexa," he said softly, "I apologize again for touching you. You're a beautiful woman, but you belong to someone else. I'm having a hard time remembering that, but I promise to respect it from now on."

Don't respect it, she wanted to cry out. *I don't belong to Vane. I only belong to myself. Help me.*

Instead, she managed to smile at him. "It wasn't your fault. I guess I'm getting cold feet about marriage."

The boat ride back to the Hideaway seemed to take forever, despite Alexa's continued tour-guide chatter. And yet, when they arrived at the dock, Alexa felt they had gotten back much too soon.

Once again, John helped with the mooring. Alexa led Phantom out of the boat. John went below for the basket.

They stood beside one another on the dock for a moment. She wanted to say something airy and sophisticated. A cute parting shot to ease their discomfort with one another.

She could think of nothing.

"Thanks for a great day, Alexa," John finally said. "You, too, Phantom." They both bent at the same time to pet the dog—

They were interrupted by a strange blasting noise. "Damn! Alexa, get down!" John shouted.

Part of the dock splintered beside her. She felt herself being shoved toward the ground and propelled by John's large, forceful body into the shelter of the tiny boathouse.

Stunned, the breath knocked out of her, she wound up lying on her back in the shadowed interior, John's full, substantial weight on top of her. "Alexa, are you all right? Alexa? Are you hit? Talk to me."

"I'm fine," she whispered.

That sound—it had been a gunshot. He had saved her life.

"I can't lose you," he muttered. "Damn it, I can't. You are the sky to me, Alexa. No matter what, you are still my sky."

She froze.

His words. She recognized them. So long ago—

With a sob, Alexa pulled back as much as she could, with his body still, unyielding, on hers. She tried, in the darkness of the boathouse, to see deep into eyes that were both familiar and unfamiliar.

"Oh, my Lord," she whispered hoarsely, tears cascading down her cheeks. *"Cole."*

Chapter Seven

"Alexa! Are you all right?"

The shout came from outside the boathouse. Quite possibly from the shooter, Cole thought, recognizing Vane's voice.

He leapt up, dragging Alexa with him. He plastered his back against the boathouse wall, pinned Alexa against it, too, with his outstretched arm.

For this outing, Cole hadn't brought his gun. It was too difficult to hide while wearing a T-shirt and swimsuit. He'd decided to risk being unarmed for the day.

It could have been a fatal mistake, damn it. And not just for him.

The boathouse door burst open. Vane stood backlighted in the doorway. But even in the shadows, Cole could see that his hands were empty. Cole relaxed, just a little. Alexa slipped from behind his arm.

"Are you all right?" Vane demanded. He went to Alexa and took her hands.

"I'm fine, Vane," she said, though her voice wobbled. Vane hugged her against his side, and she seemed to welcome his support.

She didn't look at Cole.

"What are you doing back here so early?" she asked her fiancé.

"We finished what we needed to do faster than anticipated."

"Did you see anyone else outside?" Cole demanded.

"No." Vane sounded angry. "I heard the shot but couldn't tell where it came from. If I'd seen the shooter, I wouldn't be here. I'd be after him."

Unarmed?

But he wore a sports jacket again today. There were any number of places he could hide a weapon beneath its loose folds.

"We'd better go call the police," Cole said. He forced himself to rein in all his habitual take-charge, investigative instincts. To Vane, he was still John O'Rourke, home improvements salesman.

Maybe he could still convince Alexa—

Not likely. She darted him a glare that spoke volumes, then allowed Vane to help her out of the boathouse.

Cole followed. He automatically checked out their surroundings. No boats were close by on the lake. Nearby docks were empty, as were the vast, sloped yards that were all separated by hedges up to the path that meandered along the edge of the lake.

The sound had apparently carried, or maybe their quick reaction had been seen at the dock. Several concerned neighbors were running toward them along the lakeside path, including the woman who'd been at the grocery store when Cole had run into Alexa.

Cole squinted in the bright sunlight, scanning windows of nearby houses that weren't obscured by vegetation. Some windows were open, but he saw no movement behind any. He couldn't see the street, nor could he see any motion aside from swaying branches on the trees covering the surrounding mountainsides.

If any of the people converging on them was the shooter, Cole wouldn't be able to tell without interrogation or inspection. Or at all, since he would blow his cover if he attempted to investigate.

To the extent it wasn't blown already. He'd never be able to convince Alexa now that he wasn't Cole.

He didn't intend even to try.

That meant Vane would know, too.

Cole had to talk to Alexa first. He couldn't trust her, of all people, with the truth—or at least, not all of it. But maybe he could convince her it was in her own best interests to cooperate with him and not to tell her fiancé.

She bent to hug Phantom. The dog was evidently all right, for he was still standing and wriggling at his owner's attention. Vane stooped at the edge of the dock, examining the area where the bullet had splintered the wood.

"Hadn't you better wait till the police check that out?" Cole asked. At Vane's glare, he shrugged and grinned. "I'm an addict of TV police shows. I know not to disturb a crime scene before it's been investigated."

"Right," Vane growled.

One of the neighbors, a white-haired man with a large silver belt buckle emphasizing his paunch, pulled a cell phone from his pocket. "I'll call 9-1-1," he said.

There wasn't much Cole could do while they waited for the authorities. Alexa ignored him. Vane made light of the incident, pointing frequently to the nearest mountainside. "I don't see him," he said, "but I'll bet twenty bucks that there's a red-faced, butterfingered illegal hunter up there somewhere."

When the police finally arrived, they acted quickly and

efficiently. They took statements, extracted the bullet from the dock and checked the area. They promised to contact the victims as soon as they had something to report. They didn't allow anyone to see the bullet, so Cole couldn't tell what kind of firearm it had come from.

Cole doubted they'd locate the shooter, even if they tried. And unless Vane got more excited about the incident, Cole suspected that the very deferential local police would not put much effort into their investigation.

They all appeared to know Vane. Two years ago, Cole had found that money had been spread liberally to prevent local authorities from getting too curious at the Kenner Hotels. Everything else so far had come close to following the earlier pattern. This, too?

When the police left, Cole trudged up the path toward the inn, following Vane and Alexa.

As they reached the building, Minos Flaherty emerged from the kitchen door. "What was going on down there, boss?" he asked Vane. The short, bulky man was dressed in black sweats. There was a sheen on his forehead, as if he had been outdoors. Maybe even running.

Cole had suspected that he'd been the shooter. Now he was all but certain.

What he didn't know was whether he had been the target—or Alexa. And why shoot at either of them now?

Since Minos had missed, it had most likely been a warning. But what had it been intended to warn them of?

Had Vane set it up to make certain they didn't go off alone again? If so, he could have made the point when he'd first joined them.

Perhaps he figured Alexa would understand without being told.

All the more reason for Cole to get her alone. He had to talk to her. But first, he had to decide what to say.

VANE KEPT HIS ARM around Alexa while they walked up the path. She did not try to pull away. If she had, she would have stumbled and fallen.

He stopped to talk to Minos in private as they reached the kitchen. That was all right. She was able to hold the doorjamb for support.

Once inside, she managed to get to the steel-topped central island and lean against it. Phantom loped through the room and took his usual place in the pantry next door. He sat and watched her with his anxious, alert doggy eyes.

"Are you all right, Alexa?" Vane asked. She was uncertain whether his irate frown resulted from concern for her—or from the fact he had found her returning from an outing he might consider forbidden. "You're certain the bullet didn't nick you? Or a splinter from the dock? You look pale."

"I'm fine, Vane," she said. *Except that a dead man just saved my life.* She made a show of glancing at her watch. Her arm trembled. "Oh, my. It's late. I'd better start dinner, or we'll have an inn full of hungry guests."

"Fine. I'll leave you alone." But instead of leaving, he drew close and grabbed her. Kissed her hard on the lips. The pressure of his mouth obliterated any remaining sensation from the sweetness and shock of being with Cole.

"I don't know why you decided to disobey me, Alexa," Vane said, still holding her tightly against him. He was shorter than Cole, but he, too, was strong. A faint scent of beer on his breath indicated he had drunk a draught or two. "You understood my orders. Maybe I'll just call one of my government friends, mention I've found something interesting…"

She'd thought at first that he wouldn't dare contact the

government with the evidence he'd manufactured against her parents. It would only call attention to what he was doing here.

She'd dared to tell him so, and he had laughed, told her he'd just move up his timetable, send his guests on their way. He'd tell his government friends that *she* had brought the terrorists to their inn, make sure there was evidence implicating *her* this time. That way, he would get both her parents and her without interrupting his own plans.

Sure there were flaws in the idea, he'd said. The feds would know he wasn't stupid, that he'd have seen what was going on. But he'd come up with enough information and excuses to keep them investigating until it was too late for…whatever it was he was doing.

He claimed he loved her, wanted to marry her. Seemed obsessed with her.

And yet, he would ruin her parents—and her—without blinking.

He had to be mad.

Right now, she wanted to shout at him. Instead, she only managed a whisper. "I—I didn't disobey. I'd every intention of being here when you got back, but I thought you'd be gone longer. You didn't say I couldn't leave at all. It was just such a perfect day, and Mr. O'Rourke was so—"

She had been going to say "insistent," but she didn't want Vane to turn his wrath on Cole.

Not until Alexa had gotten her explanation.

"I'm sorry," she finished lamely.

"I suppose you wanted to spend some time with the bland Mr. O'Rourke because he's a refreshing change from me, is that it?"

If he only knew…

She could tell Vane. Maybe she *should* tell him.

But she couldn't. No matter what, she would not betray Cole, at least not until she understood why he had done this.

"I have no interest in John O'Rourke except as a guest at this inn," she replied in as forceful a voice as she could manage. "You know how much I dislike your demands, Vane. I needed to get away for a little while and had no idea this one small outing would upset you, especially since I planned to beat you back here. I'd no idea the day would end so...so violently." She raised her chin and studied his unyielding gaze. "You wouldn't happen to know who shot at us, would you?"

She was certain that he knew but that he would not admit it.

"Too bad whoever it was missed your Mr. O'Rourke. Watch your step, Alexa." Vane turned and left the room.

Alexa grabbed the counter as her legs nearly buckled. Her entire body felt deflated, as if she were a balloon with the knot in its neck untied.

For a change, it wasn't just Vane's wrath that had upset her. Fortunately, though he apparently did not like what she had done, he wasn't going to take it out on her parents or her—this time.

But Cole was alive.

He had been alive for two years without letting her know he was all right.

You son of a bitch, she thought.

She felt like sobbing but her eyes remained dry. She hurled herself toward the sink, an urge to throw up overwhelming her.

But she didn't. She just stood there. "Why, Cole?" she whispered.

As if on autopilot, she began her supper preparations.

She decided to prepare a spicy, curried Indian dish, with meat and potatoes and chana dhal—a type of lentil. She got out her amchur powder, made from unripe mangoes, to add a sour tang.

"Hi. Anything I can do to help?"

It was John O'Rourke. *Cole.* He had changed into a navy-blue denim shirt tucked into his ever-present, snug jeans. Over it, he wore a lighter denim jacket. His dark hair was damp again, as if he had just showered.

Or swum in the lake with her.

The expression on his utterly handsome face—the face that was not Cole's—was wary.

He looked so different. Why? And how could a disguise be that deceptive, that perfect? It hadn't even washed off in the lake.

Alexa had been playing in her mind the scenarios that might occur when she first saw Cole again. Should she act indifferent and cold? Should she vent her rage?

The one thing she had not planned on was for tears to spring to her eyes.

She looked down. A mesh bag of onions sat on the counter not far from where she had been peeling potatoes, and she grabbed it. She would not allow him to believe she was crying over him.

As she used a sharp knife to slice at an onion, she replied to his question. "There is not a thing you can do that you haven't done already."

She had meant her words to be a dismissal. Instead, he drew closer.

"We have to talk, Alexa," he whispered.

She kept her voice low, too. "We have nothing to talk about." *Except the fact that you let me believe you were dead.*

She heard a footstep at the doorway and turned. Minos

was there. His arms were crossed, and he was scowling. "Vane told me to help you." He did not sound the least bit pleased. And Alexa figured that Vane had wanted Minos to act not only as her kitchen assistant, but as her guard dog.

"Fine," she said brightly. "I need about ten more potatoes peeled, plus a couple of onions diced." She gestured toward the counter on the center island, where she had been working. "And that means you, Mr. O'Rourke, are dispensable. Go away and practice for tonight's quiz show."

The smile she leveled at him held no humor.

"Okay," replied Cole Rappaport from John O'Rourke's mouth. "See you later."

THAT NIGHT, Alexa lay in bed, her eyes wide open. Phantom's gentle snores sounded from on the floor beside her. Though the breeze wafting through the open window was warm, she wore a flannel nightgown.

She still felt cold. But the chill had little to do with the weather.

She had seen Cole later, as he had promised.

She had seen him as an ordinary guest at dinner. She had seen him slip into the parlor to mingle with the others watching television and discussing the news.

She hadn't seen him in the kitchen again. He had made no show of helping with the dishes so they could talk.

After weighing the wisdom of going out onto the balcony, in case he appeared there, she had done so, but only for ten minutes. She hadn't seen him there, either.

Maybe he was taking her at her word, that they had nothing to talk about.

But she had been wrong. They had a lot to talk about. Even though no explanation he could ever impart would be enough to ease the agony he had put her through for the past two years.

Nor enough to make her stop hating him now, as intensely as she once had loved him.

She pulled the covers up tightly beneath her chin and sighed deeply into the dark. She had to sleep.

It was the only way to turn off the dark, angry—and incredibly sad—emotions that pulsed through her as surely as her blood was pumped by her heart.

Suddenly, Phantom's snoring ceased. The dog rose.

"Alexa? Are you awake?" The whisper punctured the stillness.

She hadn't heard the door open, but she saw the faint light from the hallway and a backlighted figure silhouetted before it. The light disappeared as the door shut.

She knew she had locked her door.

She sat up, beginning to shake. "Who's there?"

As if she didn't know.

Phantom's toenails made small skittering sounds on the uncovered part of the wooden floor as he merrily greeted their intruder.

Traitor! Alexa thought. But the dog wouldn't understand.

The trespasser didn't answer her. Instead, her mattress suddenly sagged beneath his weight as he sat at the edge of her bed. She hadn't heard his footsteps as he crossed the wooden floor or the rug that lay on top of it.

He was still a phantom.

"Go away, Cole," she said, not meaning it. She kept her voice low. There were many reasons she did not want him to be discovered here, in her bedroom in the dead of night, in the darkness, not the least of which was that her controlling and ruthless—and quite possibly insane—

fiancé just might not understand the presence of John O'Rourke.

He certainly wouldn't understand that his closest friend in the world, Cole Rappaport, wasn't, after all, dead.

Neither did she.

"I'm not leaving without some answers," Cole replied to her demand, his voice also muted.

"What!" Of all the things he could have said, that was the last thing Alexa had anticipated. She moved then, stretching up to turn on the reading light on the wall behind the bed. The light was unlikely to be noticed by anyone outside the room. Even if it were, there would be an obvious explanation for its being on.

Cole was still dressed in denim shirt and jeans. He sat stiffly, without moving toward her, but there was a stony glint in his dark brown eyes. He ignored Phantom, who rubbed against his leg for attention. The pup settled down at his feet. "Don't worry about your fiancé hearing our conversation on his monitor and rushing in to your rescue. I swept the room for listening devices right after dinner, when everyone else was downstairs. I found yours, right there in your jewelry box where your ring is." He mentioned her engagement ring in a tone as full of distaste as if he spat worms from his mouth. "The device was hidden in the box's lining. It's now subject to an unfortunate malfunction."

Alexa was speechless. She hadn't even considered that Vane would have bugged her room. She had a phone extension in here. Had he tapped it, as well?

Cole continued. "I want to know exactly what the scheme is, Alexa. The one that went dormant two years ago after the explosion, and that's been put back together now."

"And exactly why do you think I know what it is?"

she replied coldly. She studied his face in the golden glow of the light. She still saw little resemblance to the man she had known in the breadth of his jaw, the sculptured cheekbones, the cleft in his chin, the rugged, straight brow.

But the eyes. They had looked familiar from the first moment she'd seen him. They still did.

Except that, before, there had been a softness in Cole's gaze. Caring.

Love.

She couldn't think about that, or how she had felt about him. She had to deal with the current situation.

"I was injured in that damn explosion, Alexa, but unfortunately for you my mind remained intact."

Of course. He must have had plastic surgery after the explosion. She hadn't been able to tell.

"So-called guests were planted in your family's hotels two years ago. Our investigation proved they were terrorists—mine and my dear friend Vane's. The investigation ended, or at least was put on hold, when I was nearly killed. Now, lo and behold, two of the original cast of characters just happen to be in the hotel business again, as partners. No, more than partners—lovers. Foreigners similar to the last batch—people highly trained in the use of explosives—are being taught U.S. customs and idiomatic language, right here. Of course you know what's going on. And I want an explanation."

Icy fingers of fear inched up Alexa's back. But they didn't strangle her growing anger. "And you think that I'm part of this plot? That I was part of it back then, too?"

"I may be a fool, Alexa, but I'm not stupid. Of course you've been part of it all along."

"I see." She wished she could erase the hoarseness in

her voice. It spoke of the emotions welling within her. She didn't want to cry. She wouldn't cry in front of this man whose purported death had all but destroyed her, and whose words now were shattering what was left of her. "And that's why you let me believe you were dead."

"No, Alexa. I let you believe I was dead because I'd thought you an innocent victim, and that by staying out of your life, I would protect you." His laugh was an ugly sound, full of bitterness. "And it gets even more ironic. I didn't contact Vane, either, since I figured you both would end up like my father, who was murdered even before the blast. And like me—or at least as dead as I was supposed to be."

"Your father was murdered?" Alexa was even further appalled. "You only told me he'd died. But of course I know now there was a lot you didn't tell me." She managed a glance at him. "What about Warren Geari? Did he survive the blast, too?" Warren had been the general manager of Kenner Hotels. In the nightmare of accusations that had been hurled at her family after the explosion, it had become obvious that Warren, a longtime trusted employee and friend of the family, had orchestrated the involvement of the hotel chain.

"No," Cole said. "I was the only fortunate one."

Alexa cringed at the continued acrimony that flowed from Cole's mouth.

But *she* was the one entitled to be bitter. He had judged her without even speaking with her. Had hidden from her for two years—two years in which he had been alive—and she had suffered because she had thought she had lost him in the explosion.

She *had* lost him in the explosion, she reminded herself. The only difference was that he hadn't died.

She had loved him so...and her love had become a

victim, just like Warren Geari. Only it had just died. Today, as she had learned the truth.

She sat up farther in her bed, resting her back against the headboard. She crossed her arms over her chest to still, as much as possible, the shudders of unrestrained emotion that passed through her.

"All right, Cole," she said quietly, hating the shakiness in her voice. "Believe what you want. But I have to assume that, since you're here, you've come to investigate this alleged plot all over again. Right?"

"That's right." His voice was cold. "I'd been given other assignments, but kept my ears open. I only recently started hearing rumors again in the intelligence community, and the trail I picked up ended, so far, at this inn— with Vane and you. And this time, it won't be enough to stop the latest group of infiltrators you have staying here. This time, I intend to find out what is planned, who else is involved. The scheme will be thwarted, Alexa. Believe me."

"Good," she said. She saw his eyes widen in disbelief. It was her turn to make a pretense at a laugh. "Let me tell you my version of the truth, Cole. You don't have to believe it. And I don't care if you do, as long as you promise to help me protect my parents."

"Your parents?" Confusion knitted his straight, dark brows together. Alexa had an urge to reach over and smooth them....

What was she thinking? This man was her enemy. If nothing else, he wanted to put her in prison.

Perhaps, instead, she could use him. And just maybe she would not need to escape after all.

"I'll cooperate with you, Cole," she said. "Tell you everything I know, which isn't much. Help you get whatever information I can, although I have to tell you that my own attempts to learn something useful have been fruitless so far. In return, I want you to help me find some trumped-up documents Vane created to implicate my parents. With luck, we'll get enough to put Vane in prison for a long time. And if you don't railroad me, maybe I can just go back to running my inn. Myself.''

''Without your beloved fiancé?''

''Myself,'' she reiterated, not bothering to tell him that she had never loved Vane. That she had become engaged to him out of gratitude—and even lethargy. She had known she could never love another man after Cole.

The old Cole. Not this cold, angry, accusatory stranger.

''I didn't know what was going on back then, Cole. In fact, if you remember, you lied to me from the first. I thought that Vane and you were army officers on leave, not undercover Special Forces investigators.'' She sighed. ''I'll make this short. After you…after I thought you died, my parents were accused of being in on the plot with Warren Geari. Vane helped to clear them. He told about your special unit, your investigation assignment together—at least what wasn't classified. I was grateful to him. My parents sold most of what was left and scaled down their hotel operations, and I decided to go into business myself. I remembered this inn…'' She remembered it because of what she had shared here with Cole, but she wouldn't mention that. ''Vane had decided to leave the military and offered to go into partnership with me. He'd supply some of the funds and legwork, and I'd supply the knowledge and experience.''

''And you weren't lovers before?'' Cole sounded insultingly incredulous.

''No!'' They had kept their voices down before, and this word came out louder than Alexa had intended. More softly she repeated, ''No. It's not your business why we decided to get engaged, but we had a nice establishment here for over a year, until—''

''Until you decided enough time had passed and you could bring the terrorist infiltrators back.''

''Stop it!'' Alexa hissed. ''I didn't know who these people were. Vane brought them in. I realized right away that something wasn't right, but Vane changed. He wasn't kind anymore. He threatened to destroy my parents if I didn't play along. He threatened me, too, but that didn't matter.''

Tears had started flowing down Alexa's face, but she didn't care. She was finally able, for the first time in these terrible, frightening months, to tell her story. Even if he didn't believe her, she couldn't stop.

''I recognized from the first how much this looked like what had happened two years ago. They'd investigated my parents, and I knew the authorities thought there had been a terrorist plot, but all the truth hadn't come out. I wanted to stop it. Mostly, I wanted to understand it, for maybe if I did, I'd understand why I lost you.'' She glanced at Cole through the veil of wetness. The fuzziness of her own ability to see must have shaded his features, for they no longer looked as hard. As remote.

Was there a suggestion of sympathy in his eyes?

She had to be mistaken. She inhaled shakily. ''I tried to get answers but I couldn't. I couldn't leave without the evidence Vane devised to incriminate my parents. I couldn't—''

''Damn it!''

Before she could react, Alexa found herself drawn into Cole's arms. She tried to pull away, but his grip tightened around her.

''Damn it,'' he repeated softly. And then his lips ground down on hers.

Chapter Eight

The kiss devastated Cole. And revitalized him.

At first, she felt as rigid as a cardboard cutout in his arms. But then she yielded.

No, she threw herself into the kiss with all the passion he recalled.

"Oh, Alexa," he whispered against her.

She made small whimpering noises as her mouth opened to welcome the plunging exploration of his tongue. The sound nearly drove him crazy.

Or was it the sensation of her soft, pliant body against him once again, after so long, that made him feel lost and found at the same time? And hard. Very hard. Almost painfully hard against the unyielding fabric of his jeans. Especially as she fitted her body along the length of his on the bed, her hips pressing against him. When had they lain down?

He hadn't intended to touch her.

And he certainly hadn't intended to believe any lies she told to defend herself.

But...those very realistic lies. The way she reacted to seeing him again. The intoxication of her soft citrus scent.

His continued feelings for her, despite all good sense.

They had all crashed together into one incredible surge of irrationality and need. Need to be with her. Need to be *in her*—

He groaned as she pulled away, swinging one leg over the far side of the bed from him and curling the other on the mattress for balance as she continued to face him. Her lips were swollen from their contact with his. Her chest heaved, the swell of her high, firm breasts visible through her long and prim nightgown. Lord, she was still the most incredibly sexy woman he had ever met. But, sitting again at the far edge of the bed from her, he resisted reaching for her again.

He couldn't touch her now. Not as he watched the unrestrained heat in her eyes grow chilly. She took a deep breath. Her eyes did not leave his. "All right," she said, her voice hoarse. "We just learned something. The attraction we felt for one another—it's still there. Even with me knowing you are not the impostor John O'Rourke, but yourself."

"Yes," he agreed. "And—"

"And nothing. We're not going to act on it. You don't trust me, and I certainly don't trust you." Her expression blazed. "I loved you, damn it! And you died. The pain—" Her voice broke and her head drooped. Her lovely, honey-colored hair draped about her face, hiding her features. Obscuring any tears. But her shoulders shook.

He couldn't help himself. He extended his arms toward her. She must have seen the movement, for she looked up once more with glistening, angry eyes, stiffening her body against his impending touch.

He dropped his hands. He replied to her words in a monotone. "I had hoped that you would mourn me but get on with your life, Alexa. Your *life*. I thought I was ensuring you still would have one. My father had been murdered because of my involvement in that investigation. I'd been warned that everyone else I cared about was at risk, too.'' That had been Vane and Alexa. His mother had died when he was young, a fact he had revealed to Alexa back then. ''It took a long time after the explosion before I could think at all, and even longer before I could think logically, but staying away from you was the only way.''

She studied him for a moment before her expression softened. ''You were in pain, too,'' she finally said. ''Physically as well as mentally, I expect.''

He shrugged.

''Does it still hurt?''

''Sometimes,'' he admitted, though he would never describe the shooting stabs in his back, the cramps in his hands, the aches deep within the bones of his face.

''I assume you look so different as the result of cosmetic surgery.''

He nodded.

''Couldn't they reconstruct your face the way it was before?''

Shrugging, he said, ''They weren't sure, and I told them not to try. In my line of work, a new appearance can be an advantage.'' Especially since he'd had every intention of picking up this investigation again as soon as he could. And if no one involved knew that Cole Rappaport had survived, so much the better. Even now, most members of his Special Forces Unit still didn't know the truth.

''I see.''

He could tell she did, too, by the combination of sympathy and dismay in her eyes. With his new identity, he had fooled her, at least for a while, the person who had known him best—the better to scrutinize her and her involvement.

"I really liked how you looked before," she continued in a small voice, "but this way is good, too."

"Just good?"

Her smile was wry. "Are you fishing for a compliment, Rappaport? Okay, it's great. And I can't even tell it's not natural."

He had allowed his hair to grow much longer than his previous military cut, and he pulled it back on one side. "They did a good job with the cosmetic surgery, but there are still scars along the edges."

She leaned toward him, appearing to study his face even closer in the glow of the reading light. "They don't show much."

"No," he said. "The damage is still much more obvious on my back."

Her head rose sharply. "That was why you didn't take your shirt off at the beach."

He smiled. "And you thought it was just my boyish modesty."

She made a small snorting sound, but the edges of her full, sensuous mouth curled slightly in an ironic answering grin. "Yeah, something like that." She hesitated, then asked softly, "Who else knew you survived, Cole?"

"My boss, Forbes Bowman, pulled me out of the rubble just in time. He'd been on his way with some others to the garage that exploded. We'd intended to—never mind. That part is classified."

"And you didn't tell him to contact me." There was no inflection in her tone, but he sensed both question and sorrow.

"For a long time, I couldn't tell anyone to do anything. And when I regained consciousness enough to discuss it with him, we concluded it was in your best interest not to know I'd survived.''

''Oh.'' Alexa's voice was subdued.

Maybe he had been wrong. If she *had* been innocent, he had left her alone to cope with his death and the accusations against her parents. Had left her vulnerable to Vane's encroachment on her life.

But he hadn't known of Vane's involvement then, either. And he still did not know whether she was a world-class actress, or if she was telling the truth.

Phantom, who had been lying on the floor, suddenly stood at attention. Cole froze, listening.

''What—'' Alexa began, but he held his hand up to silence her.

Cole didn't hear anything, but all his senses were on alert. What if Alexa had been feeding him a line? Was Vane coming in here to see his beloved? To make love with her?

Even when Phantom settled back down again, Cole felt his skin crawl. He had kissed Alexa. Had begun to joke with her.

And he still could not buy that she wasn't in on the plot he had come to investigate. He didn't *dare* buy it, not if he wanted to stay alive…this time.

She was engaged to Vane.

''I'd better go,'' he whispered. He knew that his mistrust had turned his voice cold once more.

''No!'' she said quickly. ''Not until we have an understanding.''

''I'm listening.'' But he wasn't about to consider a bargain that would let her off the hook. Not if she was as involved as he still suspected she was.

''I need your help. I'm a virtual prisoner here—I *am*!''

This last must have been the result of his deep-seated

skepticism being reflected on his face. She bit her luscious and tempting bottom lip—the way he'd do if they were making love.

And then her face took on an imperious expression. "You don't need to believe me. But if we work together, maybe we can get the answers you need to stop whatever is going on. I will do what's necessary to help you with that. In exchange, I want you to— You do still work for the government, don't you?"

He nodded curtly. Was she going to grill him for classified information, assuming he'd blurt it out because he wanted her so badly?

"That same secret agency? Never mind. You didn't tell me about it then, so I don't expect you to now. But I'll need for you to help me locate the file Vane put together to implicate my parents, and to guarantee that someone will watch over and protect them. And you'll keep an open mind about their innocence, no matter how realistic Vane's documents appear to be. Also, if I can somehow prove that I'm not involved, that I wasn't involved before, you'll leave me alone here, at the Hideaway. *Alone.* Without Vane. If you find the evidence you need about this plot, Vane will probably go to prison for a long, long time."

"And if I don't agree? Assuming you're right and your parents and you weren't involved, what can you give me that I can't get on my own?"

She lifted her fingers to enumerate items. "Easy access to the guest rooms. Vane's and Minos's, too. Printouts of information about the guests. And I can keep them occupied while you search. I can tell you what I've heard so far, though I admit it isn't a lot. They've been careful. I haven't been able to get into Vane's computer yet, but you can do that. And—"

"And you're not going to tell Vane who I am?" he interrupted.

"Of course not," she said scornfully. "What good would that do either of us?"

"All right, then," Cole said. Maybe she was playing him for a fool once more, but just possibly she could be of assistance. And if he found he had begun thinking with the wrong parts of his body again, he could always call it off—as long as he remained alive. But for now... "You've got a deal."

"I'M HELPING YOU again this morning."

Alexa whirled from the counter where she was whisking eggs in a metal mixing bowl in preparation for making Spanish omelettes. The voice had not been the one she had been anticipating. And, yes, hoping for.

Minos Flaherty's muscular girth filled the doorway. He wore black sweats, his usual morning garb, for she knew he went out jogging on mountain paths at dawn.

His dark scowl told her he hadn't elected to be her breakfast assistant.

"That's not necessary," she replied with a forced smile. "You can let Vane know I have everything under control and don't need assistance."

"I'm helping, anyway." He walked in and planted himself at the sink, staring at her with his beefy arms crossed.

Alexa gave a groan deep inside. She was being watched even more carefully today. Why? Did Vane suspect something was different between "John O'Rourke" and her? Or maybe he was still just angry about her outing yesterday.

She had put her ring back on first thing that morning. She would have to maneuver herself back into Vane's good graces if she was to be of use to Cole in his investigation.

Thank heaven she no longer felt alone—at least, in the quest to understand what was happening. She knew, from the earlier fiasco, that there could be earthshaking repercussions from the mission Vane's guests were being primed for—whatever it was. She had already hoped she could ferret out the goal and somehow thwart it—once she was able to protect her parents. Now, with Cole's participation, they would succeed. *He* would have the attention of appropriate authorities. Perhaps this time, she could even assist in saving a few lives.

And maybe, just maybe, she had some hope of breaking free of this dismal situation.

But how was she to hide that her despondency was no longer so deep?

She had even gotten a better night's sleep last night than she had for a long time. And she had risen early and taken Phantom, who was now watching from behind his gate in the pantry, for a brisker walk than usual along the water.

She had hoped to see Cole—John—on his morning run, but he hadn't appeared.

She turned to Minos. "Well, great. It'll be nice to have your company. Let's see—there are some fresh tomatoes there, by the sink. You can wash and slice them for me."

His scowl grew even uglier, if that was possible, but he said, "Fine." He turned to study the sink area. Finding the tomatoes, he took them out of their plastic bag and began scrubbing them under the tap.

"Not too hard," Alexa admonished. She kept her sigh low as she returned to her whisking.

"Good morning."

The bowl of eggs was the recipient of her smile, for

she didn't want Minos to see it. When she looked up, her expression was friendly but remote. "Good morning, John," she said.

Cole entered the kitchen with that stride she had remembered so well, the stride she had recognized in the gourmet store just a few days ago. Heavens, he looked wonderful in his T-shirt—sexy, muscle-hugging black this time—and jeans.

She was glad that she had dressed in slacks and a matching sleeveless sweater in a flattering shade of yellow. Of course, she had put on one of her ubiquitous lacy aprons to protect her clothing. She had used a plastic clip to pull her hair back from her face.

"I see you have help this morning," he said, stopping beside her at the kitchen's center island, "but if there's anything I can do, just let me know." His liquor-brown eyes appeared controlled and neutral. She studied that new cleft in his strong chin again, wanting to touch it, to stroke the silvery strands of hair at his temples.

She groped for something, anything, so that he would stay here. She didn't care for him the way she had...or at least she didn't want to, after the way he had deceived her, the way he had mistrusted her. But to her dismay she realized she had anticipated seeing him again this morning just as she had looked forward to each time they were together in the past, and it wasn't only because he represented her one shred of hope for a real future.

"Er, coffee. The beans are in the freezer, and the grinder is over there."

"You got it. If I weren't the world's best home improvements salesman, I'd be its best coffee brewer." He winked broadly at her, and she smiled. From the corner of her eye, she caught Minos's irritated stare.

She tried to recall if she had ever seen him smile.

For the moment, she didn't care. Her heart was lighter than it had been in months. Years.

Two years.

She even caught herself starting to hum as she gathered onions for the omelette, glad that the loud grinder noise hid it.

And then Vane entered the kitchen. His gray plaid shirt was open at the collar, and his long sleeves were rolled at the cuffs. He stopped just inside the doorway. "This room is the most popular in the place," he said cheerily.

"Good morning," Alexa said to him. "Would you like a chore, too?"

"No. Minos, I'll take over for you. You go into the dining room and make sure all the tables are set."

"Sure." He didn't sound thrilled at the new assignment, either, but didn't complain.

Before Minos left the room, Vane said, "I got a call last night from Leopold Salsman." He joined Minos at the kitchen sink.

"Really? He's the local chief of police," Alexa told Cole, who, as O'Rourke, regarded them with interest. She turned back to Vane. "Did the police find who shot at us?"

"Yes, an overzealous hunter up on the slopes, just as we thought."

Alexa didn't believe that for a moment, but who could it have been? One of the guests, practicing for his undisclosed assignment? Vane would certainly cover for him, maybe even encourage the cops—pay the cops—to look the other way.

The police had certainly seemed very respectful to Vane when they'd been here after the shooting.

And the one time Alexa had gone to Leopold Salsman about the inn's odd guests and Vane's changed, officious attitude toward her, he had treated it as a boring domestic dispute. Alexa had learned then that the chief was in Vane's hip pocket. That had occurred shortly after Vane began planting his own guests in the inn. Salsman must have contacted Vane immediately, for Vane had confronted Alexa the moment she'd returned. He had warned her never to try that again. He'd told her that going to the feds would be fruitless, too. Who would believe the accusations of a woman whose parents had nearly been put on trial for terrorism against the word of a military hero like him?

Oh, and by the way, if she ever tried again, he would turn *this* over to the federal authorities.

This was a file of correspondence—copies of letters on Kenner Hotels letterhead, signed by her parents, with authentic-looking signatures. Then there were the response letters, originals signed by people whose names she had first heard during the investigation two years earlier: foreign terrorist leaders.

The letters seemed to be in code, discussed deliveries and receipt of goods that could have referred to the terrorist agents planted in Kenner Hotels. The correspondence indicated that copies were also sent to Warren Geari, manager of the hotel chain who'd been blown up with Cole, and who had been found to have had close terrorist ties.

Then there were the references to payments made to her parents via Swiss bank accounts. ''The accounts actually exist,'' Vane had told her. He had access to them, of course, for her parents would never collect the money. But he would never tell the authorities that.

Sure, Vane had manufactured everything. He might even have gotten real terrorists to sign the letters to her parents. But how could she prove his guilt, her parents' innocence?

"I'm glad the shooting wasn't anything important," Minos said, drawing Alexa's attention back to the present.

Something in the way he looked at Vane as he left the room suggested to Alexa that they shared knowledge of the truth behind the incident. But they obviously weren't going to reveal it.

"What's for breakfast?" Vane asked as he looked over the tomatoes Minos had washed but had not yet begun to chop.

"Spanish omelettes and homemade biscuits," Alexa replied. "Can you get the green peppers from the refrigerator, Vane?"

"Sure thing." He turned his back on the room while he reached in for the peppers. Alexa caught Cole's stare. He didn't look happy. Had he expected a different result from the investigation of the shooting?

"Here," Vane said a minute later. He approached Alexa. Rather than handing her the plastic bag containing three peppers, he put them on the counter in front of her. "I nearly forgot something."

Alexa didn't like the way he was smiling. There was a hint of cruelty in it.

"It's morning, and I didn't give my girl her good-morning kiss," he continued.

Alexa remembered the last kiss she had shared, not with her fiancé but with Cole. It had rocked her clear through to her unclad toes. Had made her want to strip off her too-confining nightgown, and damn the consequences.

But it had been a mistake. She had made herself draw away. Cole had had no right to kiss her.

And Vane had every right. For now.

She tried to smile in return, and she lifted her chin.

Vane drew her into his arms, pulled her roughly against him. Looking over his shoulder, she caught Cole's eyes. She was pierced by their coldness and suspicion.

Don't you understand? she wanted to scream at him. She had to play along even more now that she had made her pact with Cole. She didn't dare do anything that would make Vane suspect anything had changed.

She had already learned that she had to be good, and available and compliant in all ways—except one. She had drawn the line against anything more physical with Vane than a kiss.

But with kisses for show in public, she didn't deny him anything.

As Vane's lips captured hers, she wanted to pull away, but she stood still. She even responded.

Please understand. She tried to will Cole to hear her plea.

But she felt his stare.

He would construe Vane's unrestrained, sensuous kiss as evidence that Alexa was as involved in the conspiracy as he had believed.

"WHAT DO YOU MEAN, 'she knows'?" Forbes Bowman's raised voice was so loud over the pay phone that Cole instinctively looked around to make certain no one was listening.

It was early afternoon. The small convenience store's patrons were a couple of teenagers discussing the merits of brands of soft drinks, and a mother with two children in tow. A different college-age clerk from the one he'd seen before stood behind the checkout stand.

No one paid attention to Cole, who stood with one shoulder against the dingy wall.

"We were shot at yesterday," Cole explained patiently into the phone. "We'd been out sightseeing, though my intent was to subtly grill her." He didn't mention how pleasant the outing had been. How it had felt to watch Alexa in her wet, form-fitting bathing suit. How it had felt to be near her...

"And did she tell you anything?"

Cole pictured his boss's bulk leaning forward in his desk chair as he took in Cole's words, running his large fingers through his white mane of hair to express his exasperation. He did that often in periods of stress, when he was helpless to orchestrate what was happening.

"No, she didn't say a thing that was helpful." Not then, at least. Not while he was still John O'Rourke to her.

"Who shot at you?"

"I don't know for certain," Cole admitted. "The local police were no help."

"Paid off like last time?" Forbes demanded.

Cole shrugged, though of course his boss couldn't see it. "I wouldn't be surprised."

"So you told her who you were?"

Cole pictured what had happened. The shot. His immediate reaction to protect her. His relief that she was all right.

What he had said to Alexa...

"She guessed," he replied to Forbes.

"I won't ask how." His mentor's voice was dry, as if he could read between the lines.

Cole felt the hand not grasping the phone clench into a fist. He purposely stretched the fingers of his hand and laid them against his jeans. "It doesn't matter. I've spoken with her since then. She gave the impression that she's a virtual prisoner there, that Vane has threatened her parents to keep her in line.''

''And you believe her?''

Cole considered his answer. ''To be frank, Forbes, it's hard to completely put aside what I thought was between us before.''

Forbes went ballistic. ''Didn't you learn anything, Rappaport?'' he hollered. ''Two years ago, the Unit sent you undercover, with your buddy Vane, to uncover a terrorist plot at the Kenner Hotels. You unearthed the infiltrators planted for training at hotels all over the country, but you never learned their planned destinations. Instead of talking, most turned up dead afterward, presumably killed by their charming employers. You convinced an insider, the chain's general manager, Geari, to talk to you, and you were both blown up in a garage at the time of your scheduled tell-all meeting.''

''Tell me something I don't know.'' Cole was struggling to keep his temper in check. ''I—''

But Forbes continued, undeterred. ''Before you were blown up, you were playing house with the Kenners' daughter. The guy who'd been your father's protégé, Vane Walters, was your partner in the investigation. You were made, warned to butt out or else, and that was when your father was killed. And then came your own explosion. Now, you just learned, through your own sources, that some main members of that cast of characters are starring in a similar scheme, and you even consider that one could be innocent? Come off it, Rappaport. I don't intend to go up there and drag your sorry hide to safety this time.''

''You won't have to,'' Cole said coolly. Forbes hadn't said anything he hadn't run through his own mind last night, when he'd been unable to sleep. "The thing is, Alexa has said she'll help me find out what's going on. Whether it's to protect herself by turning on her beloved Vane or whether she really is an innocent victim doesn't matter, as long as I get the information I need. In any event, I have to pretend, for now, that I trust her."

And convince himself, he thought, that he didn't.

"But I figure Vane had something to do with the shooting yesterday. He might be spooked. I'd like you to get Bradford and Maygran up here as backup in case some of the infiltrators start getting sent into the field. Tell them they're scouting for a place for a home improvement salesmen's convention."

Forbes laughed. "Right. They'll love it." And then he grew serious again. "Be careful, Cole. Whatever Vane is up to, he's not in it alone. This plot's bigger than he is, and his controllers won't be happy that you're nosing in again."

"They won't know," Cole reminded his boss. "Cole Rappaport is, after all, dead."

"He might be, before all this is over," Forbes reminded him. "Watch yourself." He hung up.

Chapter Nine

Standing near the sink in her frilly apron over a white shirt and beige slacks, Alexa finished washing the lunch dishes. Thank heaven the mundane task didn't require conscious thought, for her mind was whirling like a waterspout on the lake.

It could all be over soon. She might be able to protect her parents, to survive, keep her inn to herself. She felt the edges of her mouth curl tentatively upward at the very thought.

All it would take was to help Cole learn what was going on.

And then the man she had loved so deeply, so completely, would disappear from her life once again.

She sighed. How would things have been, these last two years, if she had known the conniving, mistrustful, lying son of a soldier was alive but was avoiding her? Would they have been any different?

"Yes," she said aloud decisively, slapping the edge of the metal sink with her wet dishcloth. She wouldn't be engaged to Vane, for one thing.

She would have known better than to be manipulated by any man.

She let her head drop forward, her eyes close, as she

steeled herself against the renewed wave of pain. Cole's death had hurt her. But somehow it hurt even more to know he had hidden his survival from her.

He didn't trust her. Even when they had been together, he must have suspected her complicity in the scheme he'd been investigating. That was why he had stayed so close to her then, had sex with her, hoping she would reveal something important in the afterglow.

He had never loved her. It had all been a lie.

She made a small sound of agony.

At the noise, Phantom stood up in the adjoining pantry. He barked for her attention.

She lifted her head. She couldn't dwell on Cole's deception now. She had to concentrate on survival—hers and her parents'. And that required fulfilling her end of the devil's bargain with Cole.

"Okay, boy," she said to Phantom, making herself smile at the wriggling dog. "Let's get out of here." But just as she opened the gate, Vane entered the kitchen.

"Have you finished in here, Alexa?" His voice was cool and distant, which wasn't good, if she wanted information from him. But she didn't dare act too warmly, either, for he would know something was up.

"Yes," she replied. "Do you have any preference for dinner tonight?" Phantom wriggled against her leg, and she petted him, encouraging him to quiet down.

"You know I leave that in your very capable hands." He drew near to where she stood by the pantry door with Phantom, and lifted her left hand off the dog. He stroked it with forceful fingers, toyed with his damn diamond engagement ring. His dark blond eyebrows were raised mockingly, as if he waited for her to yank her hand back.

She didn't, though she had to grit her teeth against the urge. "Thank you," she said. She hesitated. "I don't suppose there's any more information about whoever shot at me yesterday.''

''It was a stupid, careless hunter, Alexa. No one shot at you. O'Rourke and you just happened to be standing in the direction the fool's rifle was pointing.''

Right. That made as much sense as if the mysteriously untraceable hunter mistook Cole or her, standing on the dock in broad daylight, for deer.

Was it possible that someone suspected ''John O'Rourke'' wasn't the innocent salesman he claimed to be—someone aside from her?

Someone who didn't want to be investigated by an undercover government agent?

''You're probably right.'' She tried to pour earnestness into her gaze as she looked into Vane's deceptively youthful and innocent face. ''You know, I really do hate it that we seem to be turning into enemies. I don't like what you're doing with our inn, don't understand it. But we are still partners. Can't we try to work out our differences?''

''Just how,'' he asked, ''do you propose we do that?'' The chill was back in his voice, and suspicion darkened his pale brown eyes. ''And don't bother singing that tired old song to me, that it's your place, too, and you want more say in who the guests are. I just allowed you to bring someone here, after all.'' He dropped her hand and folded his arms, leaning one shoulder against the pantry's door frame.

''Yes, you did. And I really appreciate your not telling John O'Rourke to leave yet. He hasn't said when he plans to check out. But he gets along well with the other guests, and he doesn't seem suspicious that there's anything different about this inn.''

''And there isn't anything different,'' Vane said

sternly. "We just encourage our guests to come from all over the world."

Alexa didn't meet his eyes. "I'm not stupid, Vane."

"We've gone over this before, Alexa."

She made a noncommittal noise, then looked up at him. "I've given up on trying to change things. It hasn't done any good. Maybe it's time for me to help instead. That way, perhaps things can move more quickly for you, and then we can go back to running a regular inn. Unless—" The thought she had been trying to keep way at the back of her mind had suddenly intruded.

"Unless?" he prompted.

"Unless you're intending for this to be the usual way of running the Hideaway By The Lake." She pretended a nonchalance she didn't feel, turning her back on him to let Phantom out the back door.

"It depends" was his cryptic and frustrating answer.

She sighed, watching Phantom sniff the lawn along the upper slope. Then she faced Vane again. "All right. I know you don't want to talk about it. But this group—is there any chance they'll leave soon? John O'Rourke has friends who want to stay here to consider the inn as a site for a small sales conference, and I'd like to accommodate them. It would make this place appear more open to the public."

"Find out when they'll want to come," Vane said. Alexa's heart leapt. He hadn't told her no.

More important, he hadn't said this group intended to stay much longer. And if they were ready to leave, that would be significant to Cole.

But then Vane said, "Of course, if they want to come soon, it won't work. Our current guests are booked for at least another couple of weeks."

Alexa's heart sank. But this, too, would be important

for Cole to know. "I'll ask John what he has in mind," she said.

"It's nice that you're finally showing an interest in our current business, rather than just criticizing me." Vane drew near her again. "If you'd like to really be my partner, that can be arranged." He took her shoulders and drew her closer. She made herself yield. Soon, she was engulfed in his arms. "Two months, Alexa. In about eight short weeks, we'll marry."

He nuzzled her hair. She closed her eyes tightly, willing herself not to pull away.

"Right," she whispered hoarsely, just as footsteps sounded on the kitchen floor behind her. She stepped back, out of Vane's arms, and turned.

Cole stood there. For a moment, she thought she saw utter iciness in his gaze. Or was it the chill inside herself, caused by Vane's touch and his reiterated demand, that made her so cold?

Had Cole heard? Did he know that Vane was setting their wedding date?

In less than an instant, Cole changed and it was John O'Rourke standing there, smiling at them. "Sorry to interrupt, folks. I just got back from Skytop Village and I'm about to do some more sightseeing around the mountains, maybe go for a hike in the woods. Is anyone interested in coming along?"

"Not me," Alexa said hurriedly, noting how Vane's shoulders stiffened. Shoulders that were not nearly as broad as Cole's. Shoulders that would never be offered to cry on. To lean on.

The shoulders of a man she just might be forced to marry as part of the charade.

Fix this, Cole, her mind yelled to him. *Get your an-*

*swers quickly. Put this deceitful man in prison—far away
from me.*

Aloud she said, "Maybe one of the other guests would
be interested in hiking, John. Try Jill Fuller. I saw her
out on the upstairs balcony after lunch."

"Good idea," said Cole. He turned back toward the
door.

He might actually get the beautiful and flirtatious
woman to reveal something accidentally, Alexa thought.

But though the rendezvous had been her idea, she
wanted to throw something at Cole as he left her alone
once more with Vane.

COLE GOT OUT of that damn kitchen as fast as he could.
He'd thought it a nice, restaurant-size room before.

Just now, it had felt as close as if it were a closet.

The heat had certainly been on in there, he thought as
he headed for the stairway to the inn's upstairs.

It had galled him to see Alexa standing so intimately
near Vane. Watching his former friend paw at her, as he
had also done that morning before breakfast. As he did
a lot, *could* do a lot.

And knowing Alexa was willingly in his arms. Planning a wedding with him in two months.

Give her the benefit of the doubt, a voice inside him
cautioned. But it was a very small voice.

You gave her the benefit of the doubt once before,
shouted the larger voice that was his sense of self-
preservation.

There could be an innocent reason for that little scene,
as well as the one he'd witnessed earlier that day. Alexa
and he had made a bargain. She was going to help him
by trying to get information from Vane. Therefore, she
would need to be close to him. Her fiancé.

Two months until their wedding? Was everything to be over by then?

Could Cole stop it in time?

Cole took the steps two at a time, hearing his own clumping footsteps on the rust-colored runner at their center. At the top, he turned toward the lake side of the inn.

As he reached the sliding glass doors to the balcony, he glanced out at the bright blue sky dotted with only occasional wisps of clouds. Skytop Lake shimmered and danced in a mild breeze. People were taking advantage of the great summer day. He heard the hum of the half-dozen visible motorboats through the thick glass.

He unlatched the door and walked out. Jill Fuller sat on a plastic chair, gazing out over the water.

"Hi, Jill," he called in his jovial John O'Rourke voice.

She started in her seat, turned toward him. The frown on her beautiful face quickly changed into a broad smile. "Hello, John," she said in her heavy accent.

Cole couldn't help comparing her with Alexa. Jill Fuller, if that was her name, had an olive complexion and black hair, an exotic look that would drive some men wild.

Cole preferred women who looked more wholesome and down-to-earth. Like Alexa. It was one of the things that had attracted him to her before. Still attracted him…too much.

"Is it okay if I join you?" he asked Jill. "I was just down at the village and intend to do some hiking this afternoon, but wanted to relax in between."

"Please." She gestured toward a chair beside hers.

Cole sat, then leaned forward, hands clasped between his knees. "Is everything all right?" he asked. "You looked a little upset when I came out."

"Upset? No. I am not upset." But there was a catch in her voice. Once again, her gaze wandered toward the water.

She looked more like a pretty woman nervous about her next date than a terrorist trained in blowing up buildings—and people.

"Even though it's obvious I like to gab a lot, I'm a good listener, too," he said. "Of course, I don't know how long we'll be in the same neighborhood. I hope to stay for another week, if I don't get kicked out first." He grinned. "How about you?"

When she glanced at him, he saw fear in her expression. But it segued quickly into solemnity. "I do not know yet. Maybe we will have more time together. But now—" she looked at her watch "—I need to go." She stood hurriedly and walked toward the glass door.

She gasped audibly when her husband walked out onto the balcony. "Oh, here you are, Jill. I was looking for you."

"I was sitting here by myself, and Mr. O'Rourke just joined me." Sounding nervous, she glanced at Cole as if requesting his confirmation.

He nodded. "I'm planning a hike for a little later. Would either of you like to join me? Of course, we'll have to figure out the best place to go. Something not too strenuous. I haven't hiked in a long time."

Ed Fuller gave him an assessing look. Still, Cole believed his salesman-like prattling disarmed the man's suspicion. Was he unhappy that his wife was flirting?

Or was he afraid she would reveal something about what was going on?

"Hi, everyone." Cole heard Alexa's voice from somewhere behind Ed Fuller. "How great you're taking advantage of the view. It's the main reason I fell in love with this place.''

And what about the memories we made here? Cole thought, feeling an irrational pang of regret. He looked Alexa full in her tantalizing blue eyes as she appeared behind Fuller on the balcony. She seemed to sense his question, and her lovely face reddened.

But her small, determined chin lifted as she reached the railing. "A day like this makes me want to go out on the lake with the boat," she said. "Is anyone game?"

No one jumped at the idea. She appeared momentarily taken aback. "Oh, well. Maybe another time."

"Maybe," said Ed Fuller. "Right now, we must go get ready for a ride we are going on with Minos. Come, Jill."

She followed him off the balcony without a second look at Cole.

Alexa said loudly, "This is the kind of day I'm sure you hoped for when you came to the mountains, John. Isn't it?"

"Definitely." He also allowed his voice to carry.

They drew closer together at the railing. He smelled her citrus scent wafting toward him in the soft breeze. Her honey-brown hair wisped becomingly about her face, and her white shirt waved enough in the wind to hint at her sensuous curves beneath.

She was a damn attractive woman. The tautness of his body didn't let him forget it.

But her sex appeal had never been an issue. Her integrity was.

"I...I was trying to get some information from Vane, when you saw us together before." She looked not at him but at the water. Their shoulders nearly touched.

One step to his left, and they would be in contact.

Two steps, and he would be right behind her. He could press her curvaceous back against him, feel her buttocks against the growing tenseness in his groin, reach for her full breasts, the way he had done on this very balcony two years ago....

He was crazy. She was talking about her fiancé, Vane.

He forced himself to stand absolutely still. "No need to apologize to me," he said. "I'm sure Vane and you have been closer than that many times. A lot closer."

"Don't bait me, Cole," she said through gritted teeth. "My relationship with Vane isn't your business—though I've already explained it to you."

"Yeah, you did. It's all over now, and you're just being threatened by him." He didn't even try to keep the scorn from his voice. "That's why you're planning your wedding, and he had his hands all over you this morning, this afternoon—"

"He didn't— Never mind. I only wanted to report to you what happened."

"Besides the little love scenes?"

She ignored him. "I suggested again that I might be willing to help him with whatever he's doing, rather than fight him. He's setting the damn wedding date, and I didn't stop him because I was hoping he'd confide in me."

"And did he?"

She shook her head, tilting it as she looked over at him. She appeared so winsome, so sorrowful, that he had another urge to pull her into his arms.

Alexa was *his,* damn it!

At least, he had thought so. Until loving her had nearly cost his life.

"No," she said. "Vane didn't confide anything. I

don't think he trusts me any more than you do." She laughed at the irony. "But when I turned the conversation to how long our current 'guests' would be around, he said they weren't leaving for a while. That doesn't help you much, but at least it's something."

"Yeah," he said sarcastically, "that's something."

Actually, it did help. There would be no need to tell Forbes to hurry to get a team together to follow these terrorists off the mountain and into their new lairs.

"I don't know yet when we'll be able to be alone together here," Alexa continued. Her eyes widened as they looked into his, and she blushed again. "To search for information, I mean. And Vane's file." Obviously she remembered a time long ago when they had been here together. Alone.

And all they had shared...

Damn! If he didn't get his mind back on business, he might do something he would really regret.

Like reenact the love scenes of two years earlier. When they had made love in their room here at the inn. In the shower.

Even in the dead of night, while all but the lake was still, up here, on this very balcony—

Wake up, Rappaport, his inner voice commanded. *Get your body back under control or you'll need a cold shower, all right. Or a dip in the lake.*

Alexa cleared her throat, then repeated softly, "I don't know when we'll be alone together here so I can get you into Vane's room to search it."

"Fine," he said. "We'll have to work on that."

And I'll have to work on not wanting you, Alexa, he nearly said aloud. He turned and stalked back into the inn.

"WHAT DO YOU WANT ME to carry into the dining room?" Minos Flaherty stood at the kitchen door, arms folded. His eyes were trained on Alexa the way they usually were—forceful. Intimidating. As if they could see through her.

She glanced at her watch. It was nearly seven in the evening. "Well, you could bring the salad bowls for each table." She pointed to the row of ten wooden bowls heaped with the Caesar salad she had just thrown together. "We don't have reservations tonight for anyone other than the inn's guests, and I'm going to have them serve themselves."

"Fine." Rather than using the tray she had left out, Minos picked up three of the large bowls and headed for the other room. He would be back in a minute. Alexa sighed. She felt terribly uncomfortable around the short, husky man with the unwavering stare.

She needed to find a way to get on his good side, too, as she was trying with Vane. Minos didn't talk much, but there was always a possibility that he'd let something slip if his guard were down.

Alexa stirred the large stockpot on the stove that contained the evening's beef stew. She inhaled the aroma. She had flavored the sauce, in which potatoes, carrots and onions simmered with the meat, with chervil, seasoned salt, her secret ingredient—German bock beer—and a hint of ginger.

"It smells good."

Alexa spun to find Cole standing in the doorway. His head was raised as if he had been enjoying the scent, and there was an appreciative smile on his face.

He was dressed in khaki slacks and a short-sleeved cotton shirt that revealed his brawny forearms. His dark hair was damp. Alexa thought of their outing on the lake, when his contours had been outlined by his soaked clothing.

Whatever the explosion had done to him, it had apparently not changed the breadth of his powerful physique.

He was still the sexiest man she had ever met.

"Thanks," she said quickly, making sure her tone was steady and revealed none of her inappropriate thoughts. "I hope it tastes good, too."

A couple of years ago, she had been fully aware of the old adage "The way to a man's heart is through his stomach." Although she had only occasionally helped the chef at the Santa Monica Kenner Hotel, where the chain had its offices, she had cooked often for Cole. In her own apartment in the hotel. In her own private kitchen. Where they could be alone.

He had appeared to like her cooking—among her unrelated skills that involved her hands and other body parts. He had allowed her to think that she had, by one means or another, gotten to his heart.

He had called her "his sky" then, as he had when he had rescued her from the shooter. He'd claimed she was his heaven on earth.

She realized she was staring into his eyes. He was watching her with an expression of…not longing, certainly. Recollection? Was he remembering, too?

Minos clomped back into the room. He muttered greetings to "John O'Rourke," whose demeanor was once more friendly but impersonal.

This time Minos used the tray to pick up all but one of the remaining salad bowls.

"You're forgetting one," Alexa called to him.

"No, I'm not. We're going to have an empty table tonight."

"Really? Is someone eating elsewhere?" Alexa was surprised. Since their arrival, the guests had gone out now and then for breakfast and lunch but had seldom missed dinner here.

"Yeah. From now on. A couple left today." Minos turned his back to her and left the room.

"Who?" she called, but he didn't reply.

"Damn!" Cole muttered under his breath. His eyes hardened. "I thought you said Vane told you they all were staying for another couple of weeks."

"He did," Alexa said, angry that she felt so defensive. But she might as well have saved her breath.

Cole was gone.

Chapter Ten

She hated this.

It was nearly two o'clock in the morning. Alexa crept along the inn's upstairs hallway, her back against the wall. She carried a pen-size flashlight. Its beam played on the wooden floor beside the long rust-colored rug that looked ash gray in this dim light.

The world was nearly silent, except for the faint, normal noises: the distant hum of the water heater. An owl hooting outside. A single car that drove by the street out front.

And Alexa wanted to scream.

Instead, she continued her stealthy journey until she reached the doorway to the room she had been seeking. She lifted her hand to knock, then stopped. No matter how lightly she tapped, the noise would sound like gunshots in the stillness.

Besides, there was precedent. She reached into the pocket of her floral quilted robe for the passkey and let herself in. She closed the door behind her.

Cole's room was dark. She knew the layout of the furniture, but used her light, anyway, to make her way to the bed. She looked down. In the faint illumination pointed toward the floor, she could barely make out the large lump on the bed that was Cole.

She drew her breath in slowly, silently. For a moment, as her eyes became used to the dimness, she watched the gentle rise and fall of Cole's chest beneath the sheet. She absorbed the mystery of his face, its new angles forming enticing, enigmatic shadows.

She resisted reaching down to smooth the dark hair from his broad forehead.

Before, his hair had been too short to form those small and adorable curls.

Before, she would not have just stood there. She would have thrown back the sheets, jumped on him to awaken him. After he'd shouted mock curses at her, they would have tumbled together, laughing.

And then the laughter would have turned to moans, as they—

With no warning, the figure on the bed sprang upward, grabbing her wrist, throwing a hand over her mouth so she couldn't scream. Instinctively, Alexa bit down.

"Damn!" The hand disappeared from Alexa's face.

"It's me, Cole—Alexa," she whispered, glancing around in concern, as if she would be able to tell if anyone had heard them.

"I know," he growled under his breath. "Otherwise, you wouldn't still be standing and conscious."

"Oh." She was uncertain how to respond. Would he have killed an intruder he didn't recognize?

With his military training and powerful strength, he certainly would be capable of it.

He remained behind her, his chest pressing into her back. His arm, as it had reached around her, had been bare. Was he naked? Her knees nearly buckled at the heat that suddenly surged through her.

"What are you doing here?" he demanded, his voice still hushed.

"I wanted to talk to you." What about? She couldn't remember. She couldn't concentrate....

He pulled away. She closed her eyes for an instant, feeling bereft. Again. It was a sensation she knew well.

She whirled to face him. He had taken a few steps away, and she could make him out, standing beside the bed. He reached over and flicked on the lamp on the bedside table. The room was bathed in brightness, and she blinked.

No, he wasn't naked. But he might as well have been. All he wore was a pair of blue boxers. And beneath them? He had apparently been as aware of her nearness as she had been of his, for his shorts bulged in front.

Alexa quickly looked upward—and saw his chest. She recognized well the pattern of dark hair that spread across his pecs and tapered downward, into his shorts.

"Do you still like what you see?" he asked, his voice full of irony.

Heat flooded Alexa's face, and she quickly sought something to say. "I—I was looking for your scars."

He turned around, and she gasped. His back was an irregular mass of pink skin interspersed with white, evidence of the severe burning. "Oh, Cole," she whispered. Without thinking about it, she drew near to him, letting her fingers trace some of the scarring. His skin was warm and only a little rough.

He pivoted and grabbed her wrist. "Admiring your handiwork?" he asked.

She pulled her arm away and stared, horrified. His dark eyes were pinpoints as they glared at her unflinchingly.

She wilted. "I know I'll never convince you I didn't

know anything," she said sorrowfully, "so I won't be foolish enough to try."

Her legs shook, as did the rest of her. She glanced around. The room was too small to have a chair. But she needed to sit down. She turned and planted herself at the edge of the bed.

"So talk," he said harshly.

"I realize this is futile, too, but I saw how you looked at me when Minos said some of the guests were gone. You blamed me, as if I hadn't divulged everything I knew. But I repeated to you what Vane told me. He indicated they were staying for another couple of weeks, and he didn't mention that any of them might leave before that."

"Mmm-hmm." Cole's murmur was skeptical.

"Tonight, after dinner, he came into the kitchen. I'd told him before that I wanted a truce between us. That I would even be willing to help him if it would mean the difficult situation here would end sooner."

Cole shifted, and crossed his arms impatiently.

She continued quickly, "I didn't want to seem too inquisitive, so... But you don't want to hear my worries. Suffice it to say that I asked, as tactfully as I could, why he hadn't told me that the Fullers were leaving."

She had learned who was missing when the rest of the guests were seated. Cole would most likely have learned then, too, that the Fullers had been the ones to depart. Alexa had been surprised. The Fullers, with their accents so thick, had seemed the least likely of their guests to assimilate into anonymity in the U.S.

And she had assumed that training for assimilation was the reason they had all come here. She simply didn't know why.

"I talked to Jill Fuller on the balcony earlier," Cole

said. "She seemed nervous, but she didn't tell me, either." His tone was more relaxed now, less accusatory.

"Vane dissembled at my question, said he hadn't realized I wanted to know chapter and verse about every guest's comings and goings. I had to assure him that I didn't, that I only wanted to know when we'd have more rooms available for other guests."

Cole looked down at her. "Did he believe you?"

Alexa shrugged. "I doubt it, although to convince him, I pushed him again about allowing you to invite some of your salesmen friends to join you at the Hideaway." She stared into Cole's eyes. "The way no one trusts me around here, I could play all sorts of games. If I tell either of you the truth, you'll believe the opposite. Maybe the only way I can get you to believe the truth is if I lie in the first place." She shook her head slowly at the irony. To her chagrin, she felt a sob rise in her throat. "I've got to go," she said quickly, swallowing hard. She stood. "Oh, I almost forgot the main reason I came. I eavesdropped on a conversation between Vane and Minos. Vane asked if Minos had seen the Fullers off all right, and he said he did. He'd made sure they got on the right plane at the nearest commercial airport in Ontario, California."

Cole took a step toward her, excitement lighting his face. "Did they say where they were going?"

"Seattle." Then, defensively, she added, "I know if you get people to check and they didn't arrive there, you'll blame me, but that's what I heard." She headed toward the door.

Before she got there, she felt strong arms turn her. She looked up into those same dark eyes that had regarded her so coldly before. Now, they were intense. "Be careful, Alexa. If Vane knows you're reporting to me, even if he thinks I'm O'Rourke—''

''Then you do believe me?'' She hadn't meant to put such joy into her voice, but the relief nearly undid her. He might not totally despise her, after all.

''Yeah,'' he growled. ''I believe you.''

Before she could say anything else, his grip tightened on her arms and his head lowered.

She trembled as his mouth met hers. The kiss was rough at first, begrudging. It suggested speed and dismissal.

But her arms went around him, as if they instinctively remembered how things once had been with this man. She pushed herself close to him, feeling the hardness of his body against her. Familiar hardness. ''Oh, Cole,'' she whispered with longing.

For a moment, Cole didn't move, as if he were deciding what to do. Whether to throw her out.

And then...the kiss didn't end, after all. Instead, Cole's lips softened. They touched the edges of her mouth, her neck. He opened her robe, and his mouth moved down farther still, his tongue touching her erotically. One of his large, rough hands moved over her breasts, then gently cupped one over her wispy nightgown. She moaned as his thumb rubbed her nipple, causing it to peak.

The most wonderful warmth flowed through her, every bit as overwhelming as it had felt two years ago. She pushed toward him with her hips, feeling his erection, hard and firm, against her belly.

She allowed her hands gently to explore his back, the new roughness. And then downward, inside the waistband of his shorts, until she felt the taut, rounded flesh of his buttocks.

He moaned, thrusting his pelvis toward her, suggesting

erotic sensations that she wanted to drink in, more and more—

A phone rang.

They froze. And then Cole moved away from her, toward the dresser, leaving her shivering. Wanting. Shocked by the sound, and his sudden abandonment of her yearning body.

It was his cell phone. "Hello?" he said softly into it.

What had she been doing? Had she totally lost her mind?

Yes, she had…two years ago. Even if he was playing games, only pretending to trust her, *she* trusted *him*. With information.

And, heaven knows, she would trust him again with her body.

But could she once again trust him with her heart?

While he continued his low conversation over the phone, she refastened her robe.

At least a dialogue had been started once more. Maybe, somehow, they would find a way to help each other. And then, just maybe, she would be set free.

But was freedom really what she wanted if it meant losing Cole a second time?

She slipped out the door and into the dark hallway.

COLE WAS AWARE when Alexa left the room, and the frustration nearly made him drop the phone and run after her.

But it was Forbes on the other end.

"So explain that e-mail a little more, buddy," his boss was saying in a mock jovial voice. Cole could almost feel Forbes's tension as he gripped the receiver.

Cole's boss was an insomniac who often got on-line in the middle of the night. Fortunately, Forbes almost never called Cole then. But after learning that the Fullers had left that day, Cole had notified Forbes as quickly as possible to enable him to get operatives on them—if the Unit could pick up the Fullers' trail. He'd sent an encrypted e-mail with as much information as he had at the time, which wasn't a lot.

Leaning on the dresser, he glanced across the room toward his luggage, where his now-dormant computer lay. "You know," he said, "I was hoping for another room or two to become available at this great inn so a couple of other guys could come and check it out for our next sales conference." Translation: Cole had wanted to notify Forbes both when some infiltrators were sent underground, and when there would be accommodations here for backup. "A married couple left today, so there's one room available."

"That's what I gathered from your e-mail. Did they like the place?"

"They seemed to. I talked to the wife a bit. I may try to contact them again and ask, but I'm not sure where they live. They said they were originally from Bolivia, but they didn't mention where they were heading." Damn! He wanted to tell Forbes immediately that Alexa had overheard that Seattle was their destination, but if someone was listening in, they'd wonder where he'd gotten that information. And he wasn't even certain it was true. Alexa may have lied about what she'd heard… although despite his better judgment he was starting to believe in her again. But Cole realized that Vane might not be giving his fiancée all the truth. If he knew Alexa eavesdropped on his conversation with Minos, he might have planted a little misinformation.

Alexa… Cole was very aware that, despite the rude

intrusion of the phone call, his body hadn't yet returned to normal after their embrace, their kiss. Their touching—

"I want more information about the place before I commit some guys to check it out." More than irritation spewed from Forbes. He sounded angry. But Cole knew that his boss's frustration was not with him. It was with their situation.

"Look," he said placatingly, forcing himself to concentrate on the call, "take my word for it. There will be one room available, at least, so send Bradford and Maygran up here, why don't you?" He would feel most comfortable with fellow agents he trusted as backup.

"Worst case," Cole continued, "they can share the room for a few days. Meantime, I'll give you a call tomorrow. Oh, and by the way, I'm considering a trip soon to the Pacific Northwest to check out a few more possible sites for the conference."

"Really? Like...Portland?"

"Maybe. Or Seattle. I haven't been there in a long time, and I keep hearing good things about it."

Good. He'd found a way to slip in that little piece of information, true or not: that the Fullers had headed to Washington State. Forbes would understand the reference, and anyone eavesdropping...well, it had been a risk, but one he'd had to take. Waiting to speak to Forbes on a different phone tomorrow would give the Fullers even more of a head start, a better chance of going underground without a trace.

"All right. We'll consider a couple more places, including Seattle. But I thought you really liked it there."

"Oh, I do," Cole said with more fervency than he'd intended. "I hate to make a decision too quickly, but I think this place has all the amenities we need, at least for now."

Like a starting point for this latest batch of infiltrators. A spy of his own, to help him get information: Alexa.

That was the heart of it all. Alexa was here. She was helping him, or at least purporting to.

If she was as genuine as she claimed—as he was beginning to believe—then he had to stay to get everything useful she could feed to him.

And to protect her, for if she was genuine, she was in danger. She had already been shot at, although that bullet had most likely been meant for *him.*

"All right, John, my boy," said Forbes Bowman. "I'm counting on you to find the right place for this conference. It's a damn important one. Never lose sight of that."

"I won't," Cole promised. He pushed the button to end the call. He wouldn't lose sight of it, for if they were right, a lot was still riding on getting this assignment completed quickly.

A lot of lives. Including his own.

And, very possibly, Alexa's.

ALEXA HAD HER USUAL morning routine down pat: walk Phantom, then cook breakfast.

She was glad the next morning, as she stood at the kitchen island preparing dough for biscuits, that she didn't have to think a lot about what she was doing, for she was thinking too much about the night before.

Her sojourn to Cole's room. His apparent about-face from total suspicion to at least qualified trust.

The knowledge that he *was* Cole, and the feel of his body against hers once more....

A phone call in the middle of the night, reminding her abruptly who he really was, and why he was there. A government operative, here to ferret out what was happening. To stop it, at any cost.

No, she had better keep her feelings for him in check. Otherwise, she could get burned again. Badly. "Right, Phantom?" She glanced toward the pantry, where her pup was sitting at attention behind the gate, watching her. He wriggled at her words, and she laughed. When she tossed her head, she felt her hair, caught in a clip, swing along the back of her neck.

"Good morning."

She twisted around. Cole strode into the kitchen as if she had conjured him by her thoughts. His dark and luminous eyes captured hers, and she smiled, then quickly turned her attention toward her white, gooey hands. "Good morning," she repeated without looking at him. "I hope you slept well last night...John." John O'Rourke. She had to keep reminding herself that he was John O'Rourke.

"No, actually I didn't sleep well at all," he replied.

She hurriedly looked around the kitchen to make sure they were alone—but she didn't forget he'd found a bug in her room. There could be one here, too.

"I hope you weren't feeling bad," she said, alarm zinging through her. Had the phone call been bad news?

He stood beside her, so close that she fought the urge to rub her cheek against his brown knit shirt.

"I'm fine now," he said, "but I had a touch of flu, I think, last night. At least I felt as if I had a fever." The sensuous glow in his eyes, the slight flare to his nostrils, sent a flash of answering heat through Alexa.

"Sorry to hear that." Her voice was husky, and she cleared her throat. "There's something going around, I'm afraid."

He gave her a sexy smile that nearly made her toes

curl inside her tennis shoes. She'd worn a pink cap-sleeved top and blue jeans that day, and wondered if she ought to change into a tank top and shorts to keep cool.

"Guess we'll just have to fight it off," he said. "Or else we can hope that the case we get doesn't do us in."

She knew he was teasing, but his words were like a bucketful of mid-winter lake water tossed in her face. "Right," she replied grumpily.

"Alexa, how's breakfast coming?" Vane stood at the kitchen door, in a white shirt, slacks and loafers with no socks. Had he been there long? Alexa felt her face flush.

"About another half-hour," she said. "I was just going to put John to work stirring rarebit cheese sauce at the stove for our eggs."

She noticed how "John" gave Vane a totally innocent, salesman's look. "I'm taking notes, you know," he told Vane. "I don't think I'll be able to hire your fiancée away from you, so I'll just steal her recipes, in case I decide to open a restaurant next door to the home improvements store I hope to establish in this area."

"No," Vane said, drawing closer, "I won't let you have her." Before she could comment, teasingly or not, he grabbed her by the waist and kissed her soundly on the mouth. He kept her close at his side when he finally ended the kiss. "Alexa, do you have any sightseeing ideas for today? I think our remaining guests want to do something new and educational." His eyes, when he looked down at her, held a warning she couldn't interpret. She had no choice but to play along—and ignore the way Cole's eyes had narrowed as he watched them, two apparently happy fiancés with a world of deceit between them.

"Let's see," she said. "There's always Big Bear Lake. We could take them there, show what the competing neighborhood looks like." She wanted to throw a look of apology, one that begged for understanding, to Cole, but she couldn't. She would have to trust him to understand.

"Big Bear is a great idea," Vane said. "Not too far, but someplace I haven't taken them yet."

Alexa turned to Cole and asked, "John, would you like to come along?" She knew what his answer would be before he spoke. Staying here, hopefully alone, would be an opportunity he would not want to miss.

If only she could help him search.

As anticipated, he shook his head. His gaze that moved from Vane to her and back was blank, and Alexa wanted to shake him. *I'm playing along partly to help you,* she wanted to cry to him.

"Wish I could come," Cole said, "but with that fever I had last night, I think I'll hang around here and sleep."

"Okay," Vane said. "Suit yourself."

"I hope you'll feel fine by the time we return," Alexa said.

To her relief, his glance warmed a little. "Me, too," he said.

COLE DID FEEL PRETTY GOOD right after Alexa, Vane and Minos left the inn with their entourage of guests. But he could have felt better.

Alexa had told Cole, at breakfast in front of everyone, that she would make up his room first so he could lie back down and rest. He'd found her at the door to his room just as she was finishing. "Look under your pillow later," she'd whispered, then said aloud, "I'm all through here. I'll tend to the other rooms that Minos didn't get to, then we're going to leave. See you when we get back."

He'd hated seeing her being pawed yet again by Vane that morning. But despite how it made him feel, he understood it was part of her act, the one she'd taken on even before Cole had arrived. The one that had become even more important now, to keep Vane off guard about how she was helping.

When he'd locked the door and checked under his pillow, Cole could have kissed her. She'd left him a printout of the names, addresses, phone numbers and credit information of all the inn's current guests. He knew it all must be fake, but even tracing the origins of false IDs could have some use.

There was also a set of passkeys to all the rooms.

After everyone left, Cole used the keys first to get into Vane's suite. It comprised a bedroom, office and bathroom. The place hardly looked lived in. Smelling of pine cleaner, it appeared as impersonal as any of the guest rooms, with generic wallpaper and furniture, and nothing to indicate it was occupied by someone other than a transient.

Except for the computer.

Cole had donned surgical gloves for this foray. It was unlikely that Vane would check his room for fingerprints, but Cole had been surprised by the man's eccentricities and mistrust before.

He flicked the switch and waited for the computer to boot up. The screen soon demanded a password, but Cole had anticipated it. He plucked a CD from his pocket and inserted it. The software it contained should find the password promptly.

But it didn't.

"Damn!" He kept his voice low but pounded one fist into the other hand. The software had been state-of-the-art. But Vane's password had managed to defy it.

This degree of secrecy shouted to Cole that something he'd want to know was definitely hidden on this machine.

Wanting to smash the impenetrable computer, he instead turned it off. He riffled through the files in Vane's desk drawers, but like his furnishings, their contents were sparse and of little value.

It was as if Vane had already stripped them, pending pulling out of here. Was this an indication that the meat of the operation was about to begin?

"I'll find out another way, you bastard," Cole muttered.

There was, of course, no sign of the mysterious file Alexa had mentioned, the one that would tie her parents to the earlier plot. He wasn't surprised. If it were here, Alexa would already have found it.

Rather than waste his remaining time alone, he used Alexa's keys to get into some of the occupied guest rooms. As in Vane's room, there was nothing useful.

There was one more place he wanted to scour: Minos's room. But before he could, he heard vehicles pull up outside. A horn sounded.

His back against the wall to avoid being seen, he turned his head slightly to look out the nearest window. Alexa slid from the driver's seat of one of the SUVs. Immediately, Vane got out of the other and sped over to her. Minos stood behind him, appearing equally irritated.

Cole couldn't hear the words, but their gestures and scowls, right in front of everyone else, told him what had happened.

Alexa had honked to warn him of their return. Vane hadn't liked it. Cole was sure he would complain that her action had disturbed the neighbors, and Alexa would claim accident or a signal to a cat that had gotten in her way....

Good girl, Cole thought as he hurried from the guest bedroom and locked the door behind him.

He would find a way to reward her—even as he asked her for more help.

Chapter Eleven

That evening at dinner, Vane stuck close to Alexa. Too close. He made her sit at his table with two male guests, right beside him, though she couldn't even touch the spicy Cajun chicken dish she had prepared. Her appetite had vanished, replaced by alertness, nervousness...and anticipation.

Vane hung on to her shoulders, her waist. Stroked her arm, bare beneath the sleeveless peach shell she wore tucked into her denim skirt, until he raised goose bumps of alarm and distaste.

Kissed her so much she wanted to scrub her face with antibacterial soap.

Not that he had helped, before dinner, to cook or to serve the guests. Oh, no. That remained too menial for him.

But Minos was with her every second that Vane was not at her side.

She felt Cole's chilly stare on her the entire time.

Don't you know what this miserable charade is doing to me? she wanted to yell at him. *I'm doing it for you.*

And for her parents, herself...and, she was afraid, for the entire United States. For although she still did not know the plans, she had overheard Minos and Vane laughing together about what was about to happen all over this country—and the rest of the world.

She wanted to tell Cole.

More important, she had news for him.

She managed to let him know as he helped her clear the dishes from the table. Minos assisted, too, but he was still collecting flatware when Alexa, her hands wet from rinsing dishes at the kitchen sink, stood on tiptoe and whispered into Cole's ear, "We have to talk. Tonight."

"Your room," he managed to say, just before Minos stomped into the kitchen.

Never before had she felt the time she took to wash the dishes, walk Phantom and get ready for bed drag so much.

And when she had turned out the lights, she lay there sleepless beneath the sheet, every muscle keyed to tautness. The moon over the lake was bright that night, thrusting light in between the slats of her miniblinds enough to turn the furnishings in her room to eerie, shadowy outlines.

The back of her head felt heavy upon her pillow, and she wished she had kept her quilted robe on over the warm nightgown she had worn to bed—a nightgown that, although it had lace at the wrists and neck, was shapeless and unsexy.

She would want no distractions from what she needed to discuss with Cole tonight—certainly not his heated stare that could stoke the tiniest spark inside her to forest fire dimensions.

Minutes dragged as she lay there, listening first to Phantom's restless changing of position on the floor near the foot of her bed, then his heavy doggy breathing. How long had passed? An hour? Two?

And then came the faint sound she had been waiting

for. Her door opened and closed. The edge of her bed sagged.

"Alexa, are you awake?"

It was Cole. Her breath left in a whoosh of relief. "Yes," she whispered. She sat up beneath the covers.

She had feared that after the show of caring Vane had made, he might decide this was a good night to reestablish whatever rights he believed he had as her doting fiancé. She still would have to make this brief, for if Vane were to find Cole here, the havoc could be lethal.

"I'm so glad you came," she said. Cole didn't move, except to reach down to stroke Phantom's ears, as the pup nuzzled against his leg. Alexa closed her eyes for a moment, feeling incredibly lonely. She wanted Cole to hold her, for she was scared.

"What did you want to talk about?" he asked. His tone was neutral, and she was afraid that all the barriers between them that had begun to come down were now even higher and more impenetrable.

Maybe it was better that way.

"I needed to let you know what I learned today," she said. "Some of our guests are leaving tomorrow. I gathered that at least half will be going, maybe more."

"Do you know where they're heading?" Excitement burst from Cole's still-low voice. She wished she could see him better in the dark, but she could barely make out the crags and planes of his features in the faint moonlight.

"No," Alexa replied.

"Damn." This time, she heard frustration in Cole's tone. "I tried to get into Vane's computer today, but I couldn't break the password."

"I think I know where to get it," Alexa said.

"Really?" He had moved without her realizing it, and

his strong hands suddenly gripped her shoulders in the near darkness. "How? Where?"

Alexa laughed at his renewed exhilaration. "He's got a handheld organizer. He always carries it with him, but one day last week he left it behind. I downloaded its contents into my computer into a file labeled 'recipes.' I've checked it out. It contains a couple of long strings of letters and numbers that I assumed were passwords, but either Minos or Vane is always around and I hadn't yet had an opportunity to try them."

"Why did you want to?" Cole asked. He had loosened his grip on her shoulders, and his thumbs were stroking her over her nightgown, just above her breasts. Warmth seemed to spread from the area of contact clear through her, down, down to end in a throbbing of her most sensitive parts.

She was with Cole, the man who had driven her to peaks of ecstasy two years ago.... It was all she could do to continue the conversation matter-of-factly, as if she didn't want to pull Cole into the bed with her. "I hoped to find a reference in his computer about where he put his evidence against my parents, or at least something about the Swiss bank account. I also hoped for enough information to get the authorities' attention about what was happening here—federal authorities. You're aware of how our shooting incident was shrugged off as a stupid act by a reckless hunter. The local police chief, Leopold Salsman, is one of Vane's close buddies, probably on his payroll, like Minos."

"Yeah," Cole said. "I figured."

"From what I could tell, all the guests are going down to the airport tomorrow. I don't think everyone is leaving, but I doubt Vane will want me along. Despite his attentions to me today—" She hesitated as she felt the hands that had continued to caress her withdraw, leaving her as alone as she had felt before. "I didn't invite them," she said in a small voice, then continued more forcefully. "Despite his attentions, he doesn't trust me. He's already lied to me by saying that the guests would all be around for another couple of weeks. He won't want me to know who's leaving, or which planes they board. I'll promise to stay here, alone. You'll need to make up an errand, preferably one he'll think will take you far away for the whole day. Then, we can search together."

Together. For a day...of intrigue and espionage. That would be all they'd engage in *together,* Alexa knew. All she would dare.

"Thank you, Alexa." Cole's voice was soft and it held a warmth she hadn't dared to hope for.

She gulped, for she had felt tears fill her eyes. There was no time for emotion, not now.

"One more thing," she said hurriedly. "I overheard part of a conversation between Vane and Minos. They were kidding one another about the wealth and power they'd have in just a few weeks."

"Did they say how it would come about?" Cole demanded.

"No." Alexa sighed. "But they were talking about the entire world becoming their toy to play with as they pleased." She bit her lower lip. "They sounded so certain. So...*smug.* It scared me. Do you have any idea what they plan, Cole?"

"Not yet," he said grimly. "But I'll find out. *We'll* find out." He shifted once more upon the bed—and Alexa found herself engulfed in his arms. She threw her own around him, resting her head on the firm muscles of his chest. She wanted to feel his flesh against her, but his

T-shirt was like a barrier, preventing her from the direct contact she craved.

She felt suddenly afraid.

"Will it all be over soon?" she whispered against him. She inhaled the scent of soap and musky male. It *had* to be over soon. She couldn't continue to live the way she'd been.

But that meant Cole would be out of her life once more. And this time, it *would* be forever.

"It will," Cole whispered against her hair. "You'll be safe. So will your parents."

And you? she wanted to ask. *Will you be all right this time?*

"Thank—" she began, but her words were smothered in the sudden crush of his mouth against hers.

She didn't think, just reacted. She kissed him back with every ounce of passion within her, wanting him.

Wanting Cole.

Loving him…

His lips felt familiar, yet different. He tasted her with his tongue, taunted her, made her remember. Made her need.

He moved his hands between them, began to rub his thumbs around and around her nipples, causing them to grow and strain. Causing her to yearn for more.

"Cole," she whispered hoarsely against him. She shifted, allowing him free access to all of her, with only a minimum of effort.

But he pulled away. "No, Alexa," he said gently, though his breathing was uneven. "This isn't the time."

But there will never be a time for us, she wanted to cry out. If they were successful in thwarting Vane, Cole would leave. He would be triumphant, would leap into other assignments, a hero.

And if they were unsuccessful… She didn't want to think about that. But the one certain thing was that they would not be together, even if one or both of them survived.

"All right," she said, trying to sound calm and accepting. "We'll just wait and see what happens tomorrow."

COLE STOOD IMPATIENTLY in the convenience store, ostensibly regarding the shelves of soft drinks. Instead, he kept his attention on the pay telephone. A teenager stood there, apparently arguing with his girlfriend.

Cole couldn't wait much longer. He needed to call Forbes on as secure a line as possible under the circumstances, but not all his calls needed to be made that way. Sure, it'd be better if he could talk to his boss first, but they'd already discussed bringing in backup. He'd obtain Forbes's final authorization in a few minutes. But in the meantime… He pulled his cell phone from his pocket and made a couple of quick calls, one to Jessie Bradford and the other to Allen Maygran. They knew his cover, so it wasn't difficult for him to explain to them both over the non-secure connection that the place where he stayed was a great locale for their next conference. It was time for them to come and look it over.

Finally, the pay phone was free. Cole hurriedly called Forbes. "It's time," he hissed into the receiver, when his boss answered. "More of them are leaving today. Maybe all of them. Do you have agents prepared to follow?"

"Yeah. There are a bunch in the hotel at Arrowhead. I'll get them started right away looking for the SUVs you described. But where are they going?"

Cole wanted to pound his fist into the wall. "I don't know yet. I might be able to find out later today, though.'' He didn't take time to explain how. ''But I still don't know the goal of this exercise. I've already called Bradford and Maygran. They're on their way here. If I can't get the information by stealth, I'll get it by force, with their help.''

''You've already called them?''

''Right.''

''Good going. I'll call the guys at Arrowhead right away. How much of a head start do Vane and his alien infiltrators have?''

''Not much. I left while they were still packing—oh, about half an hour ago.''

''Great.'' Forbes paused. ''You know that the key to this isn't running these guys to earth.''

''Yes, I know. Unless we figure out what the greater scheme is, we won't be able to stop them again. We don't even know if this is the only team of infiltrators being planted, let alone their assignment. But I'll get that information. You know I will.''

''Yeah. Good luck, Rappaport.'' The receiver clicked. Forbes was gone.

Cole was again on his own, at least until his backup arrived.

But then he realized with a start that he *wasn't* on his own. He had Alexa to help him.

He was beginning to believe in her.

But heaven help her if she betrayed him this time.

WHEN COLE RETURNED to the inn, Alexa and Phantom were running along the lakeside beach. He parked and hurried toward them. He wanted to shake Alexa. Didn't she know better? Being out in the open like that could be dangerous.

But everything seemed fine. He couldn't help watching

them for a minute. Alexa appeared so lighthearted, laughing with her puppy. She was dressed in shorts and a halter top, and he felt himself respond to her natural and uninhibited sexiness. As her golden-brown hair swayed about her shoulders, its auburn highlights glinted in the sunlight.

Maybe he should have taken advantage of their solitude in her bedroom last night. She certainly had seemed willing....

But he had been right in his restraint. That was not the time.

And *this* was not the time just to stand gawking at her, growing hard with a need he couldn't satisfy.

He walked onto the beach and held up his hand in greeting. "Hi," he said, when dog and mistress ran up to him, both out of breath.

Alexa smiled. "Phantom needed a little exercise, and so did I."

"Did it occur to you," Cole said with an angry frown, "that you make an easy target?"

She looked edgily over her shoulder, toward the ponderosa pine-covered slope from where they had been fired on. "But they're all gone for now."

"Maybe. And maybe it was just a ruse."

"Oh." Alexa chewed slightly at her bottom lip as if she considered whether he was right and she should worry. But then she looked up at him defiantly. "No. You're wrong. They'll be gone now for hours."

"How can you be so positive?" Cole demanded.

"Relax," she said with a half smile. "I know it's your job to be suspicious, but listen. The Fullers left already, and there's been an undercurrent of excitement among the remaining guests, as if something is finally about to happen."

"That doesn't mean anything." Cole was scornful.

"I've been here with them for weeks. The atmosphere is definitely different. Trust me. And knowing Vane and his attention to detail, I'm sure no one will be back till late tonight. He'll get everyone who's leaving to the airport early, make sure they're checked in and that they actually get onto their planes. But he won't trust them. Minos will be his extra pair of eyes to make sure things happen as they should. He'll make the rest of the guests stay at the airport, too, as a lesson in how things are supposed to go. So, let's take advantage of this window of opportunity, shall we?"

Without waiting to see whether he followed, she started up the path to the house.

He hurried along at her right side. Phantom loped at her left.

Inside, they went upstairs and booted up her computer first. She opened a file and printed a page that held several strings of letters and numbers, the information she had downloaded from Vane's handheld organizer. If these were possible passwords, Cole was uncertain why his software had failed to capture them.

Alexa shut Phantom in her room and, using her pass-keys, she let them both into Vane's room. Cole handed her a pair of medical gloves. "No fingerprints," he said briefly.

"But he wouldn't—no, I won't say that. I have no idea what Vane would or wouldn't do."

Cole sat in front of Vane's computer, the printout from Alexa's in his hand. When a password was requested, he entered the first string of gibberish.

Nothing happened.

He tried the next. Still nothing.

"Damn!" he exclaimed. He turned to Alexa. "They're

on the move. Members of my unit will follow the infiltrators, but that's not enough. To stop them, we have to
know what they'll be up to, and if there are any more of
them.''

Alexa lifted her gloved hands in a sad gesture. ''I
know. And I know how important this is to you.'' She
looked over his shoulder to the paper he held. ''Maybe
if you combine these. Do you know how many characters
the password has?''

''No, but it's got to be a lot or my software would
have gotten it.'' He did as she suggested, typing all the
characters from the page onto the screen.

Still nothing.

''Try it backward,'' Alexa suggested.

He looked at her and shrugged. ''Why not?'' He began
typing the characters in reverse order, pushing the Exe-
cute button after each one. ''Bingo!'' After entering
about three-quarters of them backward, the machine per-
mitted him access. He stood just long enough to give
Alexa an intense but brief kiss.

Cole quickly scanned the computer's contents. There
were a lot of files. Reviewing each could take all day. Or
more.

''You don't happen to know what he would call a file
that contains all the information about his criminal activity, would you?'' he asked Alexa dryly.

Her laugh held no humor. She watched him scroll
through the possibilities. ''There,'' she finally said, pointing to a document labeled ''Tomorrow.'' ''Try that one.
Vane loves that song from *Annie,* and he's always talking
about how great the future will be.''

It wasn't the right one. Oddly enough, it contained the
song's lyrics.

And Cole didn't know whether the actual file might be

encrypted so that it would appear as innocuous as this one. The computer didn't hold a zip drive or recordable CD, so he couldn't download all its contents to study at his leisure.

He had to find the right one now.

They opened one file after another. There were others with similar names: "Future," "Prospects," "Opportunities."

And then they came across one labeled "Kenners."

"Let me see what he put in there," Alexa said, her voice shaking.

He wished he had time to hold her, to ease her tension. But they had to continue. Quickly.

He did as she asked and opened that file. There it was!

"Oh, no," Alexa cried, gripping his shoulder.

"Damn!" he said. He grabbed the cell phone from his pocket. There wasn't time to get to someplace secure. They appeared to be alone. And he had to get this information to Forbes immediately.

"It's me," he said, when his boss answered. "This isn't a secure connection, but I needed to report right away."

"What's up?" Forbes sounded alert and ready.

"I found the computer file. I've a list of all the terrorists from last time, and that might help with a conviction on murder charges if we catch their killers, since they were all found dead. Then there are the current ones who were here, along with the places they're to be sent. They're all areas with strategic military facilities, including the Pacific Northwest, California, Florida and Texas. And our infiltrators aren't the only ones. There are three other training installations, though from what I gather their people should just have arrived and are probably too green to be planted at their final destinations yet. In any event, write these down.''

''Can't you fax or e-mail them?''

''I will when I can, but you need to know this now.'' Cole rattled off the training locations and destinations of the Hideaway's agents, as well as the target listed for destruction at each of the group's intended sites. They included military headquarters buildings; airports and air-fields; large barracks; and officers' quarters.

A lot of important property would be decimated.

A lot of lives would be lost.

''Destruction?'' Forbes demanded. ''When?''

''There's no date given, but it's clear they're all to be done concurrently.''

''Damn. The pandemonium all over the country could be catastrophic.''

''That's not all,'' Cole told him.

''What do you mean?''

''It's clear that as soon as the damage is done and the military's on alert at all of these places, there are landing places—air, sea and land—where terrorists from other countries will be brought in.''

''Why? Where? What's the goal?''

''Washington, D.C. All of this is to be a decoy while the U.S. government is seized.''

''What! Impossible.''

''Think about it,'' Cole insisted. ''All that chaos? It'd be a perfect opportunity for a coup.''

''You could be right,'' Forbes said slowly, as if taking time for the idea to sink in. ''Look, how did you get into Vane's computer?''

''Alexa. She found the password, let me into his room.'' He glanced toward her proudly and gave her a wink. "She even suggested that I enter the password backward when it didn't work at first."

"Alexa Kenner." There was a sneering note in Forbes's voice. "The woman who's engaged to marry our clearest link to the conspiracy? The woman who was working with him before? This information is a plant, Rappaport. You've been had again."

Cole froze. He turned slowly back toward the computer…away from Alexa. His thoughts churned.

His entire Special Forces Unit would be mobilized if Forbes gave the word. Perhaps the entire military of the United States. They could all be off on a fool's errand if he were wrong.

If this wasn't the actual scheme, the real one could be carried through this time. Whatever it was….

He couldn't afford to be wrong. The country couldn't afford it.

Once more he turned to look at Alexa. Her expression was quizzical. She hadn't heard Forbes's accusations.

She was beautiful.

And treacherous?

She had claimed always to have been innocent. A victim as much as he was. Could he believe her? *Did* he believe her?

Yes. The answer was both as simple and as complicated as that.

He smiled at her. Though her lovely blue eyes still appeared puzzled, she smiled back.

Without removing his gaze from hers, he said slowly into the phone, "You're wrong, Forbes. I've talked with Alexa. She wasn't involved before, and neither was her family. And she's only going along with things now to protect her parents. She didn't plant anything on Vane's computer. She didn't bring me here to con me. What we found here is the real thing.''

When he began this speech, he watched the shock come over Alexa's face, turning her complexion waxy.

As he continued to speak, tears came into her eyes. She knelt on the floor beside him, placed her head in his lap.

He could feel her shake as she silently cried.

''You're not thinking, Rappaport,'' Forbes barked into the phone.

''Yes,'' Cole replied, ''I am. And I would suggest you get our forces mobilized. You'll need a lot of troops to stop the destruction of all those military installations—and to greet our unwanted visitors when they arrive to invade the capitol.''

''And you?'' Forbes's tone was derisive. ''I'm sure you've got a great excuse to stay there and play house while this Armageddon plot you've unearthed is foiled by the rest of us.''

''That's right, I'm going to stay here,'' Cole agreed. ''And I will protect Alexa. But I'm also going to continue to play the game with Vane Walters until I can see his face when he's stopped yet again.''

''He'll kill you...again. For real, this time.''

''No, he won't. I'm warned. Besides, Bradford and Maygran will be here this afternoon. We'll keep an eye on the infiltrators who are still here—as well as getting whatever other evidence we can on Walters.'' He paused only momentarily. ''Better get busy, Forbes.''

''Yeah,'' he said.

For a moment after Cole pushed the End button, he just sat there. Forbes Bowman was his boss and his friend, the man who had pulled him from the burning garage after the explosion that had killed Warren Geari and had nearly killed Cole.

Forbes believed Cole was being set up again.

And Cole? Well, his gut told him there *was* something that didn't ring true in this situation. He couldn't put his finger on it…yet. But things seemed both too easy and too complicated. Still, he didn't think the problem was Alexa.

He looked down at her. She still knelt with her head on his lap. He touched her soft hair, and she looked up at him, her eyes shimmering. "Thank you," she whispered hoarsely.

"For what?" He kept his voice gentle, not allowing himself to show any doubt.

Did he feel any?

No. He didn't. He was certain that Forbes was wrong.

"For believing in me," Alexa said.

He smiled at her. "We'd better finish up and get out of here."

She nodded.

"Here," he said, pointing to a couple of lines at the very end of the file.

"What's that?" Alexa peered over his shoulder.

"Looks like a reference to a private post office box. What do you want to bet that Vane's keeping hard copies of his file on your parents there? And this—" He pointed to a line that said "Z. Banq," followed by a string of letters and numbers. "Here's your Swiss bank account info, I'll bet. 'Z for Zurich.'"

"Thank God," Alexa breathed.

He printed the contents of that horrifying, incriminating file, downloaded them onto a floppy disk. As always, he opened and closed a few other documents, ones listed on the file of most recently opened documents. That

would make it harder for Vane to recognize that anyone
but he had been using his computer. Then Cole logged
off.

In a short while, they stood in the hallway outside
Vane's room. "There's one more place I want to see,"
Cole said.

"Where?" Alexa asked.

"Minos's room."

Alexa led him down the steps and along the hall past
the kitchen. At its end was the separate corridor that led
to a couple more guest bedrooms, and Minos's quarters.

She used a passkey to let them in.

"This is amazing," Alexa said as she stood beside him
just inside the doorway.

"Why?" Cole asked. There seemed nothing amazing
about this room. It was spartan, containing only a single-
size mattress and box springs on a frame and a chest of
drawers. The floor was bare hardwood—oak. There were
no pictures on the white-painted walls, nothing on the
top of the three-drawer dresser. The bed had no spread
on it, but it was neatly made with white sheets and a light
blue blanket. The closet door was closed.

The room had a clean odor. It didn't look lived in.

"Minos demanded that I stay out of here," Alexa said.
"He told me he'd clean it himself. I figured it was because he was hiding something, like Vane was. But I
don't see anything he wouldn't want someone else to
see—at least, not on the surface. Nothing that should
make him feel uncomfortable with me being in here, especially if I just cleaned the tops of things. He doesn't
have a computer or a desk. But I'll bet…"

She crossed the room and pulled open the top dresser
drawer. Her lovely lips pursed in distaste. For the
drawer's contents, or for what she was doing?

Cole joined her. The drawer contained several neatly folded T-shirts and that was all.

The other drawers were similarly occupied with the man's sparse items of clothing: jeans, socks, underwear. And nothing more.

"Let's try the closet," Cole said.

But it, too, was nearly empty, except for the set of barbells resting on the floor, along with heavy weights that could be added to the ends. It was apparent how the man maintained his muscles.

"Except for the weights, it's as if he doesn't live here at all." Alexa's soft voice was full of wonder. "Who is he? *What* is he?"

"A hired thug," Cole said bluntly. He had moved toward the door to the bathroom. Inside, he pulled open the medicine chest. It was empty.

He checked the cabinet below the sink and exploded with laughter. "Bubble bath!" he exclaimed.

"What?"

Alexa peered over his shoulder. She began laughing, too. "It's not mine," she said. "And I throw out anything like this that a guest leaves. It's got to be his."

They continued to look around for another few minutes, but there was nothing else in that room that indicated anything about Minos Flaherty. Certainly nothing useful. No files on Alexa's parents. No further evidence about the horrifying plot, though Minos had to be up to his shaggy eyebrows in it, just like his boss Vane.

Cole shook his head. Something about Minos Flaherty bothered him—and not just the fact he came off as a violent bully. Alexa had hit it on the head. Who was he? Why was he here? Other than attempting to intimidate Alexa and poor "John O'Rourke," he seemed to have little function.

"Okay," Cole said to Alexa, not wanting to worry her further. "I think we've got the picture, at least all we're going to get. The man isn't a collector. His room, like him, has no personality. And he has two pastimes when he's not working: he lifts weights, and he takes bubble baths."

He loved Alexa's lighthearted giggle as they left the room. It reminded him of two years ago, when they'd had little reason to worry about anything. Then, he had been able to keep his assignment separate from their time together.

So he had thought.

He tested Minos's door to ensure it was locked behind them. Only then did he remove his surgical gloves and stuff them into his pockets. Alexa did the same.

They walked side by side back down the hallway toward the reception area. Cole held Alexa's soft hand firmly in his.

When they reached the bottom of the stairway, he turned toward Alexa. She wasn't laughing about Minos any longer. Her eyes appeared scared when she looked up at him. "We still don't have all the answers," she said.

"No, but we have a hell of a lot more than we did before."

She didn't appear convinced.

"Will we be all right now?" she whispered.

"We're going to be fine," he promised. Without thinking about it, he took her into his arms.

She was warm in her brief outfit. And soft. She smelled like citrus. She smelled of memories, in this place where they had made love and promises together two years ago, before their worlds had exploded.

Gently, he kissed her.

Not so gently, she threw her arms about him and kissed him back.

"Please, Cole," she said, quivering against him.

He knew what she was asking.

Without another word, he took her hand once more and led her up the steps. At the top of the stairway, he looked into her eyes. He saw his own want mirrored there. Still, he had to ask, "Are you sure, Alexa? We won't—"

She must have anticipated the rest of his disclaimer— of promises, of any future for them—and chose not to hear it. She put her index finger against his mouth to silence him.

He sucked it inside, licked it…and she moaned.

With a soft moan of his own, he swept her into his arms and carried her to his room.

Chapter Twelve

In the haven of Cole's strong arms, Alexa couldn't think. She didn't want to think. She only wanted to feel.

Cole believed in her. They were together.

She rested her head against the powerful, muscular surface of his chest as he carried her.

In his room, he shoved the door closed with his foot. It slammed, but she was almost unaware of the sound.

He put her down on his bed ever so gently.

When she looked up, he stood over her with his hands at his sides. The glaze in his eyes spoke of heat and passion and need. And question. He gave her another opportunity to say no. To reject him.

She would sooner have cut off a limb, for he was part of her. He had been before. He was still.

She reached her arms toward him. That was enough to draw him down into them.

For a moment, they lay together, unmoving. Her head rested in the crook of his neck. She inhaled his male fragrance, breathed with him. He used his hand to lift her chin. Slowly, very slowly, he lowered his mouth to hers.

It was as if he had lit a fuse, for the kiss burned her, ignited her, welded her to him. She bit at his mouth, even as his hands tore at her clothes.

She helped him remove her top, her shorts, her under-garments. She lay against him, naked, while he remained fully dressed. The vulnerable, exposed sensation nearly drove her crazy with desire. His hands kneaded the skin of her buttocks, her back, then burrowed between their bodies until he held her breasts. Again, he circled her nipples with one thumb, then the other, over and over, endlessly until she moaned and thrust her aching fullness into his grasp.

He bent and took one breast into his mouth, sucking gently, teasing the straining nipple with his tongue. All the while he stroked her other breast while it waited for the same lavishing treatment.

The feelings were familiar, yet so different that she opened her eyes. She wanted to watch him as he plea-sured her. To drink in the expressions on Cole's new face, as they learned each other's bodies once more.

She wanted to feel him. All over.

She unbuttoned his shirt and tugged it until he moved enough to shrug it off. And then her hand went lower. She touched him outside his pants, felt the hard bulge of his arousal. Heard his gasp of pleasure as she gently squeezed. She undid a button and his zipper, and tugged. In moments, he was as bare as she.

His hand slipped lower, cupped her most sensitive area. One finger, then two stroked her, teased her until she arched against his touch.

She, too, teased. She rubbed his maleness, caressed him, felt him grow and throb until she could not wait any longer. "Please, Cole," she managed to say.

But he was already moving. His weight was sheer wonder as he lowered himself onto her. Into her. She nearly cried out, but his mouth swallowed the sound as he kissed her and plunged his tongue into her even as his body penetrated hers, stroked hers, fed hers sensations that she had thought never to experience again.

"You are still my sky, Alexa." His voice was ragged, his mouth still against hers. "Always."

She rocketed higher and higher until she feared she could soar no more. And then she exploded into a million pieces, even as she heard his groan, felt him grow still, then pierce her one final, fantastical time.

SHE MUST HAVE fallen asleep. She lay on her side, with a man's arms crossed over her chest. Behind her was the warmth of a body curled around her.

Cole's body. Her lover's. The man she would be with forever....

She wiggled her behind, feeling the immediate response of a growing hardness against her buttocks. She purred...then opened her eyes with a start, realizing her disorientation.

For a moment, she had thought this was two years ago, when Cole and she had made love over and over, as if they hadn't a care in the world. Before he had died...and come back to her.

But this time, Cole's wonderfully welcome words of love had been said in the heat of passion. They weren't real, could not be relied upon. There would be no forever for Cole and her. And what they had now was tenuous. Ephemeral.

She rolled over and opened her eyes, to find Cole watching her. He smiled lazily, looked her still-naked body up and down, and she felt desire curl through her all over again.

"Hi," she whispered.

"Hi," he replied, then bent down to kiss her. But even as she threw her arms about him, he drew back. "Alexa, we can't stay here. Vane and Minos will be back soon. We have to be ready for them. And we also have to get rooms ready for other guests—my backup.''

She nodded. Everything rushed back to her now, engulfing her with trepidation. ''Is Vane really involved in a plot to overthrow our government?'' The horror of it made her shudder.

''Yeah,'' Cole said succinctly. He climbed out of bed, leaving Alexa feeling even more alone and afraid. But she nevertheless watched with appreciation as his muscles flexed while he pulled on his jeans.

His back was to her. His poor, scarred back. He had been hurt, badly. Even though she hadn't done this to him as he had previously believed, she would still do everything she could to make it up to him.

If she was given the chance.

As he pulled on his shirt, she rolled off the other side of the bed and picked up her clothes from the floor. She dressed hurriedly.

Looking into the mirror over the dresser, she scowled at the reflection. She opened the top drawer and lifted out a black plastic comb. It was just where she'd thought it would be. Where Cole had always left one. Her frown softened into a fond smile. Some things didn't change.

His face appeared beside hers in the mirror. His new face, perhaps more handsome, definitely endearing. She caught his eye.

His expression was worried. ''I'd send you away from here if I could, Alexa, for your safety. But if you leave, Vane will be angry and might suspect something. We can't let him disappear. We need him to be able to stop the plot.''

''I understand,'' she said. ''And I wouldn't go anywhere, even if you wanted me to. For one thing, he might harm my parents.''

A hardness flattened Cole's mouth before he spoke again. ''We'll take care of them, I promise—clear them of suspicion. I don't want him to run. I don't want the son of a bitch to get away again.''

Alexa turned and hugged him. ''I don't, either,'' she said. ''Not after what he's done to me—and most especially what he did to you.'' She let one hand gently rub his back through his shirt.

She felt his slight wince, could only imagine how excruciating the pain had been when he had been injured, for clearly he still hurt now.

He put his arms around her and nuzzled her hair. ''I don't care about what happened to me. It's my father. I doubt I'll ever find any evidence, but I'm sure Vane killed him. I was warned to back off the investigation of the terrorists in your family's hotels or face the consequences. I didn't give up.''

''Of course not,'' Alexa said, reveling in his continued nearness. He *wouldn't* give up. No matter what, Cole would fulfill his assignment.

Even if it took him years.

''My father,'' he continued, ''was a Special Forces operative himself. Because I didn't back off, he was killed. He'd always been careful, taught me to be cautious. For someone to get to him, it had to be a person he trusted.''

Alexa nodded against him, not wanting to release him. Not wanting him to let her go. ''I'm so sorry,'' she said softly. ''Vane was his protégé, wasn't he? It would be easy for him to get close.''

''Yeah. I didn't mind sharing my father. I liked Vane, and he had no remaining family. We were like brothers.'' His laugh was mirthless. ''Brothers don't murder their families.'' He pulled away from her. ''But I'll get him now, even if I can't pin my dad's death on him.''

''Yes,'' Alexa agreed. ''*We'll* get him.'' Before he could protest, she pulled gently away and left the room.

First thing, she released Phantom from her bedroom, where she had locked him while Cole and she were on the prowl. She let him romp outside for a few minutes, keeping a close eye on him. Then she returned to her duties, with Phantom keeping her company.

She had already cleaned the room previously occupied by the Fullers, to get ready for future guests. It was next to Cole's. She chose a nearby room for Cole's other friend. The previous guests had taken all their things, so they were apparently among the group that left that day.

She was vacuuming, when Cole appeared at the room's door. She turned off the machine.

''I'm back in character as John O'Rourke,'' he said with a wink. ''My fellow 'salesmen' just arrived.''

Alexa accompanied him downstairs to the reception desk. Two men stood there chatting amiably. Cole introduced them, while Phantom circled and sniffed them.

Jessie Bradford was a tall man. Very tall. Alexa surmised he had played basketball somewhere along the line.

She smiled and offered her hand. Jessie took it in his vast paw and bent deeply to kiss hers. She laughed aloud.

''How charming,'' she said. ''I bet you sell a lot of home improvements to women.''

''Absolutely.''

Alexa wondered if Cole had told him she knew who they were. No matter. She would play along, for soon Vane and Minos and the remaining guests would return. She would not dare act as if these men were anything but what they professed.

The other man was shorter and plumper and wore a red baseball cap backward on his head. "Allen Maygran," he said. "And I don't kiss...hands." He leaned toward her and planted a kiss on her cheek. "When we get to know each other better, maybe we can try something more exciting."

Alexa stepped back and caught Cole's eye. He didn't look pleased. "Hands off," he said. And then, back in character, he said, "Alexa is engaged to her partner here at Hideaway By The Lake. His name is Vane Walters. You'll meet him later."

All three men exchanged glances.

"Once you've checked in," Cole continued, "let's go for a walk along the lake. It's got great atmosphere, and I can fill you in on what I've learned about this place— and its potential for our conference."

"Right," Allen said.

Alexa went through the routine of having them sign registration forms and provide credit card numbers. She showed them upstairs to their rooms, then returned to her cleaning, while Cole led them to the water. He asked Alexa if she wanted him to take Phantom along for more exercise, and she agreed.

A few minutes later, she was putting the cleaning equipment away, when she heard a call from downstairs. "Alexa?"

She stood absolutely still for a second, gathering her courage.

It was Vane.

"Up here," she called. In a moment, she heard footsteps on the stairs. She pasted a smile on her face and walked down the hall to greet him.

How was one supposed to act with a terrorist planning to overthrow the government?

Normally, she told herself. She was engaged to marry this particular terrorist. For now, she had to continue to play that role. Her life might depend on it. And her parents' lives, and Cole's…and her country.

Vane was smiling as he waited at the top of the steps. He still looked youthful and carefree when he smiled like that. How did he manage his conscience?

What conscience? He couldn't have one, Alexa realized, to be involved in such a horrific plot.

He hugged her and kissed her cheek. She managed to give him a friendly squeeze in return. "Did you see everyone off all right?" she asked.

"Sure did. They're on their way." He had sent terrorists off to blow up military installations, probably prepared to kill anyone in their way, and he sounded cheerful about it. Alexa forbade herself from shuddering, for he would feel it. He still held her close. Too close.

"Great," she managed to say. "Since we had a few rooms become vacant, I told John it was all right for some of his fellow salesmen to stay here. They're the ones looking for a place for a small conference in a month or two." She felt Vane stiffen. She had to play dutiful fiancée, no matter how much she despised it. "I hope that's all right with you," she said. "If not, if you'll just let them stay for tonight, I can tell them that you'd booked their rooms without my knowing about it and send them on their way tomorrow."

He backed away. His eyes, as icy as the lake's surface in winter, regarded her angrily. "That would be better, Alexa. I know we talked about having more of your salesmen come, but I'd no idea it would be this soon. At least wait until the rest of our current guests have left."

"Sure, Vane," she said nervously. It was all right for

her to act nervous in front of him. She had been doing so for months.

"I was just about to start dinner," she said. "I'll tell them when they come up from the lake to eat. In the meantime, how many of our other guests are still here? I need to know how much food to prepare."

"There are six left," he replied. "I'll see you at dinner. Right now, I have paperwork to do."

As he walked toward his room, Alexa couldn't help feeling even more worried. Would he be able to tell she and Cole had been there? Would he know they had read his computer files?

Would he realize that they now knew exactly what kind of miserable scum he was?

She descended the steps slowly, waiting for his furious shout.

But the upstairs hallway was silent.

Alexa popped into the parlor and gave a brief hello to their remaining guests. All men, she realized.

Where had the others gone? Was that information in the files Cole had taken off Vane's computer?

Where was this group destined for?

"Do you need help with dinner tonight, Alexa?" She nearly jumped out of her skin. Minos had appeared from nowhere to stand beside her. He stared assessingly with his small and cunning eyes.

Bubble bath. But she didn't find it funny now. Nothing about this man was humorous.

She shook her head. "No, thanks. Since we don't have a full house any longer, I'll keep things simple. But I appreciate your asking." Like heck she did. But she had to stay cordial. Pretend normality.

Everything will be fine, she told herself firmly as she headed for her kitchen. *Cole will see to it.*

"GREAT DINNER, Alexa." Cole was seated at a table with Bradford and Maygran. Since he was ostensibly entertaining his friends, he hadn't offered to help her with dinner. Nor did he rise to help with the dishes.

He was glad to see Vane give a nod to Minos. The short thug with the big muscles rose from a table where he'd sat with some of the remaining guests. He began collecting dirty plates.

"So what is there to do around here after dinner?" asked Jessie Bradford as he stood and stretched his tall frame.

Bradford was dressed in a short-sleeved checked shirt and off-white slacks, but Cole had seen him most often in camouflage gear. Jessie had been a Navy SEAL, and had worked with the super-secret Delta Force before joining the antiterrorist group run by Forbes Bowman a few months earlier. Cole was glad he'd been available to help out here. Though part of the assignment Cole had wanted backup on had been completed—learning the goal of the terrorist plot—he still needed to take down Vane and his lackey Minos. Jessie would be an asset.

Allen Maygran was younger and more conservative, but he, too, knew his way around antiterrorist operations. Since Cole's return to active duty, he had had an assignment with Maygran in which they had rescued a U.S. businessman in Baja being held for ransom. The businessman was now well and happy and reunited with his family. The kidnappers had disappeared into the Sea of Cortéz.

"We've been playing along with game shows on TV after dinner," Cole told Jessie. "You want to join us?"

"No, I think I'll take another little walk along the lake. It's nice out there." Cole knew what that meant: Jessie wanted to do his own reconnoitering around the area.

"And I'm going to check my e-mail," Maygran told them. "Maybe I'll join you outside a little later." Allen Maygran was also an expert in technology, including state-of-the-art listening devices. Cole anticipated that all the walls in this inn would soon have ears. And any discussions of where today's infiltrators had been planted, where the remaining ones were going, would soon be on tape.

In the meantime, Cole would hang around in Alexa's general vicinity, in case she needed him.

For now, everything was under control.

But he wasn't so certain of that a couple of hours later. He hadn't seen Jessie Bradford return. He went upstairs and knocked on Allen Maygran's door. No, he hadn't seen Jessie.

They both went out on the balcony and looked down toward the lake.

There was no sign of their compatriot.

"I'll go look for him," Cole told Maygran. "You send an e-mail to Forbes, then join me. I'll take Alexa's dog for a walk. Maybe he can help me run down Bradford."

He found Alexa in the kitchen, preparing a grocery list. As John O'Rourke, he played jovial guest, just a little curious about what happened to his friend. "It's easy to get carried away by the great scenery at this lake," he said aloud. But he could see by the worry in Alexa's eyes that she, too, understood the potential significance of Jessie Bradford's disappearance.

No one would bother with a salesman looking for a convention site. But a terrorist would gladly dispose of a government agent out to stop him.

With Jessie's skills, it would be hard for anyone to bring him down. But if he was all right, where was he?

"I'll come, too," Alexa said with a too-bright smile. She had already reached behind her to untie her apron.

"No, everything's fine," Cole lied. "I'll walk Phantom for you, though. Ol' Jessie's going to be embarrassed enough if I discover that he's gotten lost and can't even follow the lake back." He warned her with his steady gaze: Stay here. Be careful.

The way she gnawed on her lower lip told him she understood. "Okay," she said cheerfully. "Good luck."

Cole was afraid he would need it.

But he didn't get it, for about half an hour after they'd set out, Phantom whined and pawed at the door to a neighbor's boathouse about a hundred yards along the lakefront from the Hideaway.

"What is it, boy?" Cole asked, though he already knew.

He opened the door...and stood absolutely still, except that his hand reached below his jacket to his shoulder holster, where he had stuffed his Beretta before leaving the inn.

He needn't have bothered. It was too late to help Jessie Bradford.

He lay there in a pool of blood, a knife stuck in his gut.

Cole checked for a pulse, just in case. There was none.

He turned and raced back toward the inn.

Chapter Thirteen

Cole reached the house in time to see one of the SUVs disappear down the driveway. He gave chase but couldn't catch it. He couldn't even tell for certain who was in it, although it seemed packed.

Where was Alexa? He had to warn her. And Maygran. Allen needed to know what had happened to Jessie. They had to contact Forbes. But first, Cole needed to make sure Alexa was safe.

His hand inside his jacket clutching his Beretta, Cole burst through the kitchen door. Vane stood inside, smiling insidiously at him. His left arm was around Alexa. He aimed a Glock at Cole with his right hand.

It was too late for Cole to draw his gun, too risky to drop to the ground, pull it out and fire, with Alexa standing there.

"Welcome back, *Cole*," Vane said.

Cole's breathing was irregular and deep, as much from emotion as exertion. He felt enraged. Powerless.

Frightened for Alexa.

But Alexa moved, unhindered, away from Vane and closed Phantom behind the pantry gate. She appeared nonchalant, in control. Not scared in the least.

Why?

Vane approached Cole, the Glock still trained on him. He patted Cole outside his jacket, then removed the gun from its holster, checked the safety and stuck it into the back waistband of his own pants. Then, slowly, he backed away till he stood where he had been when Cole had come into the kitchen.

Alexa returned to Vane's side.

"How long have you known who I am?" Cole directed his demand to Vane through teeth clenched as tightly as his fists.

"All along. Haven't we, darling?" He squeezed Alexa.

She was smiling at Cole now, too. But it wasn't the loving smile he had come to treasure again. Instead, she looked as sinister as her fiancé.

But beautiful, in her softly clinging shirt, her tight jeans. Her golden-brown hair hung loose, a halo that framed her lovely face.

How could innocent-looking beauty like that obscure such evil? Cole shook his head slowly, as if in denial.

Alexa, however, denied nothing. "Of course. Did you think I would keep anything so important from the man I love?" She stretched enough to throw her arms around Vane and kiss him. But she didn't distract the man Cole had once thought of as a brother. Vane's eyes remained open as he regarded Cole with triumph.

Cole wanted to smash something, preferably Vane's smug face. And Alexa's, too—even though he had never even considered striking a woman before.

She had done it to him again. Betrayed him. And this time he had allowed it, with his eyes wide open.

His mind taunted him now with epithets worse than "fool." He had been a dupe, an idiot, a besotted SOB who'd thought with his sex organs instead of his head.

His sky. That was what he had called her in the heat of passion. But he knew far better. She was his hell.

Unable to bring himself to look at her any longer, he demanded, "Where's Maygran?" Maybe there was hope that his fellow agent lurked somewhere, ready to come to his aid.

"Poor fellow had a small accident," Vane said. "Somewhat similar to his friend Bradford's, I'm afraid."

Then Maygran was dead, too, damn it.

Bradford and Maygran had been Cole's friends.

At least he had learned early enough to get information to Forbes about what the plot was intended to achieve. With luck, Forbes would be able to thwart it.

For Cole knew he wouldn't be allowed to live.

But he would stay alive as long as possible. Perhaps he would find an opening, a way to save himself.

And if, instead, he was to die, he would try to take Vane with him. And that damn faithless turncoat Alexa, too.

His instincts had told him there was something else he should see in this situation, but he had turned his back on the most obvious explanation: Vane and Alexa *were* in it together.

"Sit down, Cole." Vane used the gun barrel to motion Cole toward a chair near the kitchen's center island.

Cole had little choice but to comply. Seated, he felt even more vulnerable.

"Tie him up, Alexa."

She moved toward him, then disappeared behind his chair. In moments, one arm was jerked behind him, and then the other. His wrists were tied tightly together, then Alexa stepped back. He felt cold metal pressed under his chin, as Vane tugged on his bonds, assuring himself they were tight.

"Why, Vane?" he asked, when Vane faced him once more. Cole wanted to buy time. He tried to be surreptitious as he strained at the cord that bound him, but it didn't budge. He wondered whether there was any blood circulation at all in his hands.

Alexa had done her job well.

"Why did you betray our country? And my father—"

"Your father was a worthless bastard who couldn't see the truth when it hit him in the face." The bitterness in Vane's shout was almost palpable.

Cole blinked, absorbing it. "What truth was that?"

Vane stood before Cole, regarding him coldly. "I joined his elite little group three years before you did. I threw myself into it because I believed in it. But then, you got out of school and he insisted that the Unit take you in. No nepotism, though, he said, so he allowed himself to be promoted to another Special Forces Unit. But he still had power and authority. Even though your friend General Forbes Bowman was put in charge of our unit, my dear mentor General Carter Rappaport, your father, made certain that *you,* his flesh and blood, were given the most prestigious assignments, that *you* were promoted on the fast track. I'd been there longer. I was more highly trained. I liked the old man. Loved him like a father. And yet, you—" His voice had risen until it was an octave higher than normal. He calmed it suddenly. "I was easily recruited by my current employers." Again he regained his evil smile. "More money and more power than you could ever dream of, and revenge to boot. Who could ask for more?"

"Did you kill him yourself?" Fury raged within Cole, but he kept his voice utterly toneless.

"Of course." Vane leaned carelessly against the counter, crossing his legs at the ankles. "But that was your fault, you know. You'd been given the assignment of finding out what all those foreigners from unfriendly countries were doing in Kenner Hotels throughout the country. *I* was given the assignment of preventing you from finding out. But you were getting too close. You had to be stopped, and so you were warned.'' He put his face right in front of Cole's, so close that Cole could smell the garlic Alexa had put in their chili at supper.

Had they been doing something so mundane as eating dinner, only a short while ago?

''But you didn't heed the warning,'' Vane finished, drawing back. ''So I had to show that my threats weren't idle. And it felt good, very good, to demonstrate to Carter Rappaport at last who was better—his dear, inept son or me. He didn't believe I would actually kill him, you know—not until I pulled the trigger. His look of astonishment was priceless.''

Pain threatened to turn Cole into a howling mass of anguish, but he squashed all emotion. He forced himself to stare over Vane's shoulder toward Alexa. She looked pale, the beautiful demon who had betrayed him once again. But her expression was neutral, as if Vane had merely been giving a weather report.

''You killed him.'' Cole's voice was hoarse. He made himself clear his throat. ''And you damn near killed me.''

Cold fury washed over Vane's face. ''If only I had, we wouldn't have had to go through this miserable scene today. I knew you'd convinced Warren Geari to spill what he knew, that you were meeting him in the Kenner Hotel garage. He'd been vital to our plan, in its incarnation at that time. As business manager of all the Kenner Hotels, he'd been in an ideal position to make rooms and other amenities available to our guests, while we trained them and before we sent them off on their well-armed covert assignments all over the country. I figured a well-timed explosion would get rid of both that squealing rat and you.''

''But thanks to Forbes Bowman, I survived.''

Vane did not reply for a moment. ''That was a damn shame,'' he finally said.

Cole knew he had to keep Vane talking as long as possible. The moment he stopped, he was likely to shoot. ''But tell me why you got involved with this plot to over-throw our government. What's in it for you?''

Vane approached Cole, his gun still leveled at his chest. ''You believed that? I knew Alexa would help you hack into my computer. It was part of the plan. But you can't really think that what you found there is actually what's going on.''

Cole's heart sank. He had at least believed that the information he had imparted to Forbes was correct. If so, Forbes could get the military on alert and stop the entire plot.

But if they were sent off on a wild-goose chase in-stead…this time Cole *would* be killed, and his death would be for nothing.

Forbes had suspected another ruse. Had Cole con-vinced him otherwise? He sure as hell hoped not.

''Tell me,'' Cole said as nonchalantly as possible. ''Since you've managed to fool me in so many ways, won't you let me die knowing the real goal of your in-genious scheme?''

''I don't think so.'' Vane laughed. ''And you're not going to die just yet. I suspected all along that you had survived the explosion. And I knew who you were the moment you arrived. Do you realize, I've purposely dis-obeyed orders to keep you alive this long? Minos was trying to speed things up. He's the one who shot at you, you know. I've had to rein him in over and over.''

"Why did you bother?" Cole growled.

Vane shrugged. "After all you did to me, I wanted to see you suffer. And the best way to do that was to make sure you saw exactly what Alexa and I mean to one another. I figured you'd show up here eventually, since I had her. You'll die soon, but not just yet. As soon as Minos returns to keep an eye on you, Alexa and I are off to Las Vegas to be married. When we get back, that's when you'll die. I'll make certain that Minos understands that.''

Cole glanced over his shoulder at Alexa. Her smile was fixed on him. She didn't deny a thing.

Without thinking, and notwithstanding the way his hands were fettered behind him, he leapt toward her, dragging the chair with him. "You damn—"

He didn't finish that thought. Pain exploded through his head, and the world went black.

PHANTOM BARKED AND SNARLED, but his lunges did not budge the gate that held him in the pantry.

Ignoring Vane's angry commands to back off, Alexa knelt at Cole's side. Blood trickled from the side of his head, into the silvery edges of his dark hair. She touched his neck, felt his pulse. It was strong. He was still alive.

Thank heaven.

That meant she had to continue with this awful charade, but she would do it. For Cole. Even though he believed all that Vane said and despised her for it.

For if she hadn't gone along with it, Vane had made it very clear that he would shoot Cole the moment he came back into the house, or the first time Alexa failed to agree with something Vane said.

"Get up!" Vane raged, and dragged Alexa to her feet.

She whirled to confront him. "We had a deal. I would do as you said, and you wouldn't hurt him."

"Wouldn't *kill* him. There's a difference."

"Not to me." Her hands were on her hips, and her entire body trembled with anger. "If you hurt him any more, I won't go along with you at all." She paused. "You're going to kill us both, anyway."

Vane didn't deny it. So much for his obsession with her. He was *more* obsessed with obtaining revenge against Cole for being better than him, for having a loving father. Alexa knew that all she could do was to buy Cole and her some time.

Buy *Cole* time. For she would do anything to get him out of this. No matter what he thought of her, she loved him. And even though she wasn't sure what the purpose of Vane's plot actually was, she knew it was evil, and Cole had to stop it.

She just prayed he would also do as he'd promised: protect her parents. For as part of Vane's coercing her to play along with him, he had begun to threaten not only her family's freedom, but their lives as well.

She turned her back on Vane and went to the sink. There, she dampened a paper towel and returned to Cole's side. She gently sponged off the blood. "I'm so sorry, Cole," she whispered low. But he was still unconscious, couldn't hear her.

A cell phone rang behind her. Vane answered. "Hi, Minos. Where are you?"

He listened, then said, "Good work. Then they're all on their way? Great." Another pause, then he said, "I'll have to go upstairs to get that information."

Alexa didn't look up until Vane kicked Cole's side. Cole did not awaken but moaned slightly.

"Why did you do that?" she demanded.

"I just wanted to make sure he was still out. And he'd better still be there when I get back. This'll only take a couple of minutes."

He turned and left the kitchen. His voice grew muted as he continued to talk on the cell phone.

Alexa grabbed a knife from the butcher block near the sink and quickly but carefully sliced at the ropes around Cole's wrists. Then she shook him gently. "Cole? Cole! Wake up."

He stirred, but just barely.

She stood and drenched a paper towel at the sink. When she got back, she squeezed water over his face. Would this work? It *had* to.

Cole's eyes opened slightly. "Thank heaven," Alexa exclaimed. "Get up. Now."

He shook his head, then flexed his hands and raised one to the wound.

"You'll be fine," Alexa said. "But you have to get out of here before Vane comes back."

That apparently spurred Cole to come fully awake. "Where is he?" he spat, pulling himself to his feet. Alexa helped him.

"He's upstairs. But he'll be back, and Minos is on his way, too. You need to get out of here."

"What the hell kind of new ruse is this, Alexa?" He was entirely conscious now. In his fury, he grabbed her arm and squeezed, hurting her. "I'm sick of your mind games." He stared into her face, his expression furious and feral.

She swallowed. She wanted to explain, but there was no time. "Fine," she said. "Now shove me away, quickly. Preferably against a wall. I need to say I thought you were unconscious and tied, but you were faking, and somehow already free. I mustn't have tied the ropes as tightly as he and I thought. You overpowered me, then ran out of here."

"The plot, damn it. I'm not leaving until I get the whole story."

"You'll never figure it out if you're dead."

He didn't move, didn't release her now-throbbing arm. "Cole, leave. Quickly. Vane killed your friends, and he'll kill you, too. Please take the rope so he can't see I cut it."

He glanced toward the kitchen door. "Is someone out there ready to shoot if I try to get away?" His voice was little more than a growl.

"No. Minos isn't back yet."

"Why should I believe *you?*" He stared down at her coldly.

His iciness made Alexa shiver. She wanted to cry. She'd done the only thing she could to save the man she loved: she had made him hate her. But it would be for nothing if Vane caught him now.

"You have no reason to," she agreed pleasantly. "But think of your options—stay here and wait for Vane to shoot you, or make a break for it and see if you can get away."

"You're coming, too." He dragged her a few steps toward the door. "I want to hear the rest of the story from you."

She wanted to go with him. God, how she wanted to. But she couldn't. Not now. "I'll only slow you down," she whispered. Then, more strongly, she insisted, "Now push me."

"No."

"Then just leave."

He hesitated just one moment more. "I suppose I

should thank you for letting me go—assuming I'm not shot the second I step out the door."

"No need—" she began, but it was too late. He couldn't hear her. He was gone.

At least he had grabbed the severed rope.

She glanced outside in time to see him hurry off toward the property next door, and its stand of sheltering white pine trees.

Were those the last words she would ever hear from Cole? Probably, Alexa thought, her grief threatening to overwhelm her. Unless, someday, he was the one to arrest her for treason—assuming she survived that long.

She had to try, at least. Steeling herself, she threw her body against the nearest kitchen wall, gratified at the loudness of the *thud*. She screamed, made herself crumple to the floor—in time to hear Vane's running footsteps as he reentered the kitchen.

She whirled. "Oh, Vane, he was faking, after all. His hands weren't tied tightly enough. He jumped me just after you left the room."

"You expect me to believe that, especially after I was careful to check the way you tied him?" Vane said. *He* had no compunction about shoving her. He knocked her, once more, against the wall. "You liar. I'll take care of you and your parents as soon as I get back."

Phantom snarled again and hurled himself at the gate. Thank goodness, it held, for Alexa had no doubt that Vane would shoot the dog in his frustration.

"Which way did he go?" Vane demanded, towering over her menacingly.

Wincing from the pain in her side, Alexa thought fast. Vane wouldn't believe what she said, for he knew she would be trying to protect Cole. "Toward the trees," she said.

As she suspected, Vane ran down the path to the lake.

This was *her* opportunity! She had to get out of here, then call her parents. Warn them.

Alexa let Phantom out of the pantry. She ran upstairs for her purse, then down the steps toward the reception area.

And stopped. Minos was there, his gun pointed at her. Of course. Vane must have known he was this close, or he would never have left Alexa alone in the house.

"Where are they?" Minos demanded.

"Outside," Alexa said. "Cole got away." She heard the triumph in her voice and hoped that what she said was true. Vane hadn't returned yet. That just might be a good sign for Cole.

Minos grabbed Alexa's purse from her hand and took her arm, the same one that Cole had squeezed. "Let go of me," she demanded loudly through her pain, unwilling to show Minos any sign of weakness.

Phantom leaped on Minos, and he kicked the dog away. Phantom yipped and curled up on the floor.

"Let me go to him," Alexa said, her panic obvious in her shrill tone.

But Minos ignored her, dragged her up the stairs. He locked her in one of the guest rooms. "You'll stay here till one of us lets you out."

FROM BEHIND ONE of the thickest of the young white pines, Cole watched the inn. He'd seen Vane race down the path toward the lake and been pleased that he had a little more time.

But then Minos had pulled up in the missing SUV. Damn! One against one would have been easier.

At least Vane hadn't taken his cell phone. "Forbes," he hissed into it. "Listen. I need more backup. Bradford and Maygran are dead." He quickly related all that had happened.

"But you're all right?" Bowman demanded.

"For now. Hurry." Cole pressed the End button.

If only he had his Beretta. But he could survive without it...he hoped.

His head ached like the devil. But he hadn't time to pamper himself. Too much was at stake.

He saw Minos exit the kitchen door. He talked on a cell phone—to Vane, Cole presumed.

He headed directly toward Cole.

Cole scanned the area toward the lake. There was no sign of Vane now. At least he was unlikely to show up at this moment. Maybe it would be one against one.

But the wrong one was armed.

At least Phantom wasn't with him. Cole wouldn't have a chance if the dog, no matter how well-meaning, pointed him out.

He crouched, his shoulder hard against the tree. He remained absolutely still, clutching the trunk, feeling the bark scratch his skin. He inhaled the scent of fresh mountain air mingled with pine. Perhaps for the last time.

He had always believed he would speak Alexa's name with his dying breath. Now, he wondered whether, if he did, it would be because she had killed him.

No. He didn't dare allow himself to think about Alexa and her duplicity now. He had to concentrate.

But Alexa...she had released him.

Apparently Minos wasn't concerned about being seen. He stomped into the thicket, his footsteps crunching on dead needles.

Cole waited, holding his breath. It was around 8:00 p.m., not yet dark outside on this summer evening. If only he had worn camouflage. Would he stick out, be entirely obvious in his jeans and jacket? Probably. His plain white T-shirt would be even worse.

Minos hadn't shot at him yet, but he did draw closer. Too close...

"Might as well give up, Rappaport." Minos pointed his Smith & Wesson, tipped with a long silencer, directly toward where Cole knelt. "It's over."

"Is it?" Cole remained cool, though he started to rise.

Minos drew closer. The gun was leveled right at Cole's gut. "What do you think?" He laughed.

"Maybe." But Cole ducked and lunged forward, all in one motion. The gun went off with a low thudding sound. The shot missed him.

But he didn't miss Minos. He tackled the short, muscular thug. It was as if he dove into a cement-filled swimming pool. But he had aimed at Minos's legs, and the goon fell to the ground, lashing out with his arms and the gun.

Sitting on Minos's knees, Cole used a karate chop to his unprotected throat. The smaller man gasped, but he grabbed Cole's wrist and began twisting until Cole feared it would break. He hit at Cole with the gun clutched in his other hand. It struck Cole's shoulder, causing pain to shoot through his body.

And then Minos hit him in the head, in the same spot Vane had struck him before.

Cole's vision grew blurry and black at the edges. *No,* he commanded himself. This time, he had to stay conscious—or he would never wake up.

He shook his head briefly. Fortunately, his vision cleared. But Minos had not ceased his struggle. He was trying to roll out from under Cole. His knee was free now, and he was trying to damage Cole's privates.

Cole used his left hand to gouge at Minos's eyes until

Minos screamed. Then, abruptly, Cole rolled, tugging his wrist away and grabbing at the gun. He wrestled for it, but Minos, still clutching it, had the advantage. Ever so slowly, he got it pointed toward Cole's face.

Cole swallowed hard. He paused, as if awaiting his fate. And then he lunged, grabbing the gun and planting one foot firmly on Minos's throat once more. This time, he was able to get the gun, as Minos tried unsuccessfully to throw him off. He pressed hard for a moment until the man was still.

Cole got off, stood and aimed the Smith & Wesson at his beaten adversary. But Minos had no intention of admitting defeat. He leapt toward Cole.

Cole shot him, point-blank. Minos's massive chest muffled the sound of the shot even better than the silencer had.

He fell to the ground, bleeding. Beaten at last. Dying.

Cole waited for just a minute, then checked Minos's pulse.

One down, Cole thought. Two more to go.

He looked up again toward the inn. He definitely had some unfinished business.

Chapter Fourteen

Alexa paced back and forth between the window and the door more times than she could count, along the same straight line at the edge of the floral area rug.

If only Minos had locked her in her own room. There, she could have gotten out onto the balcony and escaped, something Minos had obviously considered. Of course all guest rooms at the inn could be locked from the outside, but each also unlocked from the inside, too, for the customers' convenience and safety. All but this one. Had the locks on this one been changed by Vane and Minos to make it a prison for her or for some recalcitrant guest? Whatever the reason, she could not unlock it now.

She tried everything she could think of, but the lock was a dead bolt, and she had no tools in this room to remove the thick oak door from its hinges.

She could open the window, but she was on the second floor, nowhere near a balcony. The flower garden was beneath. There would be nothing to break her fall. And the bed had been stripped; she couldn't even try to plait sheets together for a ladder.

She was stuck.

Vane had gone down toward the water, away from the direction Cole had taken. But from the window she had seen Minos head for the wooded area next door. Had Cole gotten away?

She prayed so. She grasped the doorknob and turned it, then rattled the door again. It wouldn't budge. She sank down onto the floor beside it, resting her face against its hardness, ignoring the tears that ran down her face. She had to get out of here. She *had* to.

She heard a noise outside. Footsteps, coming up the stairs.

Cole's? No, he had to be far away by now. Minos's? Maybe. She braced herself as the footsteps drew nearer.

A key rattled in the lock of her door. Now she wondered if she should have hidden. Too late. Not that it mattered. There was no place worth hiding in this small room and its adjoining tiny bath. Nor could she find anything to use as a weapon. Alexa braced herself behind the door, giving herself an extra second.

"Come on out, Alexa," Vane's voice commanded. He pushed open the door so hard that it struck her shoulder. And then he reached behind it and grabbed her.

"Did you find him?" she asked, not bothering to complain about how Vane had hurt her shoulder, how his grip now caused her pain. He pulled her with him along the upstairs hallway toward the stairs.

"No," he said, "I didn't. But I talked to Minos on the cell phone. *He* found Cole. That's why I gave up my search and slipped in around the front. By now, I'd imagine, your sweetheart is fish food."

Alexa swallowed hard. She wanted to scream, to hit this man who had created so much havoc, so much despair, in her life. But he was stronger than she. And she knew he'd have no compunction about hitting her back, might even throw her down the stairs they now descended.

Besides, he didn't know for certain that Cole was dead, or he would have told her so. Gloated about it.

"So what are we going to do now?" Alexa asked, although part of her didn't want to know.

"*I* am going to get rid of a lot of evidence," Vane said. "*You* are part of that evidence."

"What do you mean?" Alexa's voice was hardly more than a choked whisper. They had reached the bottom of the stairs, and Vane towed her toward the kitchen. She looked around for Phantom but didn't see him. Had Minos killed him?

No, thank heaven. The pup paced in the pantry behind the closed gate. He whined anxiously when he spotted Alexa. She managed to break away from Vane and run toward the gate, then pulled it open and knelt beside Phantom, who licked her cheek.

"What a loving scene. You and your dog together in life...and death."

Alexa stood, terror gripping her. "Vane, please—I can't do anything to hurt you. I've helped you, in fact, and—"

"Not because you wanted to. And I can't take the chance on your getting in the way now."

"But— But what is this big plot, if it isn't what we discovered on your computer? Will you at least tell me that?" Alexa was stalling for time. But all the time in the world wasn't going to get her out of this.

Vane grabbed her again. She fought him, but he was too strong. How could he look so boyish and innocent while tying her to a high-backed chair? He still was dressed in a white shirt and khaki trousers, the outfit he had worn to meet with the guests before they left that morning. Phantom growled at him, and he shoved the angry dog back into the pantry, fastening the gate.

"Oh, Alexa, my darling, you did learn exactly what the plot is—although I suspect you didn't find the additional file that tells its true intent. We are planting our agents—the delightful guests you met here—as well as some others, all over the country near key military posts. There are other groups, too, doing the same thing. When the signal is given, they'll blow up some strategic installations. That'll direct attention from our nation's capital, where a coup will be undertaken."

"That's what we learned," Alexa admitted hoarsely. "But that's not all? Isn't that enough?"

"It's merely a decoy from our true intent," Vane said. He was doing something near the gas stove, though she couldn't quite tell what.

"Which is...?"

"Which is none of your business," he said with an evil rictus of a smile, "for you won't be around to enjoy it. Or revile it, for that matter." He drew some wire from his pocket, along with something that appeared to be a clock.

"What are you doing?"

"This is a timer," he explained. "And that is gas. When the timer reaches the time I set, it'll emit a spark. If you happen to be alive despite all the gas that'll fill this room and your lungs, you will go up in a ball of flame, you and your cute little puppy dog and this inn you find so wonderful. Along with my computer and fingerprints from all our guests and any other possible evidence."

"But, Vane, you put up a lot of the money for this place." Alexa was desperate for something to get him to change his mind. Anything.

"Ah, but when everything is finished, I will have more money than you can dream of."

"But—"

"Enough questions. I need to finish up here and go look for Minos. I expect he's already disposed of your friend Cole. I had hoped to blow Cole up with you, you know. Poetic justice and all, since he escaped from the last explosion I rigged, due to some unfortunate twists of fate."

He cut off some of the wire, then turned back toward Alexa. "In any event, in the remote chance that he survives, he'll know what happened to you. Maybe he'll even be happy about it, since he believes you turned on him, betrayed him from the beginning—"

"No, actually I don't."

Alexa drew in her breath at the sound of the beloved voice. She turned her head.

Cole stood in the doorway that led from the kitchen to the rest of the inn. How had he gotten there? His jeans, T-shirt and jacket were dirty and torn, his dark hair unruly. There was dried blood on the side of his face, contrasting with a shadow of beard visible beneath his skin. He had never looked more forbidding—or more handsome.

"How the hell—?" Vane began. He reached behind him—for a gun, Alexa figured—but Cole already had a weapon pointed at him.

"I wouldn't do that, if I were you," Cole said. "And by the way, I've been listening for a while. I gather that the information Alexa and I found is real, though possibly not complete. And Alexa's pretense at even liking you, let alone loving you enough to run off to marry you— well, I figured even before that it was false."

Alexa sagged in relief. She'd wanted him, for his own sake, to believe her pretense of siding with Vane. Otherwise, Vane would have killed him on sight, when he'd come in after finding his fellow agent's body. But for her own sake, she had felt the depths of despair to think that, after all she had revealed to Cole, all they had been to one another—again—he could accept their lies as true.

"Where is Minos?" Vane growled. He had stopped moving.

"In hell, I expect," Cole said cheerfully. "He's dead, at least."

"Damn! I should have listened to him. He was under orders to kill you immediately, but I wanted you alive. I wanted you to suffer for a while, watch Alexa with me as my fiancée."

"You got that wish, at least at first," Cole acknowledged. "I hated the idea that she was with you, had been with you two years ago. But it didn't take me long to realize she was as much a victim as I was, and that she continued to be one. You nearly had me convinced otherwise a little while ago. But I'd gotten to know Alexa again. When I'd a moment to think, after that blow to my head, I suspected she was under duress. And I don't like having people I love in bad situations. I'd some unfinished business here—getting her out of your control. So here I am."

People I love? He loved her? Thank God, Alexa thought. But Cole still hadn't looked toward her. She realized he had to keep his attention on Vane, but she wished she could let her own love, and her gratitude, show.

But that would come. First, they had to get out of this situation.

"Cole, he's rigged that timer to blow up the entire inn. There's already gas flowing from the stove."

"You don't think I'd do something as foolish as blow myself up, do you?" Vane grumbled.

"Only if that were the only way to exact your revenge. But I won't allow that to happen. I want you to pay for what you did to my father and even to Warren Geari. And for what you've put Alexa through. Most of all, I want you to watch while this scheme of yours fizzles."

Vane lunged at him then. Cole seemed to expect it. He didn't fire the gun. Instead, he turned sideways, which caused Vane to fly off balance. As Vane caught himself, Cole grabbed at his immaculate shirt, tearing it. He wrested Vane upright and clipped him hard under the chin. Vane sagged and fell to the floor.

"Are you all right, Alexa?" Cole said. He strode toward her, that wonderful, familiar stride that suggested he had the whole world under control. But he didn't—

"Look out behind you!" she screamed as she saw Vane rise and lunge toward Cole's back.

Cole turned. Very calmly, he raised the hand that still held the gun.

Vane stopped. He looked at Cole. His breathing was heavy and ragged, and the expression on his face was that of a trapped and ferocious wild animal. "Do it, you bastard. Kill me."

"I don't think so," Cole said.

Vane turned and grabbed the timing device he'd left on the stove. "You'll be sorry," he said with a cackle.

But before he could push the button, Cole fired. Vane's eyes widened as if he truly hadn't expected Cole to shoot. The timer fell from his hand as he slid to the floor, a red flower blooming in the center of his chest.

Quickly, Cole hurried over and turned off the gas. He opened the door to the outside, as well as the windows beside it. He picked up the timer from where it had fallen and tossed it out the door. "I'd better get you out of here, just in case," he said. As Alexa had done for him earlier, he took a knife from the butcher block and slit the rope binding her to the chair.

"Phantom," she managed to remind him. The pup was leaping at the gate from inside the pantry.

"Can't forget my good friend," Cole agreed. He opened the gate, then laughed as Phantom leapt toward him with a bark.

Taking Alexa's hand, he led her out the door.

FORTUNATELY, A BRISK breeze was blowing from the lake. Alexa went around to the front door and unlocked it, propping it open for ventilation through the inn's first floor. Dusk painted the street outside in shades of gray.

While they waited a safe distance from the kitchen door, Cole made a call on his cell phone. She gathered it was to his boss.

"He'll be here soon," Cole said when he hung up. "I caught him on his cell phone. He'd already started up the mountain and should arrive at any minute."

"Shouldn't we call the local authorities?" Alexa asked. Vane was still inside. From what she had gathered, Minos's body was somewhere in the thicket next door. Then there were Cole's co-agents...

"Do we know where Allen Maygran is?" she asked hesitantly.

"No, but I can guess." Cole's voice was grim. "In a few minutes, I'll take Phantom in to look for him."

"But—"

Her objections were stifled by a kiss that made her even more wobbly than the events of the day. Cole held her tightly in his arms, and she clung to him for support and comfort. And because he was Cole.

No matter what he had seen, what she had enacted with Vane, he had believed in her.

"How did you know Vane had coerced me to pretend to care for him that way?" she asked, nestling her cheek beneath his chin. The stubble of his beard scratched a bit, but she reveled in the masculine feel of him that reminded her he was still alive. They both were alive.

"Does it matter?" He bent his head, and his lips nibbled at hers, making her crazy. She had an urge to tear their clothes off right there, for she needed to feel him closer yet.

"No," she replied. "I'm just glad you did."

"You were pretty convincing, you know."

"I had to be," she said, not permitting her lips to leave his. "He'd have shot you the second you appeared otherwise."

"I figured." The kiss Cole gave her then made her heartbeat race. He reached up beneath her shirt and gently rubbed her sensitive, yearning breasts. But he drew away. His sexy laugh, coming from deep in his throat, drove her nearly crazy. "This isn't exactly the time or place."

"I know." Alexa turned to look around them. "But at least the backyard is secluded. Otherwise, the neighbors might be concerned about the bodies littering this place." She shuddered.

"Bradford's body is in a neighbor's boathouse," Cole said.

"Poor Bradford," Alexa whispered.

Cole nodded grimly. "I'd imagine any residual gas in the house has dissipated by now," he said. "Come on, Phantom."

Alexa didn't want to wait outside, but could not bring herself to go in—not with Vane's body in the kitchen, and Allen Maygran's probably there, too, in some unknown location.

She watched her boat floating gently at the side of the

dock. She noticed a few other boats glide by in the middle of the lake. She avoided looking at the boathouse several docks down, where Cole said he had found the body of Jessie Bradford, and the stand of trees next door where he had had his confrontation with Minos.

She tried to look beyond the hedge of bougainvillea that separated her yard from her other neighbor's, but saw no activity there. Good. She didn't want to have to deal with any questions she couldn't answer.

A large black sedan pulled into her driveway. It appeared to be some kind of official car. Could it be the police? If so, she would simply have to deal with it.

She went around the side of the house. A husky man with gray hair emerged from the car. He wore a blue buttoned shirt and black slacks that looked like a uniform.

Alexa guessed then that this was Cole's boss. But what if it wasn't? What if this was someone from Vane's plot come to check up on him?

She hurried into the kitchen and sped through the room, not looking toward where Vane had died—though she couldn't help glimpsing the spot from the corner of her eye.

Vane wasn't there, thank goodness. Cole must have moved him.

She allowed herself to breathe again, smelling just a hint of the odor of gas.

She went down the hallway toward the reception area and called up the stairs, "Cole? There's someone here."

Before she heard any reply, a strange, brusque voice sounded from behind her. "Are you Alexa Kenner?"

She turned slowly, with trepidation. She had left the front door wide open, of course, for they had been airing out the inn. The person from the car had just walked right inside. "Yes, I am," she admitted, half expecting the man to do something violent.

"I'm—"

"Forbes!" Cole came quickly down the stairs, Phantom at his heels. He held out his hand, which was quickly grasped in the other man's.

Alexa noted that Cole had changed clothes. He now wore the loose green shirt in which she had first seen him in the store at Skytop Lake Village—the shirt that had made him appear like an old-fashioned swashbuckler. And now she knew that the man who wore it *was* a hero.

He turned to her. "Alexa, I'd like to introduce my boss and friend, Forbes Bowman."

"I'm delighted to meet you," Alexa said in relief. She studied him. This must be the man who had saved Cole's life after the explosion two years earlier. She owed him a lot.

Forbes Bowman appeared to be in his early sixties. He was thick-waisted, and had a chin or two to spare. His shaggy brows were as silvery as his shock of white hair. He looked like a kindly grandfather, but she knew he was the head of a military Special Forces Unit, the secret counterterrorist outfit to which Cole belonged.

"And I'm pleased to meet you, Ms. Kenner. I've wanted to get to know you for a long time."

She smiled at him, then said, "I'm sure Cole and you have got lots of arrangements to make." She turned to Cole. "Does he know—?"

"—about Vane and the others?" Forbes interrupted. "Yes, I do. It's a shame, of course. But these things sometimes happen in war."

"War?"

"Anything in which our national interests are involved can be considered war," Cole explained. His look turned grim. "Phantom and I found Allen's body upstairs in a closet."

"Too bad," Forbes said, shaking his head. His impressive white mane rippled at the motion.

Alexa closed her eyes for a moment, swallowing hard. This might be an ordinary occurrence for men in military special operations, but the horrors she had been through this day were unnerving her.

"Well," she managed to say brightly, "I should make myself scarce while the two of you talk over all that's happened here and what you're going to do now."

"That won't be necessary, Alexa," Forbes Bowman said. He drew a small gun from his pocket and fired point-blank at Cole, who fell silently to the ground.

Chapter Fifteen

The zinging of the silenced gunshot reverberated through Alexa's head like the blast of an atomic bomb. "No!" she screamed. Cole's body slammed back, and his head smashed into the wall beside the stairs. Alexa tried to run toward Cole, but Forbes grabbed her arm. She tried to wrest it free—unsuccessfully.

Phantom leapt down the steps and growled ferociously at Forbes, who held the gun in one hand and Alexa in the other. "Make that animal keep quiet, or I'll shoot him, too."

"Sit, Phantom," Alexa cried out through her sobs. "Sit!"

The pup must have sensed her panic. In any event, he sat down directly beside Cole's body.

Cole had landed facedown at the base of the stairway.

"Let me go to him," Alexa cried.

"I don't think so," Forbes said. "It's time for us to go."

He dragged her toward the door. She tried to dig the rubber of her tennis shoes into the wood of the floor, but he managed to move her, anyway.

"Come on, Alexa," he said impatiently. He swung the gun to point it at her. "Quickly. I didn't intend to kill you now, but you're trying my patience. You can't help your lover, so move it. Now.''

For an instant she hesitated. Without Cole, she wasn't sure she wanted to live.

She shook that thought aside immediately. Maybe she couldn't help Cole now, but she could accomplish his goal for him: she would thwart the damn terrorist plot.

She would avenge his death somehow.

She wasn't the one who had betrayed him, but the man he had trusted with his life apparently had.

Was Forbes Bowman a terrorist? Why had he shot Cole?

Alexa would find out. And he would pay for it. Damn it, she would see to it: Forbes Bowman would pay.

FORBES'S BLACK SEDAN drove at a teasing pace along the winding mountain roads, not too fast for conditions in the increasing darkness, but much too fast for Alexa to jump out.

In the passenger seat, Alexa sat hunched into as small a ball as she could within the confines of the seat belt. She remained alert, watching the narrow lanes, the tall surrounding trees, the restaurants and residences they passed, praying there would be someone to whom she could signal, some obstruction that would stop the car and let her run.

But how would she outrun a bullet? For Forbes kept his gun on his lap, pointing at her. His left hand steered the car; his right hand seemed poised to grab the gun at any moment.

Oh, Cole, her mind wailed as she pictured how that same gun had taken his life, pictured him on the floor, Phantom beside his unmoving body. But she didn't dare grieve for him now.

The inside of the car reeked of this evil, arrogant man's aftershave. Alexa felt as if she wanted to throw up. She didn't allow herself to. She had to keep control of every aspect of her being, if she wanted to survive.

If she wanted to avenge Cole.

They turned a bend, and Alexa stiffened. Parked at the side of the road was a police patrol car.

How could she get the cop's attention?

"Don't bother, Alexa," Forbes said mildly, apparently realizing her intent. His fingers stroked the gun butt almost lovingly, but he didn't aim it at her. "Even if the cop were to come to your aid, you'd be dead first. And remember, I've been at this game a long time. Plus, my credentials are impeccable. I could easily make it appear that *you* were kidnapping *me,* and that the sight of the police car was enough of a distraction to tip the upper hand to me. After all, you're one of the Kenners who was involved in a vile terrorist plot two years ago, and I had you under investigation for a similar scheme today."

"You did that to my parents. You helped Vane." It was a statement, for Alexa knew the answer.

"He helped *me.*"

They passed the police cruiser without Alexa making a move.

"Why?" she demanded as her hope dimmed. "Why would you get involved in something like this?"

"Because it was a challenge." He grinned without taking his eyes off the road. "Because it was fun and potentially lucrative, and I'll soon have all the power I could ever imagine."

"Are you going to get a position highly placed in the new government after the coup?" Alexa asked scornfully. Her fists were clenched in her anger and impotence.

Forbes's chuckle was malevolent. "Oh, I nearly forgot.

That's what you understand the plot to be. And although Vane suspected the rest, that's all he knew for certain, too."

Excitement pulsed through Alexa. Was she actually about to learn the true goal of this entire malicious plot? "So you didn't even tell your flunky all that was going on? How interesting. Then you don't intend to overthrow the United States government?"

The glance Forbes shot her was cunning. "Are you trying to interrogate me subtly, my dear? Don't bother. I know more tricks to avoid spilling information than you could ever imagine."

"Then just tell me."

They rounded another curve. Ahead was a stop sign. Would he run it? If not, could she open the door and—

Again, he must have figured out how her mind was working. He picked up the gun and aimed it at her.

She yearned to grab it and use it on him. *He had shot Cole.*

But he would have no compunction about killing her. And dying now would serve no purpose. She settled back into her seat, swallowing her anger.

"That's better," Forbes said. "And as a reward for your being a good girl, I'll tell you what's really going to happen. Yes, my group is going to overthrow your ineffectual government while your military is busy mopping up its losses after the explosions our agents are going to set in key installations everywhere in the country."

Your government? Alexa wanted to throw his words back in his face. This damn traitor was an American, too. She was certain of it. Cole would have told her otherwise.

He had cared deeply about this man.

But she didn't contradict the despicable Forbes Bowman. Instead she nodded calmly. "That's what we found on Vane's computer."

They were on a main highway now. Soon, they would be headed down the mountain toward San Bernardino.

What would happen to her there? Why hadn't he killed her yet?

"But that's not all." Forbes apparently appreciated having an audience. His smile was distant and smug. "With all that is going on in its own backyard, the mighty U.S. will be much too preoccupied to worry about stopping a little takeover of Kuwait once more, plus another small Middle Eastern country or two. And all that lucrative oil will be in my group's hands."

Alexa closed her eyes, imagining all the people who would fight and die for the greed of this man and his allies. "Who is your group?" she finally spat out.

Again he shrugged. "Does it really matter? Just say we're a well-funded multinational conglomerate."

"Then—"

But Alexa was interrupted by the ringing of a cell phone. Forbes reached into his shirt pocket.

Was this her opportunity to run, while he was distracted by driving and conversing?

But they were going too fast.

"Hello, Cole," Forbes said into the phone.

Alexa gasped. Her heart started racing. Cole? But—

"Yes, I knew you'd call. I simply wasn't sure when, since you hit your head. I have to say, you made a quicker recovery than I anticipated." He listened for a moment more, then said, "Yes, she's here and she's fine. For now." Again he listened. "Of course I knew you wouldn't die when I fired at you. Why else would I have told you to put on your body armor? You'll be bruised for a long time. No, no others from my nasty little terrorist group are on their way there now. I did lie about that. Oh, and none of your good guys were stationed at Lake Arrowhead, either, to follow our trainees as they left or to help you. I haven't told anyone about your suspicions that our plot has been revived. Only your overseas contacts suspect, and they're too far away to do anything about it. Do you realize that the only reason Bradford and Maygran had to die was that you were foolish enough to contact them directly? Yes, yes, I told Vane from the first that you were still alive. He was expecting you.'' His grin grew wider and more malevolent with every second. "All right. All right. Shut up. Listen. Here's what you must do to keep your dear Alexa safe.''

For the next few minutes, Forbes rattled off instructions. Cole was to call the local authorities and make certain they knew the location of all four bodies at the Hideaway. He could give whatever rationale he wanted, except the truth. He was to tell no one outside about this alleged terrorist plot.

Meanwhile, Forbes would call in a report to his own military superior at the Pentagon, explain about the deaths, and assert that they were the result of an unplanned showdown between Vane and Minos, and the Unit's men. But the result was favorable, Forbes would say, since he had just learned about a possible terrorist plot that had already been stopped.

Cole was to back him up for at least twelve hours.

And then, if Cole had done as he was told, Forbes would release Alexa. As soon as the first military installations were destroyed, it would be too late for either of them to make enough noise to trip up the plan. But for the moment, Cole and Alexa were alive because Forbes needed time and backup—willing or not.

Alexa listened in horror. To save her, Cole would have

to turn his back on all he believed in. He would not be able to help stop the terrorists.

But Forbes Bowman was lying. He would never free her. He would kill her.

They were nearing a sharp downhill curve. She grabbed at the steering wheel and the phone at the same time. "Don't do it, Cole," she screamed.

"Alexa!" His voice was faint and distant, even as Forbes Bowman hit her in the head with the gun.

Alexa's consciousness faded.

"ALEXA!" Cole shouted into the phone, but it was too late. That damnable traitor Forbes had already broken the connection.

He had heard Alexa cry out to him. At least she was still alive—or had been just seconds ago.

But he wouldn't put anything past Forbes.

Damn it, this had been the problem his instincts had warned about. Things were too pat here at Skytop Lake. Vane had seemed to anticipate Cole's moves. Minos had been too rebellious toward Vane to be in his employ.

Forbes. He had been behind it all.

Cole hurriedly looked around. He was still in the inn's reception area, standing and leaning against the desk. His chest hurt like the devil. He might even have a cracked rib or two. The body armor had protected him from the bullet, but not from the force of its impact. The wind had been knocked out of him, and he'd lost consciousness when he hit his head. But he hadn't time to baby himself.

Phantom was snuffling around uneasily. The poor pup obviously knew something was very wrong. "It's okay, boy," Cole said. "I'm going to find Alexa."

He hoped.

He shut Phantom behind his gate in the pantry, then

glanced around outside before he exited the inn's door. The street still appeared quiet. Good. Somehow, the neighbors must not have heard anything. Either that or they were hiding inside, awaiting the police—the police whom Forbes had said Cole must deflect from the truth for a while, in their investigation of the four killings.

Both of the inn's SUVs were in the driveway along with his own car, which, fortunately, wasn't blocked. He reached into his pocket for his keys and found them there. His Beretta, retrieved from Vane's room, was in its holster, too, beneath the jacket he'd hastily donned. Obviously, Forbes didn't believe Cole would be much of a threat, for he hadn't searched and disarmed him.

And that worried Cole.

Forbes would expect him to obey his instructions. Otherwise, he would kill Alexa. And there were a few things that Cole had learned about Forbes over the years: he was ruthless, and he never made idle threats.

But Cole had thought his boss's single-minded determination had been in furtherance of the country's interests.

And he had saved Cole's life after the explosion.... Now, Cole wondered why.

Sirens suddenly sounded in the distance. Ignoring how it hurt to move, Cole thrust himself into the driver's seat. In moments, he sped away from the inn.

And toward Alexa.

He drove at a breakneck speed on the dimly-lighted roads, taking curves as fast as an amusement park ride. It was his best chance to catch up with Forbes. For unless Forbes was doing something uncharacteristic, Cole knew his boss was a cautious, uneasy driver who seldom sped.

But there had been a lot he hadn't known about Forbes

before. Maybe caution on the road was just part of his act, too.

It didn't matter. Somehow, Cole would catch up with them.

There was only one good road down the mountain from here—unless Forbes was attempting to lose him by heading, not directly toward civilization, but toward Big Bear Lake.

Cole swerved into the left lane around a slower car, then pulled back into his own lane, narrowly missing a head-on collision.

Two horns blared behind him. He ignored them, listening only for sirens. As far as he knew, the police weren't following him…yet.

Forbes had told him to remain at the inn and do a tap dance about the four dead bodies. It seemed very convenient that the police would arrive right about the time Cole woke up.

Forbes must have called them, to make sure they kept Cole occupied while Forbes got away with his hostage—effectively forcing Cole to go along with his plan or risk Alexa's murder.

He passed the turnoff for Lake Arrowhead and headed toward the town of Blue Jay. In a short while, he reached the four-lane road that would take him down the mountain.

How far ahead were Forbes and Alexa?

He continued his carefully controlled speeding as the roadway headed downward…and then he spotted them, on a switchback down below.

He sped up even more.

Fortunately, traffic coming up the mountain was sparse that day. But Cole was uncertain what to do. If Forbes were alone, Cole would have had no compunction about running him off the road. But Alexa was with him.

He needed to think of something that would not endanger her life, that would not cause Forbes to shoot her out of malice, because Cole had not obeyed him.

An idea came to him. He called Forbes back on the cell phone. "The police are here at the inn," he said, "and you forgot something." Since they were using cell phones, his boss would have no way of actually knowing Cole's location.

His former boss did not sound pleased. "What the hell are you talking about, Rappaport?"

"I'll tell you. Just let me talk to Alexa first."

Forbes argued for a few seconds, but his curiosity caused him to comply.

"Cole? Are you all right?"

He pictured her soft and lovely features pinched with fear—for him. He wanted to hug her, to hold her close. Make her safe.

"Never mind about me," he said. "How are *you?*"

"Okay." She seemed to hesitate just a split second. "They're using the coup as a decoy," she said in a rush, "so they can—"

He heard a harsh sound he could not identify. He had been making progress catching up with the car ahead of him, and he saw it swerve just a little.

"Alexa!" he shouted.

"You talked to her." It was Forbes's voice that next came over the line. He sounded furious and out of breath.

"Is she all right?"

"She's fine. Now tell me what I supposedly forgot."

Cole wanted to reach through the air, grasp the man's throat in his hands…and squeeze.

But instead of using his strength to conquer this foe and save Alexa, he had to continue using his wits.

"The thing is, you didn't check to see whether our friend Vane was dead. Frankly, I just assumed he was, too. But though he's not going to be lifting weights or doing anything else strenuous for a long time, he's lucid enough to be telling these guys what you both have been up to. And the police chief—the guy Vane paid off—well, he knows he's in way over his head. He's sent for the feds down in L.A. They should arrive by helicopter in San Bernardino any minute, if that's the way you're heading. A roadblock's being readied as we speak."

"I don't believe you," Forbes growled.

"It doesn't matter what you believe," Cole said, and he hung up. For a moment, he chewed his bottom lip in an agony of contrition. Had he just sealed Alexa's death warrant? Would Forbes kill her merely out of spite that Cole hadn't responded the way he wanted?

He pressed on the gas once more. He had never been more glad that the car he had borrowed for this assignment didn't just have a luxurious interior; it had power to match. He hurtled down the mountain, weaving in and out between the cars in both lanes that were in his way.

And then he reached them. Forbes's dark sedan was right in front of him. Across the double lanes of the road toward his left was the cliff's sheer drop-off. At the other side of Forbes's car was the unyielding rock of the mountain.

How could he stop them without endangering Alexa?

But she was already in danger. No matter what, he had to stop them quickly.

Taking a deep breath, he pulled his car alongside the sedan. Forbes glanced over at him. He did not seem surprised. In fact, he seemed pleased.

And Alexa? She was still alive, thank heaven. In the split second he had to look at her, he could see that she was white-faced and frightened. Her wide eyes met his, and she managed somehow to give him a tense smile.

He couldn't let her down. He used a button to roll down his passenger window. "It's over, Forbes," he yelled, though he doubted his boss and former friend could hear.

With a grin on his face that Cole wanted to eradicate with his fist, Forbes lifted his gun and pointed it at Alexa.

"No!" Cole yelled, at the same time he turned his steering wheel hard toward the car beside him. Toward the man who had betrayed him, who now threatened the life of the woman he loved.

With a shriek of grinding metal, the two cars collided. Cole watched as the front of his vehicle smashed into the driver's side of the sedan and pushed the other car into the wall of rocks at the side of the road.

"Alexa!" Cole shouted. And then there was silence.

Chapter Sixteen

Ignoring the pain in his head and chest, Cole unhooked his seat belt and leapt from the car in one fast motion. He gripped his Beretta in his right hand.

"Alexa!" he called again as he ran toward the other ruined vehicle. He inhaled deeply. Although the area smelled of ground metal, there was no odor of gasoline, and he saw none on the road. At least the danger of fire seemed minimal.

Looking through the smashed windshield, he saw Forbes's bloody face. The man was motionless. But that didn't mean he was unconscious or dead. Cole had to make certain he was neutralized before he could take care of Alexa.

The side of Cole's car still dug into the sedan, which was pressed, on the other side, against the face of the rocks. "Forbes, you bastard, look at me."

The man didn't move. His eyes were closed.

Cole took his gaze off his nemesis long enough to glance at Alexa. She, too, was unmoving, her head lolling back on the seat's damaged headrest. Her loose honey-brown hair half covered her face.

Holding down his fear and panic, Cole circled to the

back of the two vehicles. There, he was able to open the driver's side rear door.

Forbes still didn't move. But Alexa, her gorgeous, alert blue eyes open, turned her head toward him. "Cole," she whispered.

"Don't move," he said. "You're going to be fine." He ignored the pounding of his heart that signaled his own terror for her. The side of her poor face that was visible was bruised, but she had never looked more beautiful to him. He scanned her quickly. Just a small amount of blood, on one leg. But she could still have internal injuries.

"I've called 9-1-1," called a voice from outside the car. Cole glanced out to see the face of a frightened teenage girl, a kind passerby who had stopped to help.

"Thanks," he called. She must have seen the gun in his hand, for she hurried out of sight.

Turning sideways, Cole snaked his body between the two mangled seats, his gun poised to shoot Forbes in the head if necessary, while he reached down for the other man's weapon. Grabbing it from where it had fallen on the floor, he threw it behind him. Then he shook Forbes.

Forbes groaned. The corpulent older man no longer looked dangerous, but Cole knew better than to underestimate him…again.

Forbes's eyes opened to mere slits, and he grimaced in pain. He glared at Cole. "I should have left you to die in that damn explosion." His voice was garbled and weak.

"Why didn't you?" Cole demanded.

"Too risky. Too many people around. Would have wondered why I didn't try. Didn't want suspicion—"

"I got it."

But Forbes didn't stop talking. "The new plot—you

weren't supposed to find out about it. When you did…
Minos. He was my man. Ordered to kill you. Vane
stopped him, damn him.''

"Shut up and save your strength," Cole commanded.
''I want you to survive, you son of a bitch. You're going
to spend the rest of your miserable life in a maximum
security prison, if you're not executed for murder and
treason first.''

He moved back in the car and put his free hand on
Alexa's shoulder for comfort. He also kept his gun
trained on Forbes, although the man appeared not to be
faking his injuries.

"Alexa, tell me where you're hurt," Cole said softly.

"I'm fine," she said, but the weakness of her voice
belied what she said.

"Just hold on," Cole said, wanting to take her into his
arms but knowing he did not dare move her.

This time, the wail of sirens in the distance could not
have been more welcome.

THE ''ACCIDENT'' had been caused deliberately by Cole
to save her, Alexa knew. It blurred in her mind with the
arrival of the paramedics, the ambulance ride, the emer-
gency room.

Now, she lay alone in her sterile, impersonal hospital
room that smelled of the usual disinfectant. The television was on, but the news from the Los Angeles station
was local and boring. She'd seen nothing about a newly
discovered terrorist plot or an accident on the mountain
road, or anything else she could relate to. Alexa kept the
sound low.

She had a lot of time now to rehash what had happened, even though her recollections were fuzzy.

Although the police had been at the crash site, too,

demanding answers from Cole, she had been aware enough to realize that he insisted on accompanying her to the hospital. As far as she could recall, he had flashed his credentials at the California Highway Patrol officers and insisted that he, and not Forbes, was in charge. After that, he refused to answer questions until he was certain she was all right. But the police had accompanied them as well, obviously unsure whether Forbes, who ostensibly had higher authority, or Cole, was the one to be believed.

He had gripped her hand, giving her comfort. He had stroked the side of her battered face and murmured words of love and courage.

She had assured him over and over that she was fine, but she could see the worry in his beloved face.

Now, her insides ached. A couple of ribs had cracked from the impact of the crash, her face hurt from where Forbes had struck her, and her right leg was cut and bruised. An IV dripped into her arm, and she had been given painkillers that she tried not to take. But she was going to be fine.

She didn't know about Forbes Bowman, didn't care. But she knew his survival mattered to Cole. Not, however, because the man was a friend and mentor, a lifesaver.

He was a spoiler, a terrorist, and Cole wanted him to pay.

In the ambulance, as weak as she had been, she had managed to explain the rest of the plot to Cole: the terrorists' goal of using the U.S. coup as a diversion to take over one or more oil-rich Middle Eastern countries. He had immediately gotten on his cell phone and called someone, though she didn't know who.

Apparently whoever it was believed him, for Cole was

not taken into custody by the local police, even after they had reached the hospital.

She heard a sound now, and looked toward the door to her room, expecting another nurse wanting to check her vital signs.

"Alexa?" It was Cole. He strode into the room with the rule-the-world stride she recognized and adored.

She grinned, ignoring the way the movement of her facial muscles hurt. "Have you come to see the damage you inflicted on me, Rappaport? You'd better learn to drive one of these days."

For a moment, a flicker of pain crossed his luminous dark eyes, and Alexa regretted her teasing.

But then he flashed her one of his cockiest grins. "You know I'm a military weapons expert, don't you? And everything turns into ammunition in my hands, even cars."

She laughed and held out her hands. She saw him glance at the line to the IV and wince. "I'm going to live, Cole," she said, again teasingly. And then, more softly, more seriously, she added, "Thanks to you." She hesitated. "And Forbes?"

"He'll live, too, though it'll take him a while to re-cuperate enough to stand trial." Cole's edgy voice was curt. "Don't worry about him, though. Don't worry about anything but getting better."

In a moment, he was sitting on the side of her bed, and she was in his strong, welcome, gentle embrace. For the first time in months—no, years—she felt alive and protected and wonderful, notwithstanding her physical pain. She laid her head against the hardness of his chest and closed her eyes, listening to the steady, soothing beat of his heart.

"I thought I'd lost you, Alexa."

His whisper against her hair was hardly audible, but she felt the caress of his lips on her forehead.

"I'm a hardy soul, Rappaport," she countered, though her voice was hoarse. "And I'd haunt you forever, you know."

"Oh, yes," he said. "I know." He hesitated, then said softly, "My sky."

She turned her head to look into his face, the face that belonged to the new Cole who had the same invincible heart and soul of the man she had first fallen in love with. She touched the cleft in his chin, his straight brows, his wide and loving mouth, his hair that was much longer than the regulation military length he had previously worn. "I liked you before, but I can deal with your looks now, too," she said.

"That's good."

"I love you, Cole," she told him.

He bent so his lips met hers, very gently.

The kiss felt wonderful and comforting. But Alexa wanted more to remind her that she still was alive. She deepened the kiss, drawing him closer. She felt the bandage beneath his shirt, knew the bullet and his vest had cracked his ribs. Her tongue touched his mouth and delved between his lips, and he took it in, testing and tasting it with his own. She felt a stirring of desire down below that had no place in a hospital room, where she was hooked up to tubes and bottles, and where someone could walk in at any time. Oh, how she wished she were someplace else with Cole. Someplace very private.

But she wouldn't be here for long. The doctor had said so. And then—

"Alexa, I'm here to say goodbye." Cole dashed her erotic and romantic thoughts with his soft but incontrovertible words.

She drew back as quickly as if she had been slapped. "Oh" was all she could manage to say. She stared in his face. His expression had turned remote, as if he had already put distance between them.

But he had told her he loved her, too, in the ambulance. Had called her his sky once more.

"It's not that I want to," he said.

She wanted to capture his lie in her hands and throw it back in his much-too-handsome new face.

"But Forbes's betrayal has left a big void at the head of the Unit. Since I'd been reporting only to him before, he had sent no one to follow and capture the infiltrators, so they have to be rounded up all over the country—there were some in training in other locations, too. Plus, there are other terrorists waiting for the signal to hit Washington, D.C., and we have to find out who was giving Forbes his orders. And we also need to alert our overseas allies about what's going on, make certain that the Middle Eastern nations are protected—"

"Yes," she said calmly, "you do."

Last time, when he had exited her life, it had been abrupt and, she had thought, final. But she had believed it had been involuntary. Now she knew better. He had claimed it was to protect her. In his mind, perhaps it had been.

But it had also been because he loved his country, and his job, more than he had ever loved her. And now he had even more important work to do.

He had already done what he could for her, saved her life. She had no choice.

She had to let him go.

He cupped her face in his hands. She wanted to turn away so he wouldn't see the moisture that leapt into her eyes.

But she also wanted to stare at him, make sure she had memorized every one of his features, from the length of his dark hair with its vague silvering at his temples, to the strength of his broad jaw and cleft chin.

"I'll be in touch," he promised her.

"I know," she said. A brief phone call here, perhaps an e-mail there… "Take care of yourself, Cole."

He bent down and kissed her hard and fast. And then he stood. "You, too," he said.

And then he was gone…again.

Chapter Seventeen

"How are you, Alexa?" Marian Shelton, her fiftyish, curly-haired neighbor from two houses down, met Alexa at the inn's front door three days later, after she'd been released from the hospital.

She had taken a cab home. With Cole gone, there was no one she had wanted to call for a ride.

"I'm fine," Alexa lied. Then, wincing, she stooped to give Phantom, frisking at her feet, a gingerly hug. Cole had let her know he'd asked Marian to take care of the pup until Alexa's return.

"That nice Mr. O'Rourke was so concerned about you," Marian continued, pulling the edges of her yellow windbreaker down. "We all were." Her expansive gesture encompassed the entire neighborhood. "That crazy man coming here and shooting people, then taking you hostage—why, I don't know how you stood it."

Alexa slowly rose again, ignoring the way her ribs and leg ached. "I'm not sure, either," she admitted. That had been the story eventually released to the media: a maniac had run amok at the inn, killed four people, including Vane, and kidnapped Alexa. Purportedly, the police had saved her, but not before the car in which she'd been taken had been wrecked, injuring her in the process.

Parts of the story, at least, had been true. Forbes Bowman's identity had remained classified. So far, Alexa had been captured by an "unidentified gunman" who was killed during her rescue.

"It's scary that such a thing could happen in our quiet neighborhood." Marian hesitated, then said, "I suppose it was the same fellow who shot at Mr. O'Rourke and you last week."

Alexa nodded. "That's the police's speculation." How easily lies came to her. But there was no sense in scaring Marian or anyone else about terrorism and international intrigue.

This story was something the neighbors could believe. And Alexa was certain that if Cole's Special Forces Unit could have easily hidden the existence of four bodies, not even this much would have made it into the news.

"Anyway, Mr. O'Rourke told me all about what happened and how sorry he was he had to hurry back to work before you were all better."

"Yes, I'm certain *Mr. O'Rourke* was very busy."

Something odd must have come through her tone, for Marian squinted quizzically at her, deepening the crease between her brows.

"I suspect," Marian said confidentially, "that after all that happened, he was too scared to stay here."

Alexa nearly laughed at that.

"In any event," Marian said, "I'm sure you were sorry to see him go."

Alexa threw a sharp look at Marian. Was her sorrow at losing Cole written on her face?

"I mean," Marian said hastily, "I couldn't help noticing that all your guests seemed to have left around the same time."

"Yes, they did," Alexa said, annoyed that her neighbor had noticed. "But they were friends of Vane's. I'm going to throw myself into keeping the inn going." She voiced her inner thoughts, speaking more to herself than to Marian.

Her neighbor nodded sagely. "Yes, it's best to keep busy to get over the grief. Poor Vane. I'm sure it was very hard for you to lose your dear fiancé that way."

If you only knew, Alexa thought wryly. "Yes," she said, then opened the inn's door. "If you'll excuse me now, I need to rest. But I can't thank you enough for watching Phantom."

Inside, she quickly locked the door behind her. Phantom rubbed against her legs, obviously glad to have her home again. "I'm glad, too," she said, bending just enough to pet the dog's smooth and furry head. *Phantom.* Her other phantom was off once more, disappeared from her life so he could rout the bad guys. In this case, the bad guys were really bad. Cole was brave. A true hero.

Her hero.

But not really *hers.*

She sighed, then straightened. "Come on, Phantom," she said. "We have work to do."

There were a lot of messages on the inn's answering machine, including one from her parents. Alexa had called them from the hospital first thing to let them know what had happened, without going into detail. She had assured them she was fine.

They had wanted to come to be with her, but she insisted that they stay home. Her inn was, for now, the center of a sensitive investigation. It was better that her parents remain far away. That way, not even the tiniest shred of suspicion would land on them—especially after the way Vane had threatened to destroy them.

She had kept in telephone contact with them while she was in the hospital. Now, standing behind the tall, familiar reception desk, she returned their latest message.

"Oh, honey, we're so glad you're out of the hospital. We were worried you hadn't told us all about your injuries, since you didn't explain everything that happened." Her mother's shrill voice sounded upset yet relieved. Alexa pictured her slender mother, salt-and-pepper hair snipped short in a pixie cut, clutching the phone in their office at the Tucson Kenner Hotel, the only hotel in their chain that they hadn't sold off to a conglomerate. "The news here today was full of that horrible situation. I know you said you were a hostage, but we didn't understand the details."

"I'm fine, Mom," Alexa said. Cole's group had been able to keep a media lid on what had happened for a couple of days. But Alexa had known something as exciting as deaths and a hostage situation in a quiet mountain community couldn't be kept quiet forever.

"The media blew it all out of proportion," she told them, "as they always do."

"Yes, they certainly do." Her father must have gotten on an extension. His wry, sad voice indicated that he was recalling how their alleged participation in planting terrorists all over the country had been leapt on in the news, until the furor had died down for lack of evidence.

Before the accusations, her father had been round-faced and plump. Now, he was gaunt, with haunted eyes.

Vane had helped to clear them before. Now, Alexa knew it had only been to get into her good graces so he could use her to restart his appalling scheme…and seek revenge on Cole.

"How are you getting along without…without Vane, dear?" her mother asked softly.

"As well as can be expected," Alexa replied noncommittally. If they only knew...

"He helped us so much... I'm sure you'll miss him a lot. *We* will. Are you sure you wouldn't like us to come for a visit to help you? Or you still could come here."

"No, I just need to be alone for a while," Alexa said. "And I need to keep the Hideaway going." She hesitated, but she still worried about them. "Is everything there all right?"

"Of course, honey," her mother said.

But her father said, "Pretty much so, although a strange thing happened here just yesterday."

Alexa held her breath. "What's that?"

"You know our concessionaire, Marty? The one who runs the gift shop in our lobby? The police arrested him. They accused him of dealing drugs. Can you believe it?"

Alexa had met their octogenarian employee, Marty. The man had sharp eyes and an even sharper tongue. She couldn't believe he was the one who'd had her parents under surveillance.

But the timing fit. Alexa blessed Cole for coming through with protection for her parents. And she knew she could rely on him to vouch for them, make sure Vane's damnable file was found, that its forged contents would not be used to hurt her family.

"I suppose the police wouldn't arrest Marty without evidence," she said noncommittally.

"I suppose," her father agreed. "Except that with us—"

"I love you both," Alexa blurted. "I'll call again soon." And then she hung up, feeling both happy that her parents were okay and apparently under Cole's protection, and sad because she was alone.

With difficulty, she shook off the feeling. She hurried

upstairs to the desk in her room. She had some ads to place, travel agents to invite for a visit…an inn to get up and running again.

FOR THE NEXT FEW DAYS, Alexa kept herself busy scrubbing the inn, particularly the room in which agent Maygran had died, and the kitchen, where Cole had killed Vane to save Alexa's life and his own.

She also found black, sticky fingerprint dust all over the place, although it appeared someone had at least made an effort to clean it.

Could the authorities identify who the guests really were? Did they know where each of them had been sent? Had they all been captured?

Alexa would never know.

Then there was her engagement ring. She'd almost wished it had been stolen at the hospital, but Cole had taken it for her, brought it to the inn when he'd come to make arrangements for Phantom. Now, it was in a box at the bottom of her dresser drawer. Someday, when she felt strong enough to deal with it, she would sell it, give the proceeds to charity.

There were agencies that helped victims of terrorist attacks. They would be the appropriate recipients.

Although Alexa watched the television news and read the *Los Angeles Times* carefully each day, there was no mention of the wide-ranging and, hopefully thwarted, terrorist plot. That probably was good. Hopefully, that meant that everything was being carried on in secret, and if capture of the infiltrators and the terrorists ready to overrun Washington was done surreptitiously, then national security remained intact.

Huge, ugly, bloody raids would have been difficult to keep out of the news.

She heard nothing from Cole—other than one brief, businesslike e-mail telling her to expect a team of agents from his unit.

Not that she expected deep expressions of affection over the Internet, but his abruptness still hurt.

On her third day at home, a young man rang the inn's bell. His credentials identified him as Tom Carville, an army lieutenant. He looked as young as if he had just graduated from college. With him were half a dozen others, all in uniform.

Alexa showed them to the rooms where the terrorist agents had stayed. Though the police had apparently been through the place to investigate while she was in the hospital, these guys started right in to check for more evidence. The crimes they investigated were much more extensive than the four murders.

"Do you know Cole Rappaport?" Alexa asked impulsively as she watched Lieutenant Carville unhook the cables from Vane's computer.

"I sure do, ma'am." The young man's eyes glowed. "He's about the smartest, bravest man... But I'm saying too much. Our unit is...well, it's classified. But General Rappaport sent me here, and he said you know what's happening, that you helped us to stop it."

"Yes," said Alexa, "I suppose I did." *General* Rappaport? Alexa had not asked about his military rank, but she'd supposed he was still a colonel, as he had been two years ago. She enquired impulsively, not expecting an answer, "Was the general just promoted?"

"Yes, ma'am." The young man sounded as proud as if Cole were his older brother. "I wouldn't tell just anyone this, but after what happened with our prior commanding officer...well, I guess I can tell you that there was a gap, and General Rappaport is filling it."

Eventually, Lieutenant Carville thanked Alexa, and he and his team left the inn. Along with the other evidence they had gathered, they took Vane's computer.

As well as all of Alexa's few remaining, but futile, hopes.

Cole had apparently stepped into the shoes of Forbes Bowman and undoubtedly filled them with much more skill, courage and commitment. He was now the commanding officer of the elite counterterrorist Special Forces Unit.

He would hold that position even when he and his allies had rounded up every last person involved with the current horrific plot.

He would never have any interest in coming back to Skytop Lake, except perhaps for an occasional visit—just another guest at the inn. He wouldn't want her to follow him, even if she considered it, for he would always worry that he would somehow endanger her through his work.

She had to stop thinking about Cole Rappaport. This time, he *was* out of her life forever.

MONTHS LATER, Alexa parked in front of a snowbank in the Skytop Lake Village parking lot.

In the wintertime, the San Bernardino Mountains received snow each time it rained in Los Angeles. Skytop Lake was particularly picturesque this time of year, she thought, staring between buildings toward the water's partially frozen surface.

Zipping up her parka and pulling its hood over her head, she got out of her SUV. Phantom barked and tried to jump out, too. "You stay here," she commanded. "I won't be inside long enough for you to get cold."

She just needed some additional vegetables and condiments for dinner that night. The inn was crowded with skiers and snowboarders, and people who just liked to escape the pounding rain of Los Angeles this time of year for the pristine snow-covered mountains.

Alexa had been working hard to regain the momentum the inn had lost. Although the Hideaway was seldom filled, the number of guests it attracted was growing.

She had nearly caught up on her mortgage payments. If only she could get rid of the additional debt incurred last spring and summer, during the months Vane's terrorist guests had not paid for their lodging. At least she and Vane had bought the inn jointly, and title had gone to her on Vane's death.

A few weeks ago, she had received a package in the mail. It contained the spurious file against her parents and a copy of a statement on a Swiss bank account. The latter was accompanied by a note in familiar handwriting stating that the funds were evidence and therefore inaccessible.

Although Alexa could have used more money, she wouldn't have touched a penny even if the account was handed over to her legally. She wouldn't even accept help from her parents.

She destroyed the forged documents. And if Vane had other copies, well, she counted on Cole to deal with them for her.

Now, Alexa hurried into the Juarez Gourmet Grocery Store, wiped her boots on the mat in the doorway and pulled her gloves off and the parka's hood from her head. Her cheeks burned from the cold even though she hadn't been outside for long.

She would hurry, for she didn't want Phantom to freeze.

The store was nearly empty—due to the weather, she supposed. She rolled her cart toward the produce first, where she picked out some bibb lettuce, spinach and radicchio for a salad. Then she headed toward the aisle of ethnic foods. She was cooking several South American dishes that night, for the spicy flavor would help to warm her guests.

She started to roll her cart down the aisle, and stopped. A dark-haired man walked by the end of the aisle. No, strode, with that familiar, confident gait of a man with no doubt about the world's need for what he would lend it.

Alexa shook her head sharply. She was dreaming.

Except…the man halted and turned toward her.

And smiled.

"Cole," Alexa whispered. She didn't move. Couldn't move.

He came toward her. There were lines of fatigue at the corners of his eyes that hadn't been there before. And those beer-dark eyes had a sad and haunted look in them, as if they had seen unspeakable things in the months he had been away.

But it was Cole. Complete with the cleft in his chin, the dark shadow of a beard visible beneath his skin, the straight line of his hawkish brows. There was even more silver at his temples now, but his hair was shorter.

Cole.

"Hi, Alexa." He sounded so nonchalant, as if they had seen each other yesterday. Still, his deep voice sent a shiver through her. Was she imagining he was here?

"Hi yourself," she managed to say. She stood perfectly still, even though what she wanted to do was to hurl herself into his arms, to satisfy herself that he was a real, solid man, and not just a wraith her mind had conjured up.

"I'm back," he said. He stood only inches from her.

247247247

He wore a black leather jacket that lent him a dangerous air. Oh, yes, this man was dangerous....

"Yes, I see that." He'd called now and then over the past few months, hurried calls in which he'd said little. They corresponded more by e-mail, but even at that their messages were short, friendly but impersonal.

"I saw a familiar SUV outside. I've already said hello to Phantom."

She refused to span the gulf between them. She had finally gotten her emotions back under control, and here he was. "Good to see you. I'm finished here. I was just leaving."

"I'm finished, too, Alexa—" he said softly.

His hand reached out and stroked her cheek. His skin was cold, and yet a bolt of lightning seemed to shoot from his fingers through her body, suffusing her with heat.

"Or, at least, I could be."

"What do you mean?" she whispered.

"The Unit has accomplished its mission. We've rounded up all the terrorists here and the international ringleaders. Even your friends the Fullers were located in the Seattle area and arrested. They weren't really married, by the way. Your other former guests are all in custody, too. And right now, I'm tired. I'm even thinking of retiring."

A humming began inside Alexa. What was he implying? "I heard that you're a general now," she said. "That you took over Forbes Bowman's position as head of your unit."

He nodded. "That's right. He'll stand trial in a few months, and the case against him is strong. But now that my mission is over, I think I'd like a partner."

"A...partner?"

"Yes. See, I've been saving my pay for a long time, since a lot of my expenses were paid by the government. There's a certain inn I'd like to buy into, if the owner is interested."

Alexa's pulse quickened. Was she understanding him correctly? Might he actually stay here?

"She would consider a partner," she said slowly.

Cole's eyes bored into her. "Not just any partner, though. A lifetime partner." He stepped forward and took Alexa into his arms.

She didn't resist. His hard, strong body pressed against hers, warming any vestiges of the cold from outside. He kissed her, long and hard, until she clung to him so her boneless legs would not give way beneath her.

"The thing is," he whispered into her ear, sending shivers through her. "The woman I want as a partner has a reputation of not setting a wedding date."

She pulled back, staring at his beloved face.

"Marry me, Alexa. Today, tomorrow, next week—but no longer. I love you. I want to stay here with you at Skytop Lake, be your partner and your husband, forever."

"No more Phantom?" she teased, though her voice was shaky.

"Only the dog," he agreed.

"Forever, then," Alexa said. "I love you, too, Cole." And melted back into his arms.

HARLEQUIN®
INTRIGUE®
and
DEBRA WEBB

invite you for a special consultation at the

For the most
private investigations!

**Look for the next installment in this exciting
ongoing series!**

PERSONAL PROTECTOR
April 2002

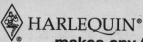

COOPER'S 🍀 CORNER

In April 2002 you are invited to three wonderful weddings in a very special town...

A Wedding at Cooper's Corner

USA Today bestselling author
Kristine Rolofson
Muriel Jensen
Bobby Hutchinson

Ailing Warren Cooper has asked private investigator David Solomon to deliver three precious envelopes to each of his grandchildren. Inside each is something that will bring surprise, betrayal...and unexpected romance!

And look for the exciting launch of *Cooper's Corner,* a NEW 12-book continuity from Harlequin—launching in August 2002.

TRUEBLOOD, TEXAS

Coming in April 2002...

SURPRISE PACKAGE

by

Bestselling Harlequin Intrigue® author

Joanna Wayne

Lost:

Any chance Kyle Blackstone had of a relationship with his gorgeous neighbor Ashley Garrett. He kept flirting, but she wasn't buying.

Found:

One baby girl. Right outside Kyle's apartment, with a note claiming he's the father! Had Kyle just found a surefire plan to involve Ashley in his life?

Ashley was determined to stay away from the devilish playboy, but the baby was irresistible...then again, so was Kyle!

Finders Keepers: bringing families together

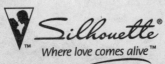

Creaking floorboards...
the whistling wind...an enigmatic man
and only the light of the moon....

This February Harlequin Intrigue revises
the greatest romantic suspense tradition of all
in a new four-book series!

Moriah's Landing
A Modern Gothic

Join your favorite authors as they recapture the
romance and rapture of the classic gothic fantasy in
modern-day stories set in the picturesque New England
town of Moriah's Landing, where evil looms but
love conquers the darkness.

#650 SECRET SANCTUARY by Amanda Stevens
February 2002

#654 HOWLING IN THE DARKNESS by B.J. Daniels
March 2002

#658 SCARLET VOWS by Dani Sinclair
April 2002

#662 BEHIND THE VEIL by Joanna Wayne
May 2002

from

HARLEQUIN®

INTRIGUE®

HARLEQUIN®
Makes any time special ®

Available at your
favorite retail outlet.

Visit us at www.eHarlequin.com   HIML